Proceed with caution!

He was the quintessential man's man, strong, rugged, independent. A beautiful example of the male animal.

She could hear Aunt Bertha's warnings, doled out in a steady stream throughout her niece's youthful years: "Be careful." "Don't take chances." "Watch where you're going." Cassie had built a safe, predictable life around all those cautions. A life that had seemed perfectly satisfactory.

What greater risk could she take than giving her heart to Eric Wagner? Eric lived his life on the brink, hanging on the edge of a cliff, constantly challenging the odds.

Had he said anything, anything at all, to indicate that he had something permanent in mind? He had deep misgivings about women, and she'd done nothing to uphold the honor of the female species. Would he simply conclude that she was just another woman with a voracious appetite for men?

Dear Reader:

Dreams, like flowers, can be fragile, but once they are pressed gently between the pages of a book, their colors and textures can be savored again and again.

This month, six wonderful authors—Ginna Gray, Lisa Jackson, Mary Kirk, Victoria Pade, Mary Curtis and Patricia Coughlin—bring you their versions of "the stuff that dreams are made of"... gently pressed between the covers of six Silhouette **Special Edition** novels.

Writer and dedicated dreamer Patricia Coughlin believes that "when you open a Silhouette **Special Edition,** you want to meet strong, compelling characters and be swept up in their unique adventure. You want to be touched emotionally, feel your heart race and ultimately be left with a sense of fulfillment. So do I," she confesses, "and I'm thrilled to share my dreams with you in the pages of a **Special Edition.**"

For bedtime reading—anytime reading—our authors and editors hope you'll choose Silhouette **Special Edition.** These romantic novels are designed to bring you sweet dreams you can savor again and again, night after night, month after month. And the morning after, why not drop us a line? We always welcome your comments.

Sincerely,

Leslie Kazanjian,
Senior Editor

MARY CURTIS
Cliffhanger

Silhouette Special Edition

Published by Silhouette Books New York

America's Publisher of Contemporary Romance

SILHOUETTE BOOKS
300 East 42nd St., New York, N.Y. 10017

ISBN: 0-373-09526-0

First Silhouette Books printing May 1989

Printed in the U.S.A.

Books by Mary Curtis

Silhouette Special Edition

Love Lyrics #424
Cliffhanger #526

MARY CURTIS,

a former Californian who now resides in Massachusetts, divides her artistic energy between writing projects and work in community theater. This author of a dozen romance novels and mother of three daughters also finds time to play the heroine herself, in musicals such as *Guys and Dolls*, *Kiss Me, Kate* and *The King and I*. When not performing, directing or writing, Mary is likely to be traveling with her husband, gathering new story and setting ideas along the way. She is also known to romance fans as Mary Haskell.

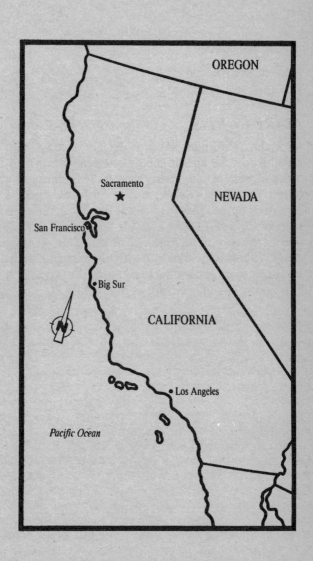

Chapter One

Cassandra stepped over the guardrail at the edge of the steep-angled cliff, stood poised for a moment, transfixed by the roiling surf pounding against the rocks eight hundred feet below, then carefully inched her way to the small ledge a short distance down the incline. She sank slowly to the ground, pushing her back against a wind-battered tree trunk and wedging her heels into a crevice in the earth just in front of her. Leaning her head back on the hard bark, she let her gaze wander, her sense of awe increasing with each passing moment. She was surrounded by magnificence. Big Sur. Her grandfather called it the front yard of God.

The fall rains had been heavy on the northern coast of California, so that now, in late November, the precipitous slopes that rose behind her, across Highway 1, were lushly flocked with green. Beneath her perch the earth dropped abruptly to the sand far below, where the waves' milky foam crawled and skipped over irregular intrusions of jagged rock along the shoreline. As far as she could see the sun-speckled turquoise water was broken only by dark clumps of floating kelp and flecks of white froth, under a dazzling canopy of original sky blue. It still gave Cassie the sense of being suspended between heaven and earth that she'd felt here as a child.

She pulled her knees tightly to her chest and rested her chin on them. Nearby, a mere two miles down the road, was Cliffhanger. The moment she thought of it, she felt its allurement, more personal than that of an ordinary house, too powerful to understand or to ignore. She recalled the time during one of her summer breaks from high school when her grandfather had first expressed his feeling for his home, a feeling now entrenched in her own heart: "I love this house, Cassie," he had told her, "and it loves me back—I can feel it. It's my sanctuary."

"Jake." She smiled as she said her grandfather's name aloud. He would be waiting for her, full of love and fun and bluster. He'd ask about her plane ride from Boston and her great-aunt Bertha, and tell her she was getting too skinny and needed to get out in the sun to lose her New England pallor. Jake and Cliffhanger. She thought of them together, interlocked and inseparable. *Her* sanctuaries.

As another, much less pleasant thought came to mind, Cassie's smile faded. Damn. She wished this was to be one of their customary reunions, full of joy and free of friction; but an argument was inevitable. Her grandfather closely fit the description of his astrological sign of Taurus, the bull. He was stubborn, independent and dogged in his loyalties, and he would not take kindly to her opinion that a so-called friend of his, Eric Wagner, was about to take him for a large amount of money. Wagner was either a first-class con man or a second-rate dreamer, Cassie had decided. Either way, he had no right to get her aged grandfather involved in a fly-by-night scheme. She must see to it that he didn't.

Cassie had heard about Wagner for years, though she'd never met him. But the lack of acquaintance had not prevented her from forming a strong impression—one she'd best keep to herself if she didn't want to set off the full force of her grandfather's renowned temper.

Cassie took a deep breath, filling her lungs with the crisp, clean air. Since she'd been old enough to drive, she'd always followed the same pattern on her visits. She'd fly to the airport in San Jose, pick up a rental car and stop here at Hurricane Point to say hello to Big Sur before going on to her destination. Cassie liked the security of ritual. She felt safer when most aspects of her life had established perimeters. She glanced down at the car bodies that lay rusting on the sand far below, silent testimony to the danger of the narrow, curving highway with its occasional landslide and frequent dense fog, and to the seductive pull of the scenic wonder that tempted eyes from the road.

She sat for about fifteen minutes, absorbing the incredible vista, allowing time for the strange shift of allegiance from the side of her that was closely attuned to the neatly girdled city life of Boston to the side that struggled free to join the vast expanses of Big Sur. She wondered if she'd ever know, really, which half of her seemingly split personality was dominant.

With a deep sigh that expressed both pleasure about the upcoming meeting with Jake and trepidation about their unavoidable confrontation, she stood and turned, ready to climb back to the road and complete her journey. She looked down as she shoved her right foot into the niche a couple of feet above the ledge. Without lifting her eyes she reached up to grasp the bush that grew just below the top edge. She gasped in shock as she suddenly felt steely fingers grab her wrist. Her head jerked up and her carefully placed foot slipped back to the ledge. "My God!"

The eyes that met hers were black and angry. "That's a damn-fool thing to do."

"What?" Cassie was so astonished she froze in place, staring up at the face that glowered down at her.

"Climbing down there. I wish you tourists would use some common sense when you come to a place like this. How do you know that ledge will stay put?"

The biting tone was insulting. Cassie started to snap back that she wasn't a tourist and that she knew the ledge would stay put because she'd stood on it at least a dozen times, but her gaze shifted from the dark, crackling eyes to the hand that held hers, and suddenly she had a terrifying vision of being pulled loose from her perch, swung free and dropped eight hundred feet to join the rusting cars. She'd never seen this man in her life. Maybe he was a maniac! She swallowed her anger and replied in a tightly controlled tone, "The ledge looks perfectly safe to me."

His hand tightened. "Looks can be deceiving. Come on, I'll help you up."

"I can get up by myself."

"Yeah? You could also fall down the cliff by yourself. Climb!"

With her jaw rigidly set she repositioned her foot in the niche and shifted her weight. Instantly a portion of the earth gave way and her foot slid loose. Cassie screamed in terror. For just a second, until her other foot regained its hold on the ledge, she was supported only by the hand that held her wrist. She glanced down at the rocky shore so far below and shuddered.

"Don't look down! Give me your other hand and step on the top of the stump." The voice, deep and resonant with authority, cut through her horror. Mutely she followed instructions, and the man pulled her up the incline with amazing ease. When both her feet were firmly planted on solid ground, his hands left her wrists to take hold of her shoulders. "Are you all right?"

Cassie was shaking all over, only now fully aware of what had almost happened. Tearing her eyes from the suddenly terrifying line of sharp-edged rocks that cut through the waves below, she lifted them to meet the dark gaze of the stranger who had probably just saved her life. The impact of the meeting shattered what small store of aplomb she held in reserve. His eyes, as dark as his thick black hair, held fathomless depths that promised dangers at least equal to those of the precipitous cliff. His imposing body—lithe, muscular, lean—looked as hard-hewn as the rocky ridge-lines of the mountainous shore. His sun-bronzed face had a haunting quality, as though something of the wild terrain had invaded his features. Cassie was shaken to the soles of her feet by a new rush of emotion so unexpected and so foreign that it held her transfixed. Unfamiliar as she was with the sensations that flooded her body, there was no mistaking the feeling. It was pure, unadulterated lust.

"I—" She swallowed, searching frantically for her vanished equilibrium. "Thank you." To her further dismay, she felt tears rolling down her cheeks. "I'm sorry—" she lifted trembling fingers to wipe away the tears "—I don't know what's wrong with me."

"You almost killed yourself. Not only a bad idea, but against the law."

Cassie looked at him closely, searching for a trace of humor. His face was unreadable. She felt intolerably gauche and vulnerable under that inky gaze, as though his eyes cut through to read her mind and found the script trivial. "Well—" she cleared her throat and stepped back, out of the grasp of those strong fingers "—I don't quite know what to say. I may well owe you my life."

The smallest twitch of a smile came to his lips but instantly disappeared. "That's a significant debt. I'll give some thought to how I want to be repaid." With that, he turned and strode to a battered Jeep wagon, climbed in and drove away without a backward glance, leaving Cassie strangely bereft. She took one last look at the benign scene below, the waves rolling peacefully on shiny white sand, shivered and got into her rented Ford.

When she reached the top of the familiar driveway, she paused, as she always did, to gather her courage before tipping the nose of the auto over the steep edge. Only when the grade finally leveled did she breathe again. She parked by the garage in back of the house. Before climbing out, she laid her head against the backrest and closed her eyes, trying to calm her still-jumpy nerves. But her peace was further shattered by the vivid picture that leapt to mind: dark, haunting eyes in a ruggedly beautiful face, a face molded by a master sculptor. With an impatient sigh she opened her eyes and got out of the car, slamming the door behind her. How had it been possible for her to be so blatantly attracted to a man under such frightening circumstances? It must have been the overreaction of badly jarred senses.

As she walked around the corner of the low sprawling house, she was sure she could hear it whisper, "Welcome home, Cassie." The very proximity of Cliffhanger had a soothing effect. When she reached the front porch she placed both palms on the oversize door, leaned her forehead against it and closed her eyes, absorbing the stored warmth of the weather-aged wood and inhaling its familiar odor, as distinct as a person's. This too was part of the coming-home ritual. With eager fingers she turned the doorknob and stepped inside. "Jake!" Her voice echoed through the big house. No reply. She glanced at her watch, mentally deducting the three hour difference in time. Two-thirty. She had told him to expect her about three.

Passing quickly through the spacious entrance hall, she stepped into the living room and stopped. How familiar it was, and how beautiful. The room was rectangular, its walls and floor crafted of wide redwood boards. The house had been built before Jake became a conservationist to whom the felling of one redwood tree was a sacrilege. Its vaulted ceiling was crossed by huge rough-hewn beams, and one entire wall was taken up by a massive stone fireplace. The polished wood floor was partially covered by an Oriental rug, richly hued in reds and blues and sandy beiges, and many of the furnishings were antiques, passed down to Jake by his ancestors. The combination of Californian casual and Eastern elegant was stunning.

Cassie walked slowly through the room, touching the small cabinet where Jake still kept the collection of pipes he hadn't smoked for years, running her hand over the alabaster sculpture of an Indian brave he'd bought at a Pueblo reservation, pausing while her eyes flicked over the collection of snapshots framed and hung on the far wall, pictures of her family. Her fingers touched the large photo of her mother and father on their wedding day then moved to hover wistfully over the shot of the two of them, laughing down at her as she hugged the tiny new puppy they'd just given her on her tenth birthday. It had been taken three days before the boating accident that had killed them, and had very nearly killed Cassie.

Her body tensed as she heard the squeak of the back door opening and the bang as it closed. "Cassie!" At the sound of the deep bellow she ran to the kitchen and into the embrace of her grandfather, who wrapped his arms tightly around her, giving her a great hug as he chuckled happily. "Well, Cassandra, so here you are, home again."

"Jake, it's so good to be here." She pulled back to look up at him. Despite his seventy-six years, Jake was a full six-foot-four. Age hadn't diminished his stature. "Where were you?"

"Down at the beach, taking my swim." His wonderful smile creased his whole face and made his eyes sparkle. Cassie had inherited her coloring from him. Although her tawny blond hair no longer matched his, which had long ago turned to gray, the vivid blue eyes were a dead giveaway.

She made a little clicking sound with her tongue before she remembered how much it annoyed him. He had commented several times that it made her sound like somebody's maiden aunt. "Are you still swimming every day? The ocean is far too rough and the water's bound to be awfully cold at this time of year." She glanced over his faded gray sweatsuit. "And I'll bet you still have your wet trunks on."

He tipped his head and scowled at her, trying to look fierce. "Good God, Cass, don't get started. I may be old but I'm not quite dead yet. I can still take care of myself." He waved a hand toward the door. "Got some stuff to be carried in from the car?"

One look at the set of his jaw inspired her to drop the subject of his daily swim and nod her answer to his question. "Yes. Two big suitcases. I'm here until after Christmas, if you'll have me."

"Humph. If I had my way, you'd be here permanently."

She gave him an impish grin. "Now don't get started. I may be your granddaughter, but I'm all grown-up and I can make my own decisions."

He laughed. "You always were a sassy kid. Come on, let's get you settled."

Cassie unpacked her clothes while Jake took a shower and changed. Within an hour they were both seated at the big round battered pine table in the kitchen, nursing cups of freshly perked coffee. Jake set down his mug and fixed her with his sharp blue gaze. "So. How was your trip?"

Cassie grinned. Right on cue. "Fine. In fact, excellent. We actually landed ahead of time."

He raised one eyebrow. "Really? Must have been a new pilot. Hasn't learned the art of stalling yet. And how about your Aunt Bertha—how's she doing?"

"Aunt Bertha is in fine fettle. Her health is good, her schedule remains hectic and her outlook is still fraught with doom. It seems almost an affront to her that the world hasn't yet been blown to smithereens or California dropped into the ocean by a killer earthquake or any one of a dozen other calamities."

Jake laughed. "Hasn't changed a bit, in other words."

"Right."

"Well, at least some things remain constant." He frowned at her. "You need to put on some weight and get some color in your cheeks."

Cassie had to laugh. "Oh, Jake, talk about constants! You say exactly the same thing every time I come here."

"Then you should start paying attention."

"For your information, I've been working on my master's degree all summer, which kept me inside, and I'm at the perfect weight for my height and bone structure."

"Humph."

"You always say that, too."

He tilted back in his chair and stared at her with indignation. "Are you accusing me of becoming an old bore?"

Cassie leaned forward and put her hand on his arm. "You? Never."

He covered her hand with his. "Ah, Cassandra. How I wish you'd forget your addiction to cold weather and snow and live here with me all the time."

"If you wanted me to be a Californian, you should have kept me here in the first place."

Jake shook his head slowly. "Yes. I've often thought the same thing. But I knew how set your parents were on having you educated in the east. And I figured my sister was better equipped than I to take on the raising of a ten-year-old girl." He smiled at her. "I have to give her her due. She did a fine job."

"Aunt Bertha's a love. She has instilled in me a rock-hard moral code, a firm sense of responsibility and an absolute dedication to avoiding doing anything to precipitate one of the innumerable catastrophes that lie in wait for us all."

Jake's face sobered. "I wish I could laugh at that, but I'm afraid you're dead right. She's the most devout pessimist I've ever known."

Cassie nodded in agreement. "It's hard to imagine how the two of you grew up in the same family."

"Has something to do with gene distribution, I suppose." His eyes squinted as he studied Cassie's face. "I'm afraid Bertha's passed far too many of her nervous-Nellie traits to you."

Cassie's eyes dropped. She knew he was right, but she hated to acknowledge it. "Oh, now come on. What do I need with daredevil propensities? Now that I've got my degree I'm going to work as an English literature professor at Boston University. It isn't what you'd call a frightening environment."

"You already have a job?"

Her head bobbed up and down. "Yes, isn't it wonderful? I start part-time in February and full-time next September." She saw the dark cloud that shadowed her grandfather's face. Well, she hadn't expected him to be pleased. The position would tie her more securely than ever to the Boston area. And she had some further news that would reinforce the knot. She took a deep breath. Might as well get it all over with at once. "Jake, I have something else to tell you." Why did she feel the need to muster her courage? "I'm...engaged."

The dark cloud threatened a storm. "What?" He slapped his palm on the wooden tabletop. "Cassie, don't tell me you're going to marry that milksop of a banker!"

"He isn't a milksop and you know it. He's a very nice man."

"Humph. Nice. Sweet, too, I warrant."

"Oh, honestly! You were determined not to like him from the moment you met him just because he's third-generation Bostonian and he wears a suit to work. You will *never* lose your chauvinistic attitudes about male-female relationships. I'm sure you'd be much happier if I wound up with some caveman type who grunted orders at me as he carried me off to his lair." She wrinkled her nose. "I met one of those guys today, and believe me, the five-minute exposure was quite enough, thank you."

Jake's shaggy eyebrows lifted. "Oh? And where have you been hanging around that you'd meet someone like that?"

The edges of her lips curled up. "I was hanging around a cliff, and he picked me up." She was surprised she could joke about it this soon, with the taste of terror still in her mouth. Before her grandfather had time to pepper her with questions, she began to tell him about the incident.

He looked more alarmed as the story unfolded. "Well, whoever this guy is, I for one am extremely grateful he happened along. I don't know why you sound so ticked off at him—sounds to me like he saved your bacon. What the hell were you doing on that ledge, anyway?"

"Now, Jake, take it easy. I've performed that little ritual for the last nine or ten years, and you know me, I'm far from being a risk taker. It's a gentle slope down to that ledge, and it always seemed perfectly solid."

He scowled. "Cassie, this is the first time in memory you've been here this late in the year. You usually come during your summer break and leave in early September, before the rainy season. Besides, if you paid attention to the national weather reports, you'd know that this area has been saturated with the heaviest rainfall in fifteen years. So *nothing* on the side of the mountain is safe right now."

Cassie glanced around nervously. "Including Cliffhanger?"

Jake shook his head. "I doubt there's any danger here. This house is built into a solid rock face on the side of the mountain." His eyes still held a shadow of fear. Her experience had obviously shaken him terribly. Jake was a man who had already suffered far too much loss. He'd outlived not only his wife, but his son. If he had any fears at all, they centered around the safety of his granddaughter. "So, you didn't get this man's name? I assume you'd know him if you saw him again. I'd like to give him my thanks."

"Oh, yes, I'd know him," Cassie assured him. She wondered if she'd ever get the memory of that face out of her mind. Or her reaction to it. Better by far if she never saw him again; just the thought raised goosebumps on her flesh.

"Cassie, you mustn't take chances like that."

She stared at him, nonplussed. "*You're* telling *me* not to take chances? That's a switch."

Jake got up and crossed to the stove to refill his cup. "I've had a lot of experience hanging on the sides of cliffs." He raised an eyebrow at her. "I never thought mountain climbing appealed to you. More coffee?"

"No thanks. One cup of your brew is enough to make me twitch." She fiddled with the mug in front of her as he returned to his seat. "Jake, speaking of taking chances..."

"Yes?"

"What's this business deal you wrote about? You know, with that man, Eric What's-his-name?" She hoped the little touch of levity made the question sound offhand.

Jake tilted his chair back on its rear legs, his expression guarded. "I figured this would come up. Bertha been chewing on it?"

"Well, yes. But I must admit to doubts of my own." Cassie leaned toward him, then forced her body to relax back into the chair. It was important to approach this subject slowly, as though she wasn't already determined to talk him out of it.

Jake's chair smacked forward onto all fours. "All right, Cassandra. Let's get at this, so we can enjoy the rest of your stay. Just what is it that's worrying you?"

Damn. He was upset already. The problem was he could smell her mood through any kind of smokescreen. Her fingers nervously turned the mug around and around. "It's just that it sounds so...iffy. I mean..." Her grandfather's eyes were darkening, not a good sign. Whatever had possessed her to get into this so soon? Her darned curiosity; she just had to know right away! She rummaged around in her mind for a tactful way to express what she had to say. Finding none, she blurted it out. "Jake, it sounds to me like this Eric person is cooking up some wacky scheme that's going to lose you a lot of money."

He frowned. "And just how much do you know about limited partnerships—or investments of any kind, for that matter?"

Her chin lifted. "I took two years of economics in college. And I own stock in a mutual fund."

"Terrific. So that makes you an expert?"

"It doesn't take an expert to be suspicious of some guy who talks a man of your age into investing a sizable sum in platinum mining in Canada, for Pete's sake!"

"My age, huh?" His eyes narrowed. "Here we go again. Too old and feeble to swim in the same chunk of ocean I've swum in for fifty years and too old and senile to make rational decisions about my own money." Cassie cringed. Stated like that, it sounded pretty awful—and very unfair. After all, she'd never said he was feeble or senile. Happily, a knock on the back door interrupted the skirmish. "Come in!" Jake shouted.

"Is that an invitation or a challenge?"

Cassie stared, her mouth agape, at the man who had entered and now stood just inside the kitchen door with an expression of surprise on his face. Jake looked from one of them to the other. "Have you two met?"

Cassie's mouth had gone so dry that her words came out in a parched rattle. "It's him." God, she sounded like a ninny! And why was she suddenly covered with a film of sweat? She cleared her throat and tried again. "This is the man I told you about, the one who...helped me." The glint of amusement that had appeared in his coal-black eyes prevented her from using the word saved. After all, if he hadn't shocked her in the first place by grabbing her wrist, chances were she'd have climbed right up to the road with no problem.

Jake smiled at the man. "Well, what do you know. So you were the one out aiding damsels in distress."

The man's smile was brilliant. His teeth, straight and white, completed the picture of physical perfection. "Bad day today. Only one rescue."

"Damn good day, as far as I'm concerned. You have my eternal gratitude. This is my granddaughter, Cassandra."

His thick brows rose as his eyes moved to her. "So this is Cassie." Cassie shifted uneasily in her chair. The heat of his gaze, she was sure, could melt iron. "Then I suppose you're glad I reeled her in."

Cassie was beginning to feel like an inanimate object, the way these two self-satisfied males were talking past her. She opened her mouth, but before she could interject, Jake said, "Cassie, this is my friend, Eric What's-his-face. Or was it 'that Eric person'?" His eyes were dancing with deviltry.

Feeling the hot rise of color to her face, she shot daggers at her smiling grandfather, but if any of them hit their target, they made no impression. She wanted to stamp her foot and tell him to knock it off, but that, of course, would only amuse these two John Wayne clones further. No wonder they were such fast friends. They were two of a kind! When she did speak, her voice emanated from between clenched teeth. "Jake..."

Much to her surprise, it was Eric who broke the uncomfortable tension. He stepped forward, his hand extended. "Glad to meet you, Cassie." That devastating smile flashed again. "Officially, that is. I'm Eric Wagner. I've heard a lot about you."

She hoped her smile didn't look as wobbly as it felt. "I've heard a great deal about you, too." Her hand met his, and as before, the physical contact was jarring. What was wrong with her?

His smile broadened. "Sounds like it. I have a feeling I'd have done better starting off with complete anonymity."

She flushed and withdrew her hand. She couldn't think straight with him touching her; in fact, his mere proximity did weird things to her thought patterns. "Well, actually..." Now what? Actually you're right? If I didn't know you were a huckster, I'd probably have fallen in love with you by now?

Jake pulled a chair away from the table. "Sit down and have some coffee, Eric." As Eric sat down, Jake went to the cupboard to get another mug. "The truth of the matter is, Cassie thinks you're about to fleece an old man."

"Really?" Eric studied Cassie's face as Jake put the steaming cup in front of him. "And just how am I to accomplish this?"

Cassie cringed. Unfair! Jake had thrown her in over her head without a life jacket. Well, she was tired of feeling like an incompetent child in front of this maddening man. If he wanted to know, she'd tell him. "I don't think you should lure my grandfather into some hokey deal involving a platinum mine—a *platinum* mine, for heaven's sake. Who ever heard of such a thing? Wouldn't it seem more logical to be going after gold?"

That unreadable expression had shuttered Eric's face. "Well now, you may have something there. I guess that might make a more believable scam at that." Without moving another muscle in his face, his black eyes shifted to Jake. "What do you think, Jake? A gold mine in Alaska sound any better?"

Jake narrowed his eyes, as though contemplating the question. "I don't know. If we're going to get into anything in Alaska, I was kind of taken by the deal in crab fishing. That sounds more original. Somehow I doubt I'd have bitten on a gold-mining scheme. Too dated."

Cassie pushed back her chair and jumped to her feet. "I hope you two are having a good time." She glared at Jake. "I don't see what's so funny. You swear you'll never come back to Boston, where I could be near enough to do something if you needed help. And now you're playing around with your financial security as though it was all some big joke. Just what are you going to live on out here all by yourself if this man—" her hand swept dramatically in Eric's direction "—has taken all your money?"

His dark eyes would no longer melt steel, but they would freeze red-hot lava. Cassie shivered. She wanted to run to her bedroom and close the door until she could regain some semblance of composure, as well as good sense. This whole thing had gotten completely out of control. Just being in his presence addled her brain and loosened her tongue. She didn't even know this man, and she'd accused him right to his face of being some kind of crook. She shouldn't have brought up this subject at all so soon after arriving, and she certainly shouldn't have fallen into this verbal sparring.

She stepped back and dropped her eyes. "Look, I'm sorry. What I said was very rude." She looked up, hoping to see a friendlier expression on Eric's face. She didn't.

Jake stood and put his arm around her. "I *was* giving you a hard time, Cass. You've always had a temper, ever since you were a little kid, and I could never resist trying to set it off. Eric didn't talk me into anything, it's entirely my decision. He's putting together a deal, and I asked to be included." He patted her on the shoulder. "You don't need to be worried about me. I'm not as close to the poorhouse as you seem to think I am."

"Jake, I didn't mean..."

"I know, honey. Let's just let it alone for now." He shifted his attention to his friend, who had stood up and was obviously preparing to leave. "Eric, sorry you got pulled into this."

Eric shrugged. "Don't worry about me. I'm far from thin-skinned, as you know." He gave a little bow of the head toward Cassie. "Cassandra. It was about time we met. Somehow we missed each other for the last five years."

Cassie felt quite sure he'd probably try to miss her for the next five. "Yes, that's true. From what Jake told me, you move to the city during tourist season, which is the time I generally come. I didn't mean to make our first meeting so unpleasant."

"Oh, I don't know. Hauling a beautiful woman off the side of a mountain was kind of a kick. Now our *second* meeting..." He was laughing at her again, and it made Cassie mad enough to spit. For some reason he completely disrupted her usual sanguine nature. "Tell you what, why don't we call a truce? The three of us could go to the Nepenthe for dinner. Give us a chance to get acquainted."

His words caught Cassie off guard. The prospect of spending the evening with him instantly brightened her mood. "You are a glutton for punishment!" Eric laughed, and the last vestige of Cassie's irritation lost its frantic grip and slid away, sabotaged by the delightful deep rumble of his laughter. "I'd love to go. Jake? Is that all right, or did you have something else planned?" It was embarrassing, really, how much she hoped he didn't.

Jake was watching them closely and he had a strange look on his face. Could it be disapproval? "Sure, fine with me. In fact, it'll work out well. Tom Shea and Gus Saunders'll be there tonight, and they wanted me to join them to settle some strategy on a conservation matter. Told them I couldn't because you'd be here, but this way I can pop over to their table long enough for a short conference."

"Is this about the new highway?" Eric asked.

Jake nodded. "Damn idiots. One fool scheme after another to try to destroy Big Sur. I can't understand how anyone with more than two marbles in his brain can even consider doing anything to damage this kind of beauty."

"That's because you're a rational man with a sensitive soul, Jake. Not too many of those left." Eric walked to the door then turned before going out. "I'll stop by and pick you up about seven-thirty. Okay?" Cassie could have sworn that as he left, his shoulders brushed both sides of the doorjamb.

When he was gone, Cassie slid back down to her seat with a sigh. "I'm sorry, Jake. I'm afraid I really shot my mouth off that time. I had no right to insult your friend."

"No, as a matter of fact, you didn't. But I know you had my best interests in mind." He went over to refill his cup, and Cassie stopped herself just in time from admonishing him about drinking so much strong coffee. She'd doubtless pushed the limits of mothering her grandfather. "But, Cassie, I wish you'd stop all this worrying about me. I'm only seventy-six. With my genes I could be riding waves for another fifteen to twenty years. And believe it or not, I can even afford to live that long!''

She smiled somewhat sheepishly. ''Obviously you've done a very good job of living on your own for a lot of years.'' Her grandmother, or Jake's wife, as Cassie tended to think of her, had died when Cassie was about two, and he had never remarried. According to her Aunt Bertha, he'd idolized his first wife far too much to find anyone else who came remotely near taking her place; so Cassie's only memory of him was living in this house by himself. ''But Brian says that people of your age tend to underestimate what they'll need to live on in the future, because they were out of the work force before the sharp escalation of costs began.''

Jake grimaced. ''Brian, huh? Your hotshot banker. Well, you tell good old Brian that I never was in the 'work force,' as he puts it. I made my money the same way Eric makes his.'' He glanced at Cassie's face and shook his head. ''No, not as a con artist, as an entrepreneur.''

She stared at him for a minute, then shamefacedly confessed, ''It just dawned on me I'd never really known *what* you did for a living. I asked Aunt Bertha once what kind of job you had, and she just gave me that look—you know, the one that lets you know she isn't going to answer your question—and said 'humph!''' She grinned. ''She says it just like you do.''

''Humph. Bertha always regarded my career path as a straight road to ruin. It's no wonder you're so suspicious of a perfectly respectable deal.''

Once again Cassie bit her tongue. ''I know this is probably a dumb question, but just what is an entrepreneur? Not the dictionary definition—I know that. But what does one *do*?''

Jake leaned forward, as though about to answer, then sat up straight and smiled. ''I think I'll let Eric explain that one to you. Might help you get acquainted.''

She cocked her head at him. "Now, Jake, you're not thinking of a little matchmaking, are you? A chance to cut out good old Brian and hook me up with a he-man resident of Big Sur?" She was irritated by the rapid rush of pleasure the idea evoked.

She expected him to laugh, but instead he frowned. "No. As a matter of fact, that is definitely *not* my intent. Eric's become one of my best friends. I like him and I respect him. Best of all I enjoy his company. But I'd sure hate to see you hang your heart out on a limb for him. He's a walking boobytrap for women."

Cassie lifted her eyebrows. "I have to admit he's very good-looking. So what are you telling me, that I couldn't hope to compete with the competition?"

"The point is, there is no competition where he's concerned. He's a fine man, Cass, but there's a deep bitterness in his soul, and it obviously took root in experiences he had with his mother and his ex-wife. I doubt any woman could get a commitment from him. He mistrusts the entire sex."

The level of dismay that bit of information brought on was downright alarming. Just one more good reason for putting Eric Wagner right out of her mind, Cassie reassured herself. It was the only proper thing to do anyway. "Don't give it a thought. Remember, I'm safely engaged to that good old milksop, Brian."

"Humph." His expression blatantly derided Brian's ability to provide a safe shield from a man like Eric. He glanced at the kitchen clock. "Maybe you should take a nap. We'll be leaving for dinner at ten-thirty, your time."

"Oh, that's right. Good idea. I think I will go in and lie down for a while." Cassie went into her cheerful room with its lifetime accumulation of paraphernalia tacked up on the walls and arranged on shelves. She paused to look out the large window that offered a spectacular view of the Pacific Ocean. God, it was beautiful here. Every time she came back, she found something new to admire. With a deep sigh of pleasure, she took the pillow from under its lilac-and-blue quilted spread and, kicking off her shoes, climbed onto the bed, pulling up the soft blanket that lay folded at the bottom to snuggle under. As she settled down to drift off to sleep, her last mental image was of the most recent Big Sur attraction. An olive-skinned man with black, black eyes.

Chapter Two

Cassie awoke from her nap in a haze that refused to clear as she showered and dressed for the evening. She tried to convince herself that its basis lay in an accumulation of the events of the day: the flight across the country; the impact of her reacquainting encounter with Big Sur, a ritual that always had an unsettling effect; her traumatic brush with disaster, enough in itself to throw anyone into a lingering daze. But her truthful mind rejected the lot. It was the abrupt introduction of Eric Wagner into her existence that had left her fuzzy-headed—a realization she found both exasperating and titillating.

Even though she knew the majority of Nepenthe's customers would be jean-clad, she chose a pair of doe-soft slacks made of "go-silk," a wonderful fabric that combined pack-and-wear ease with caressable texture. She matched it with a cashmere sweater of the same yummy shade of dusty blue, a color that brought out wonderful highlights in her eyes and set off her blond hair. As she surveyed the total effect of the softly clinging garments in her full-length mirror, she tried to salve her conscience by assuring herself that even though the outfit was an advance Christmas gift from Brian, he certainly had put no restrictions on its wear.

After slipping her feet into navy flats she ran the brush through her long hair one more time and applied another coat of pink lipstick before gathering her purse and coat and joining Jake in the living room. Her grandfather stood in front of the huge picture window, gazing out at the spectacular half-moon that sent its brilliant swath of light dancing a trail across the darkened sea. He was dressed, as Cassie could have guessed, in faded jeans and a fisherman's sweater that had long since lost any distinguishable color. At the sound of her steps, he turned, a smile lighting his face.

"Well, well. Look at you. Did I miss something? Is it the Nepenthe we're going to or the Ventana?"

She grinned. "If we went to the Ventana, you'd have to wear a tie. Do you even *own* one?"

"Of course I do—in fact, several. They're in a drawer someplace." His eyes ran over her and one brow lifted. "Guess I'll have to take them out and squire you to the ritzy folks' hangout one of these days."

She tilted her head at him. "Well, come to think of it, that's not a bad idea. The only time I've eaten at the Ventana was when Brian came out to visit last year. And I have to admit, it was wonderful."

"Humph. I've never felt comfortable in the middle of all that blatant luxury."

Cassie glanced around the room, her eyes dancing. "Oh, yes, I can see why it would offend you, since you're forced to exist in the midst of such squalor."

The slam of a car door broke up the bantering. Cassie's heart jumped as she heard the back door open and a deep voice call, "Hello." What in the world was happening to her? Her reactions were usually so steady and reliable, and here she was, at the age of twenty-six, acting sillier over a handsome face than she ever had in her teens.

"In here, Eric," Jake yelled.

When he appeared in the archway Cassie sighed in defeat. She had hoped to find him more ordinary than her afternoon's memory. After all, being plucked from peril by a handsome stranger was, without question, enough to make any woman with a bent toward drama feel like a Gothic heroine. It was certainly possible she'd registered an unreal picture of him. But no, he'd lost none of his appeal. His jeans, softened with age, clung to his muscular thighs. His shoulders looked broader than ever in his pale yellow crew sweater, and oh, those eyes!

He nodded to Jake, then looked at her. "Ready?"

Oh, yes! "Yes. All set."

She and Jake followed him outside, where Eric opened the door of a pickup truck and held out his hand to help her in. As she stepped up, his black eyes slid over her then signaled their approval. "Nice outfit."

"Thank you."

His fingers tightened for just an instant before releasing hers.

Jake slid in next to Cassie and closed the door while Eric walked around to the other side. When he settled behind the steering wheel, Cassie was acutely aware of the touch of his hip and shoulder and the increase of pressure each time he shifted gears or turned the wheel. She made no attempt to get into the conversation between Eric and Jake, all centered around some dispute between conservationists and fishermen. Her mind was kept busy chastising her senses for slipping their gears and whirling out of control.

The truck wound up the curving driveway to the Nepenthe and stopped. Jake swung his door open and got out. "What a night! Weather like this is a double pleasure after all that damned rain." He gave Cassie a hand as she hopped down to the asphalt. "Let's go out to the terrace so we can appreciate the view." He grinned at Eric. "Have to keep reminding Cass here that Big Sur is one hell of a lot prettier than Bean Town.''

When they reached the tiled terrace Cassie did have to concede the point. With just a turn of the head she could see the steep rise of velvet-coated hills to one side and the awesome drop to crashing waves hundreds of feet below on the other. She could smell the tangy salt in the air and taste it on her lips. Brilliantly blazing stars crowded the skies, and the moon was enough to inspire thousands of new lyrical tributes to its tie with romance.

''Really something, isn't it?''

She was startled by Eric's deep voice so close to her ear. When she turned her head to meet his eyes, the lure of their black depths was hypnotically compelling. He seemed to be part of all this—the towering mountains, the broad expanse of fathomless ocean. Daring, intriguing, demanding. ''Yes. Really something,'' she responded a little breathlessly, commenting on far more than the view.

''Let's go inside,'' Jake said. ''It's cold out here.''

Cassie's attention instantly shifted to her grandfather. Jake, cold? He'd always seemed impervious to the caprice of weather. She studied his face, searching for signs of frailty. There was no denying the deepened lines in his weathered skin. And his limp, the result of a wound during the Second World War, wasn't it more pronounced than it used to be? Dear heaven, Jake would be seventy-seven within weeks. Regardless of all his humphs, he *was* an old man. She felt a constriction around her heart. The thought of a world without Jake was unbearable; she must get him to take better care of himself.

Ahead of them, silhouetted against the sky, loomed the Dark Angel, a black metal sculpture that had been a trademark of the Nepenthe for as many years as she could remember. She hesitated below it, conscious of its hovering menace.

''Still spook you?'' Jake had stopped and put his arm around her.

"Yes. He still looks more demon than angel to me."

"And how do you like your angels, Cassie?" Eric's gaze was taunting. "Chubby and pink?"

"Chubby and pink is better than black and thin and ominous."

"Ominous?" He looked up at the prominent figure. "Funny, I'd never thought of him as ominous. Just arresting."

Cassie shivered, and Jake's arm tightened around her. "The first time Cassie saw this statue was just a couple of weeks after her parents' death." He looked down at her with an expression of love and compassion. "She screamed and ran away, crying her eyes out. Took me a long time to quiet her."

Cassie poked him in the ribs to forestall any further airing of her childhood fears. "So see? I'm much better than I used to be. I can look at it now and stay perfectly calm."

Eric frowned. "Why is that better? If it helps to scream, you should scream."

"Oh, Lord." Jake set out for the door. "Let's get inside before we start some deep, philosophical discussion."

Cassie fell back and let the two men precede her, her mind replaying the brief exchange. *If it makes you feel better to scream, you should scream.* The remark brought back memories of the many times she'd wanted to kick and cry and throw things—anything to vent some of the rage and abandonment she'd felt at her parents' death. She hadn't, of course. Everyone knew how unsuitable that sort of behavior was. But oh, how good it would have felt to let go of some of the pent-up fury and sorrow. It would *still* feel good. She glanced around as they stepped inside. Even the unflappable year-rounders of Big Sur might be startled if she were to fling herself on the floor and have a full-blown tantrum. She smiled at the mental picture. It reminded her of a message she'd once found in a Chinese fortune cookie. "Before you let yourself go, be sure you can get yourself back."

The Nepenthe was far from crowded, but there were a number of clustered groups sitting around the tables, lost in conversation, and a string of patrons at the bar, joking and chatting with the bartender and each other. At the sight of so many familiar faces, Cassie abandoned her morbid memories and shifted easily into a happy mood. Brenda Collier, the manager, came toward them, a welcoming smile on her face. "Well, well, my two favorite men. And Cassie! What a great surprise! When did you get here?"

Cassie returned her hug. "Just today. I'm still on East Coast time, but I took a nap so I wouldn't fall asleep at the table."

"Just curl up in the booth if you get tired, honey. You wouldn't be the first."

They followed her to a booth at the side of the colorful restaurant, returning greetings as they went. Cassie loved the Nepenthe. She had always been fascinated by the story of how Orson Welles had bought it from a hiking group for his new bride, Rita Hayworth. They'd fixed it up as a comfortable camp, but Rita was too frightened by the lonely area to spend even one night there, so it had finally been resold and turned into a restaurant. She glanced around at the heavily beamed ceiling and the windows that exposed the unique view from every angle. The center fireplace boasted a roaring fire tonight, which added to the aura of rustic romance. How wonderful to be all alone in a place like this with the man you love. She tried to picture Brian and herself curled up on a comfortable sofa in front of the fire, but she couldn't make the image focus; Brian simply didn't fit, even in fantasy, in this place. Besides, he would grow impatient with all the quiet and isolation and want to get back to town.

Cassie sat down and Eric slid onto the padded bench opposite. Before Jake could get seated he spotted two men at a small table in the back corner. "Oh, Tom and Gus are already here. Maybe I'll go over and settle our business now, before we eat."

Suddenly Cassie was alone with Eric. Tongue-tied, she glanced around the room, wishing someone would come over to the table and interrupt the silence.

"You look like you're searching for an escape route."

Her eyes snapped to Eric's. Could he read minds? That's exactly what she was doing. "Sorry, I was just checking to see if there were any old friends here." The little lie slithered out, puffy white and obvious.

"And?"

She shook her head, grinning sheepishly. "A few acquaintances, that's all."

"So, you're stuck here with the big bad scam artist."

She felt her cheeks warm. "Eric, look, I ... well, I said some things that were way out of line. I'm sorry."

"No need to apologize. If you thought I was about to bilk your grandfather, it was right for you to speak up."

"Well, Jake assures me I was wrong."

"And are you satisfied with that?"

She picked up the knife at her place and turned it over in her hand. "I guess I should be."

"But you're not."

With significant difficulty she raised her eyes to meet his steady gaze. "Maybe we should start at the beginning. I asked Jake what an entrepreneur actually did, and he suggested I ask you to explain. It might help if I understood more about it."

"Umm." Eric leaned back. "It's pretty straightforward. He searches out ways to make money." He looked at her expression and raised one eyebrow. "Legal ways."

"That sounds so vague—'ways to make money.' Isn't everyone looking for ways to make money?"

"Not really. Most people are scared to death of taking a risk. Risk is inherent to the life of an entrepreneur. If his plans work out, he makes a lot of money. If they don't, he loses."

"Sounds like gambling."

"Sure. In a way it is. Only you don't throw the dice until you've done one hell of a lot of research into the odds."

Cassie frowned. So far she wasn't reassured. "You said plans. What sort of plans?"

"Okay. Say you've worked out some computer software that you're sure thousands of buyers would want if they only knew about it, but you don't have the money to get it into the marketplace. So you look for someone like me. I come in, assess the chances of success, and if they seem good I form a limited partnership and raise the money for your marketing needs."

"So where's the risk?"

Eric laughed. "Honey, if your software dies in the market, all the limited partners lose their investment. And the general partner—that's me—can lose his a— Sorry. His shirt."

Cassie leaned forward, determined to understand this. What she'd heard so far made her more convinced than ever that Jake should have no part of it. "What are limited partners and general partners?"

He started to rearrange the salt and pepper shakers and some of the little packets of sugar as he talked. "A limited partnership is made up of investors who want to back something, like the software. In this case, you've come to me with your idea, and I agree that it would sell. So I set up the legal structure, which requires a general partner. In other words, the executive who does the work and is accountable to the investors. I seek out potential investors, who become limited partners, and when the money is raised I see to having the software effectively marketed. For doing all this I get a fee for my work and a percentage of the profit, if there is one. If there are any snafus, I'm the one with his neck on the line."

"Why? Don't all investors lose their money if it doesn't sell?"

"Sure. But if Joe Dokes from Oshkosh comes running out of the woodwork waving a previous patent on your idea, and the legal vultures start circling, it's my carcass that's up for dinner."

Cassie plunked her elbows on the table and cupped her chin in her hands. "I'm sorry, but none of this sounds like something my grandfather should be involved in. I mean, he's too old to be taking chances like that. There are plenty of safer places to put his money."

"Like under his pillow?"

Her head snapped up. "Now don't start making fun of me just because I don't want to see Jake pouring good money down a dry well!"

"Mine."

"What's yours?"

Eric smiled mildly. "It's a *mine*, as in platinum. Not a well."

Cassie was getting mad. She was losing the war of the words again, and worse, they were veering from the point, which was getting Jake out of the investment. "Damn it, Eric—"

He held up both hands. "Whoa. I give up. You can't blame me for trying to inject a little humor. You're taking this so seriously."

"It is serious!"

"Cassie—" he leaned forward, the laughter gone from his face "—it's only money, not blood."

"You must be either rich or dead broke to have such a cavalier attitude about money."

"I've been both. And my attitude has stayed the same."

She closed her eyes for a moment, wondering whether to drop the subject or try to get through to this pig-headed man. She decided to take another stab at it. "But you're still young. You've got your whole life in front of you. Jake's an old man. The most important thing for him is security."

"Security. Good Lord." Eric sat back, a look of disdain on his face. "There's no such thing, Cassie, and the more you rely on it, the farther away it gets. And as for a whole life, all any of us has is this day, maybe just the moment.

Jake may well have more time coming than I do—nobody can predict that."

Cassie sighed in frustration. "You're confusing the issue."

"And you're shortchanging your grandfather. He's old only in years. He's strong and rugged and extraordinarily astute. He's also damned independent, which he has every right to be. You shouldn't try to make his decisions for him."

"And you shouldn't try to suck him into some flimsy deal so you can get your kicks out of gambling with the odds."

Shelley, a veteran waitress at the Nepenthe, sidled over to the table. "Much as I hate to interrupt a good fight, would either of you like a cocktail? You can drink it or throw it, that's up to you."

Cassie tried to wipe the scowl from her face as she looked up at the waitress. "Oh, Shelley, you're just in time. We were about to come to blows."

Shelley nodded. "Looked like a spirited discussion." she pulled out her tablet. "What'll it be, sipping whiskey or throwing scotch?"

Eric made a "you first" gesture to Cassie. At least she hoped that was what it was. "Let's see...a white wine spritzer, please."

"Gotcha. Eric?"

"A Beefeater martini, straight up with a twist."

"Do you want to order dinner yet?"

"No." Eric gestured toward the corner. "We'll wait for the old man."

Shelley looked around in confusion. "Old man?"

"Jake."

She stared at him in disbelief. "Jake, an old man? I should be so young!" With that, she turned and headed toward the bar.

Eric settled back, a smug expression on his face. "Case rests."

"You are a very maddening man."

"Thank you."

"Oh . . . !"

He reached over to put his hand on top of hers. "Cassie, let's call a truce and talk about something else."

Much to her chagrin he took his hand away again. The simplest gestures from him caused such radical mood swings that Cassie felt terribly off balance. "All right, agreed. What subject should we try?" She felt the sides of her mouth turn up despite her intention to nurture her anger. Actually it was kind of fun fighting with Eric Wagner. Stimulating.

"Tell me how you lost your parents."

Her mouth flattened and her mood plummeted. "Boy, you don't exactly go in for small talk, do you?"

"No. Never. Life's too short." He smiled at her. "As you've been pointing out."

"I'm not sure I want to talk about that. It still hurts."

"Of course it does. But I would like to know."

She frowned in puzzlement. "Why?"

"I figure it has a lot to do with what we were just arguing about."

Shelley set their drinks in front of them and smiled. "Well, things have quieted down over here. Guess it's safe to leave the cutlery on the table."

Eric nodded. "Perfectly safe. We're at a standoff."

"Too bad. It's a slow night. I thought we were going to see a little action."

Eric grinned at her. "Maybe later."

"Okay, handsome. If Cassie here gets too ornery, I'm always available."

"Shelley, Shelley. What would Peter say?"

She laughed. "Probably 'good riddance.'"

Cassie watched the waitress walk away, her hips swinging. She wasn't at all sure Shelley was kidding about her availability. She looked over at Eric, remembering Jake's remark about his being a walking booby trap for women. She took a deep swallow of her drink, wondering why she wanted to continue their conversation—to tell him all about that terrible day, sixteen years ago. One minute she wanted to scream at him, and the next, to confide in him. He was like a magnet, sitting across from her, pulling on her emotions with irresistible force. She watched him take a sip of his martini. It seemed right, somehow—maybe inevitable—that he would order the same drink that Jake always had.

He set down his glass. "Well?"

"You really want to hear about it? It's an awful story."

"I'm not expecting to be amused."

Cassie studied his face, struck once again with his ability to blank out expression. Did it come naturally, or was it acquired? "My folks had a summer place at Cape Cod, in Falmouth. We spent a lot of time there in the summer. We had some wonderful times. We were in kind of a separate community, with a private beach, and all of us kids spent the days playing in the sand or in the water." She picked up her fork and pinged it against her glass. "We had a motorboat. I'm not sure what kind. Daddy had been having some trouble with the engine, and he'd had it in and out of the shop. One Saturday Mom packed a picnic lunch, and Dad said we should take it down the coast a ways, to see if the mechanics had really fixed it." Her fingers turned her wineglass around and around. "So we all got in the boat, Dad and Mom and I and Jeremiah, the new puppy they'd just given me for my birthday."

She could feel the tears gathering in her eyes. Why didn't she just stop this? It was silly to go through it just to satisfy the curiosity of a stranger. But when she looked up, it didn't seem like the eyes of a stranger that met hers. It seemed more like someone she'd known for years and years. Somehow she had to go on—she *needed* to.

"We went over to the marina to get gas." She stopped and took a drink of the wine spritzer to moisten her dry mouth. "There were several men on the dock, hanging around to talk to my folks while the boy filled our gas tank. Dad was laughing and joking with them, and when the tank was filled he paid the boy and said to Mr. Benson, the man who lived next door to us . . . he said, 'Eddie, that sounds great. We'll be over about six to share your lobsters.' Then he winked at me and smiled. 'Cassie here will probably eat two. She loves them.'" Cassie, filled with memories, paused. "I did, too." She took another sip of her drink. "Then Dad pushed away from the dock, waved at the men and started the engine." She stopped.

Eric reached across the table and took her hand in both of his. "It blew up?"

She nodded, using the knuckle of her free hand to push aside the two tears that had escaped down her cheek. "Yes. It was all a jumble after that. I was thrown way out in the water, and I could barely get my breath. I kept going under. I was a good swimmer, even then, but I just couldn't get enough air. Everything in front of me was one big fire. I couldn't see anybody, and I was so scared. Then someone started shouting my name, and Mr. Benson jumped in and swam out to get me."

"It must have been terrible."

"Oh, yes. All I really remember then was Mr. Benson pulling me out of the water and up onto the beach, away from the dock. He kept telling me not to look, and he was crying." Her smile was very weak. "What's that old thing about 'it's the first time I'd ever seen a grown man cry'?"

"Good Lord, Cassie, that's awful."

"Yes." She blinked away the last of the tears and drew herself up. Now that she had told him, she felt foolish and exposed. She gave a nervous little laugh and shrugged. "Now why am I sitting here telling you horror stories from my past? That isn't exactly the sort of thing I usually spill out right after saying 'how do you do?' But then, I guess you asked for it, so you have only yourself to blame."

He let go of her hand and sat back, studying her as though looking for some sudden revelation. "Yes, I did ask for it. And I'm glad you told me, so why are you so embarrassed about it?''

Cassie shifted in her seat. "What makes you think I'm embarrassed?''

He started to answer, then looked over her shoulder. "Here comes Jake.''

Cassie quickly dabbed the last of the wetness from her eyes and sat up straight, trying to arrange her face into pleasant, casual lines. How could she possibly explain to her grandfather that, although she didn't trust Eric's business deals, she had just entrusted him with a part of her past that she seldom told anyone? Especially since she couldn't answer that question herself.

"Hello, you two. Hope I wasn't too long. Are you both starving?'' Jake's smile, too, looked rather forced. He slid in beside Cassie, putting a half-finished martini in front of him.

Eric said, "You look a little tense around the edges. Talk didn't go too well.''

Jake made a sound of disgust. "Can you believe that jackass Folger is trying to push a bill through the state legislature to cut across the top of the Santa Lucia Mountains for a new, larger highway? The idiot's reasoning is that some people are denied access to Big Sur because they can't drive Highway 1.''

"How could they possibly pull that off? They'd have to go through the Los Padres National Forest.''

"Yeah, well, he's been told it can't be done and isn't buying it. He claims the government has allowed easements through national forests in the past when it's for a good enough reason.'' He swallowed the rest of his drink. "Damn jackass.''

"Don't get riled, Jake. I can't imagine his getting far with that one. It's been tried and shot down before. I think we have more to worry about with the fishermen.''

"Yeah? That's been shot down before, too.''

"True, but each time has been a struggle.''

Cassie interrupted. "Can I be let in on all this trauma?"

Jake smiled and patted her hand. "Sorry, honey. I get so hot under the collar that common manners fly right out of my head." He signaled to Shelley for another drink. She nodded, and Jake asked, "Eric? Another?"

"No thanks."

"Cassie?"

"Yes, please."

Having transmitted the order with a gesture, Jake returned to the subject. "First, there's this idea for a wider highway, led by that whiffle-brained senator, and second, a bunch of fishermen who are ballyhooing about seals eating too many salmon want the right to radically thin the herds. We went through that same problem years ago, and the scientists proved that seals eat relatively few salmon. The real problem was the area being overfished. But human beings are stubborn creatures. Once they get an idea stuck in their heads, it sits there and simmers."

Shelley put down the drinks. "Okay. Anyone ready to order?"

All three of them took a quick look at the menu and ordered their meals. As soon as Shelley left, Cassie asked, "Why would they want to build a whole new highway? I should think it would be much easier to widen Highway 1."

Eric shook his head. "Most of the so-called progress people have given up on that one. Back in the early sixties it was removed from the state freeway system and made a scenic highway. That's tough to change."

"It's so beautiful here. Why don't people just leave it alone?"

Jake frowned. "People get restless, Cass, itchy. Don't seem content to leave anything alone, even something that's perfect as is. I'm sure there've been a lot of artists over the years who figured they could improve on the ceiling of the Sistine Chapel if someone would just let them up there with a paintbrush."

Cassie turned to Eric. "Are you as embroiled in all this conservation business as Jake is?"

"There aren't many as active as Jake, but I try to do my share. When you live in a place like Big Sur, fighting off the movers and shakers comes with the territory. Besides, I've studied ecology. Every time people mess around with the balance of nature, it starts a whole ripple of side effects, none of which ever turn out good."

Jake glanced toward the entrance, and a big smile broke out on his face. "Well, look who's here."

Cassie followed his gaze, while Eric turned around to look, then stood up as a tall woman, dressed in a long, heavily beaded Indian dress, came their way. She was the most exotic creature Cassie had ever seen. Her hair was red with one silver streak running from her left temple all the way back to intertwine with the long braid that hung over her shoulder. Although the dress was loose, her body was clearly full-bosomed but slender, and she moved with cat-like grace. Intricately crafted silver earrings dangled from her ears to almost meet her shoulders. She just missed being beautiful by the sharpness of her features.

"Margo." Eric took hold of her shoulders and kissed her—a simple kiss of greeting that nonetheless caused a tug of envy in Cassie. After Jake had greeted her in like manner, she slid into the booth with Eric beside her. Eric made the introduction. "Margo, this is Cassandra, Jake's granddaughter."

"Really?" Margo smiled, displaying brilliantly white teeth. Her eyes, lighted with interest, were a startling yellow green. Cat eyes. "So, I finally meet you, Cassandra. It is a great pleasure." Her hand, lean and smooth, with long nails painted a deep rose color, was held out, and Cassie, momentarily overwhelmed by the woman's impact, quickly recovered and shook it.

"Margo," she said. "What a lovely name."

"It is, isn't it? That's why I chose it."

Cassie blinked. "*You* chose it?"

This time the smile was accompanied by a deep-throated laugh. "Yes. My parents named me Alice. It never felt right."

Cassie had to smile. "I can see why." She was trying to guess Margo's age, with no success. She had to be in her late thirties at least, but she could be older. She had the kind of features that seemed to reach a certain age and stick and the kind of looks that made age inconsequential. "Do you live in Big Sur?" After noting the way Eric was looking at the other woman, Cassie found herself hoping Margo would say no.

"Yes. It's a magical place, full of incredible vibrations. I came here for a visit five years ago. Within a month I had purchased land and put an architect to work on my house."

"Five years?" She turned to Jake. "How come I haven't met her before?"

He shrugged. "Just didn't happen, I guess." His gaze, like Eric's, was glued to Margo's fascinating face. "So, my dear, are you still foreseeing gloom and catastrophe? You were beginning to remind me of my sister, Bertha."

Cassie looked at him in disbelief. "Good grief. I can't imagine anyone looking less like Aunt Bertha!"

Jake laughed. "You're right about that. I'm not talking about looks, only about predictions." Finally his eyes turned to Cassie. "Margo dabbles in astrology and psychic phenomena. As well as a few other 'disciplines.' Her spirits have been whispering portents of doom in her ear."

Cassie glanced over at Margo, wondering if the teasing tone had offended her. Some people, she knew, took these things very seriously. But Margo's sparkle hadn't dimmed a bit.

"Your grandfather is a skeptic, Cassandra. He laughs at my revelations, silly man that he is. But I tell him anyway, so he'll be forewarned in spite of himself."

Cassie felt a chill of apprehension. "Forewarned? Do you think something bad is going to happen to him?"

"No, no. Not to him especially. But there are very disturbing fluctuations in the whole atmosphere. Whatever it is, we are all involved."

Eric, who had been watching her with an expression of affectionate amusement, signaled to Shelley as she passed by. "Before we hear any of tonight's premonitions, how about a drink? And we've already placed our orders. Maybe you should tell Shelley what you want."

The spectacular cat eyes swung sideways to meet his. "Eric, Shelley cannot give me what I want."

One corner of his mouth turned up. "No, I don't suppose she can."

Cassie, who had watched this exchange with growing dismay, tore her eyes away and looked down at her fingers, tightly clasped in her lap. Good grief! She had almost—no, she *had* forgotten about her engagement! Here she sat, turning green with jealousy because Margo was flirting with a man Cassie had only just met and who couldn't possibly have any major impact on her life. Maybe Margo was right. If there were disturbing fluctuations in the air, it might explain her own extraordinary reactions. She unclasped her hands and with deliberation put the left one on the table, where the stone instantly caught and reflected the glint of candlelight.

Eric's attention was caught by the glimmer. He looked at the ring for a moment, then raised his eyes to meet hers. "You're engaged." It wasn't a question, just a flat acknowledgment that gave her no satisfaction.

"Yes."

He nodded, as though confirming the fact. She could find no hint of reaction on his face. Had she hoped for one? Yes. Disappointment.

Jake shifted in his seat. "Cass is going to marry a Boston lawyer." He made it sound like a jail sentence. "Ah, here's our Shelley. What would you like, Margo?"

Margo ordered a gimlet and a steak, rare, then reached over to take Cassie's hand in her own. "What a lovely diamond. So, you are to marry. That's a very important decision."

"Are you married?" Cassie, to her own disgust, couldn't keep the hopeful tone out of her voice.

"No. I have never married. I prefer to keep myself open to all possibilities. A husband might interfere with the flow."

The flow of what? The question had barely popped into Cassie's head before Jake asked, "The flow! The flow of what?"

Margo turned up both palms, suspending them in the air. "Messages. Insights. The soft voice of Karma, perhaps."

He shook his head. "Margo, much as I like you, there are times when I wonder about your tentative hold on reality."

She threw back her head and laughed. "Reality, pooh! Reality itself is tentative."

Shelley appeared at their table with Margo's drink and their food. As they ate, the conversation turned to more mundane matters, such as Margo's loss of her housekeeper, requiring her to search for another, and the progress of some renovations Eric was making on his house. But at some point the subject shifted to investments, and Cassie learned that Margo, too, was putting money in the platinum mine project. Her mind grabbed hold of the information, turning it over and over. How could Eric, in good conscience, pull his friends into such an uncertain venture? But then he was a man who thrived on risk, on trying to beat the odds. She studied his face, its fascinating planes highlighted by the flickering candlelight. He had no regard for stability and only derision for security. She narrowed her eyes, picturing him as a riverboat gambler, dark, mysterious, charming. But instead of lowering his appeal, the image made him all the more enticing.

Eric, having finished his after-dinner coffee, leaned back and stretched. "How about it, Jake...Cassie, are you ready to head home? I have a nine o'clock meeting in San Francisco in the morning, which means I must be up and out very early.''

Margo's face fell. "How dreary of you, Eric! Eloise and Chad are coming by shortly. I'd hoped you'd stay.''

"Can't do it, lady. I need my rest.''

Jake glanced at his watch. "It's only nine-thirty. I'd just as soon hang around for a while. Cassie, how are you doing?''

She stifled a yawn. "I'm afraid the time difference has caught up with me. But if you want to stay, I'm sure I can keep my eyes open a little longer.''

"I'll take you home if you'd like.''

Cassie stared in consternation at Eric. She wanted to go home and to bed. But some small inner voice warned her that being alone with Eric was not going to help one bit in banishing the totally unsuitable yearnings that persisted in creeping into her head. Her mouth opened and she formed the words *no, thank you* in her mind.

"Yes, please, that would be very nice." Cassie almost jumped with surprise. How could she think one thing and say another?

Jake looked uncertain. "Are you going straight to bed?''

"You bet. As fast as I can get there.''

"Okay, in that case I'll see you in the morning.''

"Yep. We'll have one of our gigantic waffle breakfasts and talk away the morning." She turned to Margo, who was standing beside Eric, waiting to say goodbye. "I'm glad to have met you.''

"So am I, Cassandra. It's about time. You must come to lunch. How about next Tuesday? I'll cast your runes.''

"My what?''

"Runes. They were used by the Vikings as an oracle, and we can use them the same way.''

Cassie started to ask further questions, but decided she was simply too tired to comprehend anything obtuse, so she settled for accepting the luncheon date and saying goodbye.

All too soon she and Eric were alone outside in the chill night air, making their way to the truck. As they passed the Dark Angel, Eric put his arm around her shoulders and drew her close, holding his hand up by her face like a one-sided blinder. "Just pretend he's not there."

"Are you making fun of me?" The warmth of his arm traveled through her shoulders and down her back. It felt wonderful.

"Of course not. Just teasing a little. If you can learn to laugh at something, it loses its fearfulness." When she raised her head to look at him, her lips were very close to his. He stopped, his arm tightening around her, his fingers brushing her temple and cheek. "You're very beautiful, Cassandra Chase." For one heart-stopping moment she thought he would kiss her. She wanted him to, very badly. But after that brief pause he dropped his arm and pulled away, his dark eyes hooded, his expression withdrawn. "We'd better get you home—"

She knew beyond doubt that he had started to say "and to bed," and had checked himself. Maybe that phrase brought the same thoughts to his mind as it did to hers.

In too short a time she was home, saying goodbye to Eric, opening the door and going into the empty house. She could still feel the warmth of his arm on her shoulders, the brush of his fingers on her face. Good Lord. This was the man she'd determined to fight, to sever his hold on her grandfather. And here she was, relishing the still-palpable memory of his touch! She must stop this nonsense.

She stood before the big window, watching the ripples of light on the quiet water. Finally she turned and headed for her room. "Go to bed, Cassie, and dream about your fiancé," she admonished herself, refusing to listen to the little voice in her head that responded "Fat chance."

Chapter Three

Eric sat at the desk in his wood-paneled home office, staring at the telephone. Did he really need to go to San Francisco today or could he postpone it? In some ways it made better sense to wait until next week, when he could take care of several additional matters. He pushed his chair back impatiently, got up and went to the glass door that led to the terrace. He opened it and stepped outside into bright morning sunshine that was turning the quiet Pacific into a giant reflective mirror.

He stretched, savoring the pull of back muscles cramped by three hours of bending over his paperwork. It was only nine, but he was an early riser, usually at work by six or seven in the morning. He walked across the wide swath of green lawn to the split-rail fence that ran along the face of the cliff. He'd bought the house—about two miles down the highway from Jake's—seven years ago from a woman whose husband had just died. She thought it was too lonely here by herself. Eric looked out over the ever-moving sea, wondering how anyone could be lonely in the company of so much beauty.

He stood there for some time, lost in thought. He felt strangely unsettled this morning, unsure of what he wanted to do. An extremely unusual state for him—and one that made him uncomfortable. He kept thinking of the previous night, of the feel of Cassandra Chase's body close to his, of the sight of her lovely upturned face, her lips so tempting. He'd wanted to kiss her. No, more than that. He'd wanted to make love to her. Slow down, he warned himself. She's Jake's granddaughter. Not the right target for a little un-complicated sex, or even for a passing affair, which was the only kind he wanted. And in truth, even without her family tie to his friend, he would have put her on his off-limits list. After all, she was engaged. And more than that, she'd been through enough hurt; he wouldn't want to chance inflicting more.

He walked the length of the fence, the tips of his fingers riding the top rail. Damn. He'd been too long without fe-male companionship. That was probably why the Chase girl had roused him to such a degree. It was a tough time to be single, especially in the San Francisco area. In years past, when he went into the city he might have called one of the women listed in his address book and taken her to dinner, and to bed. But now, well, any sane man knew enough to be careful. He dismissed entirely the tender, sentimental emo-tions Cassie had awakened in him, the urge to protect, to comfort. He wasn't a social worker. He'd seen plenty of what a woman could do to a man when he let down his guard.

The ring of the telephone took him back inside. "Hello?"

"So, you *are* still there."

"Hello, Jake. What's this, you're checking up on me?"

Jake chuckled. "More like checking up on my memory. I wasn't sure what time you said you were heading for the city, so I thought I'd take a chance on catching you. My lawyer called and needs to see me this morning. Thought I might ride in with you."

"To tell the truth, Jake, I canceled my nine o'clock meeting and was about to postpone the other. It's too nice a day to be stuck in air-tight offices. Why not put your lawyer on hold and we can go riding? Or maybe take a picnic out on the bluffs. That rain had us housebound so long I'm itching to be outdoors."

There was a pause. "That sounds damned tempting, Eric. But Mr. Gerard P. Huggins the third tells me this matter demands my immediate attention." Jake laughed. "These young hotshots! They're so sure the world will grind to a halt if anyone puts something off. Wait till he's lived as many years as I have. He'll know by then that the whole population of California could fall into space and the world wouldn't even hiccup. Say...if you're hanging around here, maybe you could take Cassie on a picnic. I feel bad about leaving her alone when she's just arrived." Again, there was a pause. "Or can I trust you with my beautiful granddaughter?"

"Well, I'll try to behave."

"Remember, the girl's engaged."

"To one of your favorite people, right?"

"Humph."

Eric laughed. "Put Cassie on the phone. I'll invite her for a nice friendly picnic—just two chums sharing a lunch."

"You're a bastard, Eric, you know that?"

He grinned. "I know. One of the many things we have in common."

"Okay, hold on."

Eric's fingers tightened around the receiver at Cassie's soft hello. Maybe this wasn't such a bright idea after all. "Good morning, Cassie. Jake tells me he's off to the city. I thought you might enjoy a picnic on the ocean bluffs. It's a good day for it, and I have to tell you, we've had very few good days lately."

"I thought you had to go to town, too."

"I canceled. Told Jake he should do the same and take advantage of the weather, but I guess his lawyer is a mighty stubborn cuss." Eric winced. He was trying so hard for a light tone that he sounded like someone talking over background music of "Home on the Range."

"I'd love to go on a picnic. Shall I pack the lunch?"

"Of course not. This is no 'bring your own' invitation. You just be ready at noon, and I'll do the rest." As soon as he'd hung up, he dialed the River Run.

"H'lo."

"Cal? This is Eric Wagner. Can I get you to pack a picnic lunch for two?"

"Sure. What're you doing, goofing off?"

"Just that."

"Sounds like a good idea. Find a pretty girl to do it with?"

"Sure did."

"'Attaway. I'll have the lunch ready in about a half hour. That do?"

"Perfect."

At noon, to the minute, Eric pulled in behind Cliffhanger and shut off the engine. Before he could get out of his Jeep, Cassie came out the back door and climbed into the passenger seat.

"Well, hello. That's what I call punctual."

She smiled at him. "Looks like we're both compulsive on-timers."

Eric turned the key in the ignition and the Jeep rattled to action. "I didn't think there was a woman in the world with that trait."

"Oh, come on. You sound cynical about women. We're not all that different from men."

"Oh?" The look he gave her was amused and fraught with innuendo. "You could fool me."

"I very much doubt that."

This time he really turned to look at her. "You know, Cassandra. I think we just might get along very well."

That, she thought, was what she was afraid of. "That remains to be seen, doesn't it?"

He grinned. "Going to be that kind of a day, is it?"

"Looks as though." Stop it, Cassie. You're flirting and he knows you're flirting. You're going to get yourself in trouble. She fervently wished that trouble didn't sound so appealing. "Where are we going?"

"There's a spot worn into the cliffs at the Julia Pfeiffer State Park that makes a good picnicking place. It should be nice and warm—in fact, downright hot the way this sun is shining."

"That's fine. I have my bathing suit on underneath."

He drove up the driveway and onto the highway, keeping his eyes on the road not only for navigational safety but to short-circuit the urges that crept into his mind when he looked at her. She was even lovelier this morning, rested and glowing. Her honey-colored hair hung in thick waves over her shoulders, and her startling blue eyes were clear and shining. She wore a loose-fitting terry-cloth dress of bright yellow that zipped up the front. And it covered a swimsuit. A bikini, perhaps? He clamped his teeth together. This might be a very long day.

When they had parked the Jeep, Eric took the picnic basket kindly supplied by Cal and threw his towel over his shoulder. Cassie brought her canvas bag, with a yellow-and-green striped towel poking out the top. They headed for the trail that would take them to the beach. Before long they were on the bluff over the spot Eric had picked, and he led the way down the side, careful to avoid the grassy patches that were still slippery from the long rains. "Watch your step. Do you need any help?"

"No. I've been climbing over rocks as long as I can remember."

He glanced over his shoulder and smiled. "Yes. I suppose you have. You're probably a lot more expert at it than I am." It didn't take them long to wend their way to the shelf of stone that would serve as their seat and table.

"Oh, Eric, this is beautiful!" Cassie set down her carryall and devoted herself to full-scale appreciation. They were standing at the mouth of a shallow cave that had a large flat ledge as its doorstep. The ocean, about a hundred feet below, sent billowing waves crashing over sharp-toothed rocks, skipping up the piled stones of the cliff and shooting great sheets of foam into the air. To their right was a ravine where the waves completed their roll and spent themselves as gentle ripples on the sand of the cove.

"Pretty spectacular spot, isn't it?" He set down the basket and came to stand beside her. The sun caught their forms and duplicated them in dark shadow on the ledge. "I come here quite often to watch the sunset."

"Isn't it kind of scary, finding your way up that path after dark?"

"Not really. I take it slow, and I know it very well."

She tilted her face up to him, shielding her eyes with her hand. "May I come with you sometime? It sounds like a heavenly experience."

Eric watched the wind lift Cassie's golden hair and toss it around her head, watched the way the sun danced through its flaxen strands, creating little bursts of light. He thought of being here with her, alone and isolated as the sun fell into the sea and left the night lighted only by the rising moon. "Now that does sound dangerous."

Her eyes squinted in puzzlement. "Why? Because you'd have to help me back up the trail?"

"No. Once we got on the trail, the danger would be past."

He saw the comprehension in her eyes and ran a finger down the silky flesh on her cheek. "Your grandfather says I'm to behave myself with you, which would be decidedly difficult in that circumstance."

She dropped her gaze then raised it again to look directly into his eyes. "I'm extremely independent, as I have a right to be. My grandfather shouldn't try to regulate my life." An impish smile played around her lips.

His hand slid around to cup the back of her neck. "Cassandra, you shouldn't shoot sparks around explosives."

"Dangerous?"

"Very."

Cassie stood, transfixed by the black stare that bore holes through her self-control. Never in all her memory could she recall wanting to be kissed as much as she wanted it now. His hand tightened on her neck, and she relaxed her body, willing him to pull her close, to cover her mouth with his. Time stood still for long seconds, time tense with inner battles. Then he dropped his hand and turned away.

"How about some lunch?"

She swallowed the huge dose of disappointment. "Okay. I *am* hungry." His eyes met hers and one brow raised. Oh dear. It was going to be that kind of day. Even without intending to, she blurted out suggestive remarks. She took a quick glance at her engagement ring, just to remind herself.

The sun was beating down on the rocks, making it very warm despite the cool breeze. As Eric corkscrewed open a bottle of wine, she unzipped her terry-cloth cover and stepped out of it, folding it neatly and placing it next to her bag. When she stood up she saw Eric's eyes run over her body, much of which was exposed by her yellow bikini. She could tell by the expression on his face that he liked what he saw. Now why, Cassandra, she asked herself, did you choose this, your skimpiest suit, to wear today? The answer to that was both unacceptable and, as he had warned, dangerous.

She pulled her beach towel out of the bag, spread it on the rock and sat down. "This was a great idea, Eric, whoever came up with it."

"What does that mean?"

"I suspect Jake talked you into baby-sitting me while he was gone. He was obviously on a guilt trip for leaving me alone the day after I arrived."

Eric set down the opened bottle and dug two plastic wine glasses out of the hamper. "Baby-sit you?" He sat beside her on the towel and poured the dark red wine. "Honey, in case no one has mentioned it, you're not a baby anymore." He handed her one of the filled glasses. "Madam, a little Robert Mondavi Cabernet Sauvignon Reserve?"

She took the glass, raising her eyebrows. "I'm impressed. How do I rate this special vintage?"

The sunshine accented the contrast of his white smile against the deep bronze of his skin and the black halo of wind-rumpled hair. "Any granddaughter of Jake's—" He hesitated.

"Is a granddaughter of yours?"

The smile broadened and the dark eyes gleamed. "Not exactly. I was searching for a synonym for friend. None of them seemed to fit."

"I'm so glad. Friendship between a man and a woman always seems so...dead-ended." My God, what was she doing? Eric Wagner was obviously a man who couldn't be pushed too far. Was she trying for the breaking point? And if so, why? An emotional investment with him was bound to be far more risky than one involving, as he put it, "only money," and she had never been a risk taker. Was there something about him that brought out the urge to take a flier, of one sort or another, in everyone?

Eric stood up and pulled his sweatshirt over his head, tossing it back by her bag. His wide shoulders had not been a trick of padding. His torso was beautiful, the perfect V-shape every men's workout program promised and seldom delivered. Muscles rippled under taut, deeply tanned skin as he leaned over to take off his sweatpants. The lower disclosure did nothing to slow her rising heart rate. His legs—long, lean, sinewy—were connected to that spectacular torso by a set of compact hips and, as a friend of hers put it, tight buns. No wonder she reacted to him in such an unfamiliar way. She'd never seen anyone like him.

She started to take a much-needed sip of her wine, but Eric reached down and stopped her. "Wait a minute. We have to have a toast." He settled back beside her and picked up his glass.

"All right. What'll we drink to?"

Eric searched his mind for something safe. A toast had been his idea, and a pretty dumb one, at that. Both of them were skirting too close to the flame, tempting an attraction that was clearly mutual and incredibly potent. Hell, why did Jake's granddaughter have to come in such an enticing package? And why did she have to display so much of it? Hadn't she ever heard what happens when you wave a red flag in front of a bull? "How about, 'to nature, at its best'?"

"Perfect." They touched the rims of the wine-filled glasses, and drank. "Umm. Delicious." The full-bodied cabernet slid over her tongue, filling her mouth with its rich flavor. If they drank the whole bottle out here in the hot sun, they might not make it up the trail. With that thought in mind, she emptied her glass and held it out for a refill.

Eric, surprised, reached behind him for the bottle. "Hey, aren't you moving a little fast?"

"I certainly am." Cassandra, you fool, get some food in your stomach, she chastised herself. "Maybe I'd better eat something."

"Good idea." He pulled the hamper to his side and rummaged around, pulling out some sandwiches, two Delicious apples and a bag of potato chips.

"Now there," Cassie said a little giddily. "I worried for nothing. When you said you'd make the lunch I wasn't at all sure we'd eat."

He gave her a censuring frown. "Female chauvinist. Men are not all that different from women."

Cassie laughed aloud. "I'll just say ditto to your earlier retort."

Eric's smile reasserted itself, and the frown disappeared. "I cannot tell a lie—at least when it won't accomplish anything. I didn't pack the lunch. Cal Grant at River Inn did." He looked over the food. "He's good-natured and reliable, but not terribly imaginative."

"That's just fine. My favorite lunchtime food is a big, hearty sandwich." She removed the carefully folded wax paper. "Oh boy. Turkey. Looks like the real thing, too. Not that compressed stuff."

They ate their lunch silently, watching the gulls dipping and gliding as they rode the wind streams and the waves smashing against the rocks, shooting foam sprays higher and higher, as though engaged in a contest. They felt the heat of the midday sun burning into them, giving off the pleasing odor of sun-warmed flesh, as they devoured the tasty sandwiches and sipped the red wine, both easing into a state of relaxed contentment.

"Watch this." Eric pulled off a piece of his bread and tossed it into the air. With quick grace a seagull swooped down and caught it in midair.

Cassie clapped her hands. "Oh, that's wonderful!" She looked at the tiny remains of her sandwich. "Nuts. Now I have to decide whether to eat this myself, which I'd like to do, or feed it to the gulls, which I'd also like to do."

"No decision necessary. Look here." Eric reached into the hamper and brought out two plastic bags. "Extra bread and cheddar cheese. They go crazy over cheese."

They finished their lunches, then launched into a contest to see which of them could entice a seagull into the most spectacular dive. "Hey, look at that!" Cassie giggled in delight. "A double half-gainer. I think that's a winner."

"Yeah? Watch this." Eric, by balancing pieces of cheese on his hand, managed to toss four at once high into the air. "All right!" he called as morsels were caught in synchronized flight by four circling gulls. "Now that," Eric gloated, "definitely wins first prize."

Cassie looked all around her and in the hamper. "Damn, it's all gone. I can't try to top it, I guess I have to concede." She waved a hand. "So what do we do with all our expectant guests?"

Eric surveyed the scene. They were surrounded. Sea gulls stood on the adjoining rocks, hovered in the air above, swooped in from the ocean to see what was going on. "This calls for drastic measures." He stood up and let out a roar, accompanied by a great waving of arms and fluttering of hands. The startled gulls, shrieking their displeasure, flapped into the air and, after a few more Eric-histrionics, flew away.

Cassie, collapsed in laughter, lay on her back, holding her stomach. "Oh!" She rolled back and forth, gasping for air. "You looked like a giant bird trying for lift-off." Her eyes were so filled with tears of mirth that she couldn't read Eric's expression as he turned to stand over her, his shadow all but covering her.

"Funny, huh?" His voice was low with mock menace. "Find me laughable, do you?" He straddled her legs and got to his knees, bending over her and placing his hands on either side of her head. "I did not come here to be made sport of."

Cassie's body, still quivering with merriment, began a slow agitation of a far different sort. Eric leaned over her, his knees scalding her thighs, his wide chest heaving from the exertion of bird routing, his black eyes burning into hers, hotter than the sun. Her laughter died, cut off by impulses that subdued mirth. She stared up at him, begging her mind to cough up some silly banality to sustain the aura of foolishness, but her mind was subjugated by the dark gaze that pinned her. "Eric." His name came out in a strained whisper.

His lips opened, and incredibly, his eyes darkened. But still he hovered, the giant bird, waiting to swoop and claim his prize. The agitation inside her became a pulsating plea. Come to me. Come to me. She had to stop this. She couldn't. She'd gone mad. Nothing sensible remained, only this overwhelming desire.

Slowly his body lowered. She relished the feel of flesh on flesh as their legs touched. Then his hips met hers, bone to bone, need on need. He was suspended above her by his elbows, his lips moistened, slightly open, his forehead furrowed by resolutions that, outflanked, were fast beating a retreat. He trailed a finger across her lips. "You're supposed to be off-limits."

"I think I just stepped over the line."

He sighed as she slid her hands around his neck, tangling her fingers in his hair. "Unfair."

When he finally kissed her she thought she might burst with relief. His lips, first soft and questioning, hardened, took command of hers. Their mouths, greedy with a new hunger, moved together, opened in invitation. Cassie shuddered with pleasure as his tongue entered, thrust deep, then circled and tantalized. Every part of her yearned against him, her body responding to the pressure of his.

Suddenly Eric stopped. He lifted his head, closed his eyes for a moment to cement resolve, then pulled away from her and sat up, his head in his hands. "Lord, Cassie."

Cassie's body, so abruptly abandoned, shivered in protest. She couldn't believe the strength of desire that held her captive, couldn't believe she'd been willing—no, eager—to give in to it completely. Slowly desire was replaced with a tide of mortification that rose to engulf her. She rolled to one side and managed to get to a sitting position. "You must think I'm terrible."

"You! Why should you take all the blame? It isn't just one of us." He turned to her and took her shoulders in his hands. "Hey, don't look so guilty. We obviously have a pretty strong attraction going here. A *mutual* attraction."

"I'm not supposed to. I'm engaged."

His lips twitched. "You don't act like an engaged lady." At her grimace of embarrassment, he touched the side of her mouth with his finger and tried to push it up. "Come on, give us a smile."

Cassie slapped his hand away. "Stop it."

"All right, if you'll quit acting like something awful just happened. You're hurting my feelings. I thought it was darned nice." Eric kept his tone light, coated with humor. It wouldn't do any good to betray how badly he'd been shaken by that kiss. It had been all he could do to stop. He was still trying not to be sorry he had. He wondered how long it would be before he could forget the feel of her body beneath his. And what it would take to avoid fantasizing about being even closer. "Here. We haven't had dessert yet." *You can say that again, buster.* "There are two U-no bars in the hamper. Ever eaten a U-no bar?"

Cassie, her dignity somewhat restored, nodded. "They're sinful."

He smiled, his expression once again teasing as he handed her the foil-wrapped candy bar. "But permissible."

"Funny. Very funny." Cassie's sense of humor, having completely deserted her, slowly crept back. "Tell me, is this all a ploy to get me to invest in your platinum mine?"

"Yes." He nodded as he peeled back the wrapper. "That's exactly what it is. Do you have enough loot to make my sacrifice worthwhile?" He winced as she punched his arm. "Peace! Just kidding!" They were both laughing now, disarming the tension.

"Umm. This is yummy." Cassie concentrated on the delicious chocolate-mousse candy, letting her breath ease back to normal and her heart stop leaping about. Had she ever, ever gone completely out of control like that? No, she hadn't. And what did that say about her relationship with Brian? She frowned. That it wasn't impetuous and driven only by lust—that's what it said. Relationships built on the flimsy lure of sexual attraction were the ones that soon fell apart. She and Brian were well-matched, careful people who would construct a sturdy marriage, year after year. He was very good-looking and immensely appealing. She knew at least two of her women friends who would kill to get their hands on him. Her eyes strayed to Eric's profile. It was just that there was something almost . . . primeval about Eric's allure. He was the epitome of the "hunk." The ever-elusive Prince Charming, combined with a touch of Tarzan—the kind of man women fashioned fairy-tale dreams around.

The kind of man that was so often all surface charm. She wanted to dismiss him as that, but . . .

His eyes slid to the side, catching her watching him. "Why are you looking at me like that?"

"I was just wondering why I like you."

"That's easy. I'm a very likable guy."

"I came out here fully prepared to dislike you intensely. And I have to be honest, I'm still very much against Jake's getting mixed up in a business deal with you."

"Why don't we drop that subject? It could muck up a nice day."

Cassie started to say she wasn't ready to drop it, but he was getting that guarded expression on his face. Shutting down? Tuning out? Whatever it was, it signaled loud and clear the end of two-way discussion. "How do you do that?"

"Do what?"

"Your face goes blank, like you've taken out an eraser and rubbed off all expression. It's very intimidating."

He crumpled his candy-bar wrapper and threw it in the hamper. "Comes with the genes, I suppose. The look goes on just before the war paint."

"What does that mean?"

He turned his head toward her. Now he seemed downright guarded, on edge. "It means I'm half Indian. American Indian. You know, wigwams and war parties—all part of my heritage. Only now I have a different method of scalping people. Money instead of hair."

A shiver ran down her spine. His eyes were hooded, his demeanor cold and withdrawn. How had he changed so suddenly? And why? She tried for a light note. "I can almost hear the tom-toms."

"Can you." A flat tone. Devoid of humor.

"Eric? What's the matter, did I say something to make you mad?"

"I'm not mad."

"You look mad." Sort of savage? She shivered again. His gaze dropped, and when he lifted it, his face had relaxed and he had a sardonic smile on his lips. She blinked. These sudden changes were unnerving. "I wish you'd stay put."

"Do what?"

"Stay put." She waved a hand in a gesture of befuddlement. "I don't know, you seem to slip in and out of moods."

He leaned over and kissed her lightly on the lips. "It's called frustration. Hand me that wrapper and the glass. We should clean up and head back."

Cassie didn't want to head back. She wanted quite desperately to stay, to try to recapture the happy mood they'd had earlier. She frowned. Be honest, Cassie, she chided herself. You want to be back in his arms. With a sigh she gave him the wrapper and glass then stood to fold the towel. He was right. It was past time to head back. Back to Cliffhanger and back to sanity.

"And put on that cover thing."

She glanced at him over her shoulder. His back was turned and he was picking up the last of the lunch leftovers. So, she wasn't the only one having trouble with errant emotions. But she *was* the only one who was engaged to someone else, so that put extra responsibility on her to control them. She followed orders, stepping into the yellow wrap and zipping up the front, all the while watching Eric get into his sweat suit. Covering up that body would make it easier for her blood pressure to settle down—so they were even in that respect, at least.

As they climbed up the steep path, Cassie said, "I guess you're not going to invite me here to watch the sunset."

Eric, who was leading the way, stopped and turned around. "For a girl who likes safety and security you're sure pushing your luck."

"Sorry." He was right, she was still skidding around on thin ice, and it *was* completely out of character. She clamped her mouth shut and followed mutely. The trail led them to a higher plane, where the view stretched out in three dimensional splendor. "Could we stop a minute? I'd like to just sit and look, it's so lovely. It seems like ages since I was here last."

Eric spread out his towel and they sat down. "How long ago was it?"

"Well, let's see. I left Big Sur a year ago September. So it is ages."

"It's hard to imagine how you could leave this to go back to a cold, cramped city."

"I like Boston." She picked a long blade of grass and chewed on it. "It's a good environment for me. There are lots of museums and theaters, plenty of opportunity for intellectual pursuit."

"Sounds dandy."

She gave him a censuring look. "Just because you don't care about the finer things!"

He swept his hand at the scenery. "These are the finer things. Besides, you're wrong. I enjoy art and music and theater, but I can get all that in San Francisco and still be very close to this."

"Do you go to the city often?"

"Yes. Have to. That's where my office and secretary are. Also my lawyer and accountant. And, of course, my townhouse."

She turned to stare at him. "You have an office and a town house in San Francisco? And all this time you've been playing the rugged individualist from the country."

Eric raised his eyebrows. "I haven't been playing anything. You've obviously come up with your own assumptions."

Cassie turned her head to gaze out over the rippling ocean and to give herself time to regroup. Getting to know Eric was like walking through a maze, each turn leading to another puzzle. She wasn't sure she should try to know the whole man, even if that was possible. What if each disclosure intensified his attractiveness? "Maybe I have, at that. Does your ex-wife live in San Francisco?"

"How did you know I had an ex-wife?"

"Jake told me."

"I see." One side of his mouth turned up, but she wasn't sure it was part of a smile. "No, she doesn't." He volunteered no further information.

She shook her head. "I'm sorry. I don't mean to pry." She hesitated then smiled sheepishly. "That's not really true. I do. I mean, I like to know all about people. I'm afraid I get downright nosy sometimes."

He leaned back to rest on his elbows. "Do you want to know all about me?"

"Yes. But I have a feeling it wouldn't be easy."

"Oh, I don't know. There aren't many secrets. I'm thirty-three, six-foot-two, weigh one hundred and seventy-five pounds."

"All muscle."

He laughed. "Gets a little soft between the ears now and then."

"Did you go to college?"

"Yes. But I didn't finish."

"Why?"

"Because by about the middle of my junior year I'd learned I could make as much money as I'd ever need just doing my thing. So I finished the semester and left."

"Where were you brought up?"

He lay flat, his eyes closed. Cassie had to lie down on her side, her head propped in her hand, to hear him. "As much 'bringing up' as I got was done in Los Angeles."

"What part of Los Angeles?"

"A part I doubt you've ever seen. It was what is commonly referred to as a ghetto."

"You don't seem to have come out any worse for it."

He turned on his side to face her, his eyes sheltered behind half-closed lids. "Now you're making assumptions again. It isn't always wise."

"You're a risk taker. That requires a lot of self-confidence."

"Okay. I have that."

"And if you're self-confident, you're probably well adjusted."

"I'm tough. There's a difference. At least that's what I learned in Psych 1."

Cassie sat up, rubbing her elbow. "Ouch. I must be getting too old for elbow leaning."

He laughed and sat up beside her. "I'd guess there were at least a few years between you and medicare."

Eric really was very likable. At least this side of Eric. She wondered if there was another, harder side. "You don't seem so tough to me."

"I've had no reason to be tough with you. Just iron-willed."

She smiled. "There's a difference?"

"You bet." He stood up and held out his hand. "Come on, enough of twenty questions."

She took his hand and let herself be pulled to her feet. "But I haven't learned nearly enough about you."

"Enough for what? Are you collecting odd characters for a novel or something?"

"No." She picked up her canvas bag and fell into step beside him. "But you're one of Jake's favorite people."

"And you can't imagine why?"

She shook her head. "That's not it at all. I'd just like to know you better, that's all."

He gave her a sideways glance. "I'd like to know you better, too. I thought we settled that point a little earlier."

She could feel the blood creeping into her cheeks. "I didn't mean that kind of knowing."

Eric was silent for a moment, deciding whether to put an end to the questioning. He was generally stingy with information about his past, probably because it evoked memories that were far from pleasant. This was the first time within recollection that he'd actually wanted to talk about

his life. There was something about the ingenuous open-
ness of Cassie's curiosity that discouraged secrecy. Maybe
it was just as well to give her a glimpse of his background.
It was bound to be as distasteful to her as it was to him.

"Okay, what have I left out?"

"You say you're tough. Did you get that way from growing up in a ghetto?"

"Yes, among other things."

"Good grief. Talk about getting blood out of a stone."

"I didn't know that was what you were after. Was one of
your ancestors from Transylvania?"

She stopped and turned to him, frowning. "Now come
on. If you want me to buzz off, just say so."

He started to say "so," but didn't. For some unfathom-
able reason, he didn't want to stop the conversation with
quips. In fact, he didn't really want to stop it at all. "All
right. Full disclosure. The life and times of Eric Wagner."
Sometimes it was hard to associate with that lonely little kid
he'd once been. "Everyone likes to look down on someone, to have a handy 'goat.' My neighborhood was full of
the ethnic groups that are usually used for that purpose, and
because I was the only kid around who was part Indian, I
served as a natural 'looking down' target for all the other
kids. I got it all—the crummy jokes about keeping my wig
wam, the suggestions that I'd be more at home in a loin-
cloth and so forth. One of the favorites was trapping me on
the playground and forming a war-dance circle around me
and pushing me from one kid to the next."

Cassie saw the remembered anger on his face and wondered if she'd opened something that should have remained
closed. "Eric, I—"

He held up a hand. "You wanted to hear it, so hear it.
Then next time it'll be my turn to ask questions." She nodded, subdued not only by his admonition but by her own
curiosity. "I decided I didn't like to be pushed around, so I
talked a man in our building, who happened to train fighters, into letting me come to the gym and run errands for him

in exchange for lessons in self-defense. Well, that move turned into a winning parlay. I learned a lot of things in the next few years, not the least of which was how to beat the crap out of any kid in the school—or any group of kids, if it wasn't too big. On top of that I found out that I had a natural knack for making money. I soon turned errand running into a money-making proposition, then expanded into neighborhood Handy Andy, then on to organizing services—hiring other kids to work for Handy Andy, then on to organizing services—hiring other kids to work for people outside the ghetto and taking mine off the top."

Cassie was fascinated. "How old were you by that time?"

He shrugged. "Eleven, twelve. By the time I was thirteen I went into my first real estate venture. There was a lot for sale next to some people on my lawn-care list. It had been up for sale forever, because it had a deep gully running right through it, and no one thought it was buildable. But I saw what was happening to property values, even in marginal neighborhoods, so I offered the owner a thousand dollars for it, and he took it."

"Where did you get a thousand dollars?"

"Savings. I worked all the time so I didn't have time to spend it. Besides, there wasn't much of anything I wanted."

Cassie wanted to ask if he'd contributed anything to help his parents, but decided she'd better not stop the flow or it might never start again.

"Well, to get to the end of this long-winded story, I held it for a year and sold it at a profit of three thousand dollars. And I was on my way."

"An entrepreneur at the age of fourteen! I'm impressed. So you learned how to be tough and how to make money at the same time."

"More than that. I found out that money gets you a kind of power far and away greater than physical force."

She raised her eyebrows in a small salute to his enterprise. "As they say in certain ads, you've come a long way, baby."

"A long way—and not so far."

"What does that mean?"

"I still don't like to be pushed around." With that he took off down the path, and Cassie hurried to catch up with him.

Chapter Four

The trail they were walking gradually wound down to a stretch of flat beach where the sand was fine and crystal-clean. A steady stream of water from Pfeiffer Creek, which fed out of Sycamore Canyon, ran a straight course across the beach to join the ocean. Beside the flow stood what appeared to be an orderly queue of sea gulls.

Cassie and Eric stopped, both intrigued by the lineup. "What are they doing?" Cassie asked. "They certainly weren't that mannerly while we were feeding them." She cupped her hand over her eyes to try for a better look. "Oh my God, I don't believe it!"

Eric laughed aloud. "Hot damn! They're riding the current."

And so they were. One after another, the birds stepped into the stream and rode it all the way down to the ocean, where they stood up and walked back to the end of the line. Now and again a gull attempted to butt in toward the front but was scolded and pecked to the back.

Cassie and Eric slowly and quietly made their way to a rock a short distance from the gulls' water ride and settled down to watch the unique spectacle. One of the sea gulls, his wings tucked tight to his sides, stepped into the mouth of the small river but barely got started before getting stuck on a miniature sandbar. With a loud squawk of indignation he lifted into the air, flew back to the starting place and plunked into the stream ahead of the others.

Cassie giggled with glee. "Good for him. He waited his turn, by gum, and there's no way he's about to be short-changed. Oh, Eric, look at that! Two of them together. Are they holding wings?"

"Good Lord. Now she wants romance in gull-land."

"Well, why not? There has to be some preamble to the making of little sea gulls."

"Those birds are far more in need of birth-control pills than increased propagation, believe me."

"Oh, what a cynic. That looks like such fun. Do you think they'd let us play?"

Eric grinned. "I'm afraid even that nice little behind of yours would get bogged down in the sand. That water chute is definitely not people-size."

They sat for a good half hour, both well aware that this was a sight they might never happen on again. When they did stand up to leave, Cassie had a moment of overwhelming sadness at the probability that the day had held other experiences that would, in all likelihood, not be repeated. She kept glancing at Eric as they walked back to the Jeep, mystified and troubled by the irrepressible urges to which she had surrendered. *Be honest, Cassie, you more than surrendered.* She had encouraged, in fact initiated what happened. If Eric hadn't stopped... She wondered how she would feel at this moment if they had made love. Would she be consumed by remorse and guilt? To her distress she couldn't form an answer because she honestly didn't know.

She looked around at the towering hills, the massive expanse of water and the crags and crevices of rock worn to distinctive patterns by the endless pounding of the sea. Today had dramatically highlighted a truth she'd been aware of for years. Big Sur changed her. Something inside seemed to give way, turn loose, when she came here. There was a sprite in her that struggled free the moment she reached her ledge seat, where she had for so many years sat and awaited the transition. She shivered at the memory of her latest experience there, then stopped, startled by a fact that hadn't before registered. That special place had brought something new this time. It had brought Eric. And she didn't know whether to say thank you or up yours!

Eric, who had kept walking, turned and called, "Anything wrong?"

She shook her head. "No. Just resting for a minute." She hurried to catch up, giving him a wan smile of assurance.

Was she all right? She wasn't at all sure. She lost her boundaries here. In previous visits she had discovered new levels of excitement and interest and daring. Today she'd found a new, undreamed-of level of passion. But the discovery frightened her even more than its predecessors had. Cassie liked limits. She liked to be in control of her emotions and her actions. As they drove back to Cliffhanger she considered the idea of returning to Boston sooner than she had originally planned.

Cassie could hear the phone ringing as she started to unlock the back door. She struggled impatiently with the key, finally wrenching open the door and reaching the phone. "Hello?"

"Hi, honey."

"Brian!" She sank into the chair beside the phone table and sighed in relief. Just the sound of his voice brought back a sense of rationality. She could almost feel the bits and particles of Cassandra Chase contracting, pulling back into known territory where they were safe. "It's so good to hear your voice!"

"How are you, darling? I was beginning to think you and your grandfather were out."

She gulped as the memory of the day snapped into sharp focus. "Actually, Jake had to go to San Francisco, so a friend of his very kindly took me on a picnic."

"That was thoughtful. Was it one of the men I met when I was there?"

"Well, no. I don't think you did meet him. But we had a nice time. The weather is marvelous, very hot for the first week of December."

"I'm glad you had a chance to get out and enjoy it. You've been cooped up with your books for such a long time."

She tried to dislodge the guilt that accompanied the knowledge that Brian was picturing one of Jake's rather elderly companions, like the two he'd met the year before. For one brief moment she tried to imagine his reaction if he knew what this friend of her grandfather's really looked like, but she cut the thought short. It didn't invite speculation. "What have you been doing, Brian? Missing me, I hope." Just as she'd missed him? she thought cynically.

"I sure have. I went to the Caldwells' party last night, but I left early. It didn't seem like much fun without you. I'm already missing you terribly."

Her smile was somewhat strained. "That's very sweet." She swallowed. "I miss you, too." It wasn't a lie. She did. She missed the security she felt with Brian. Unlike the daredevils of the world, she had no wish to "push the edge of the envelope." Just sitting in the comfort of this warm, well-grounded house was enough cliffhanging for her.

"I wanted to let you know that I inquired about that piece of land in Wayland, and it is within our budget. When you get back we can go out and see it. It looks like a perfect spot for a house. And Wayland is supposed to have a fine school system."

Cassie nodded, fighting the sensation of heaviness that was creeping over her. She kind of wished Brian would talk about something a little less practical than housing and school systems. Of course both were very important subjects, but right now the present seemed enough to contemplate, without projecting where their unborn children would be educated. "That sounds good. Oh, Brian, you should have seen what I saw today! There was a stream running across the beach, and sea gulls were actually lining up to take a ride in it."

"Oh? That's nice. Sounds like you enjoyed your day." She heard the rustle of papers. "Before I forget, I opened an IRA account for you, as we discussed, with the check you got for teaching part-time. It'll be deductible this year because you don't have a retirement program. The bank is sending out a card for you to sign."

Cassie massaged the ridge above her brows. Brian was a perfect banker, meticulous to a fault about money management. She could just imagine his reaction to Eric's dismissive attitude about money. Brian had his entire future planned, and now he was working on hers. Usually she reacted to his interest in her affairs with pleasure, grateful for the security he was building. But today for some reason it was too much to think about. Her head was still too full of fresh air and salt breezes and majestic vistas to worry about retirement years.

"Thank you, Brian. I suppose I should have taken care of it myself before I left instead of dumping it on you."

"That's silly." He sounded surprised. "You know I'm perfectly willing to take care of those things. After all, that's what I'm trained for. By the way, I don't suppose you've given any further thought to a wedding date? Mom is dying to start planning."

"Oh. No, I've barely settled in here. I'd sort of like to just relax for a while without thinking about anything important. I've been on such a crazy schedule. I'm pretty tired."

"Sure. Of course. You rest. We'll both want to be well rested when we get back together!" His chuckle made the meaning of his remark very clear.

Cassie leaned forward and put her head in her hand, suddenly feeling exhausted. "We sure will." An instantaneous memory of her body's reactions earlier in the day flashed into her mind. That body had shown no symptoms of fatigue then. Not one.

When the conversation with Brian came to an end, Cassie went into the bathroom, stripped and stepped into a hot shower. She let the water run over her for a long time, hoping it would wash away some of the confusion she felt. But nothing disappeared down the drain but sand. It was all she could to to dry herself and get to bed for a much-needed nap.

The next few days drifted by, notable only for their lack of organized activity. Jake picked up on her need for rest, and they fell into a pleasant routine of long, chatty meals. Hours were spent in the sun with a good book.

Margo called on Monday night to remind Cassie of their lunch the following day and to give her instructions on finding her house. "I know Jake could tell you, but I always find a man's directions hard to follow. They seem to give out as few hints as possible, and I usually end up lost."

Cassie, to her surprise, was excited about the visit. She was curious about the exotic Margo and about her relationship with Eric. Eric hadn't called or come around since their picnic, and she found herself thinking about him far more than was comfortable, or suitable.

On Tuesday she headed down the highway until she passed the series of three mailboxes that Margo had described, then started to watch for the next driveway. When she reached it she took a deep breath and turned the wheel, nosing the car down the steep incline. The house wasn't visible until she rounded a curve, then the large structure loomed ahead of her, as unconventional as the woman who owned it. The house was circular, with no apparent squared-off edges. Cassie drove to the roundabout in front of the garage and parked the car.

The back of the house had high windows with trellised vines covering the wood framing. As Cassie walked around to the front door she couldn't help gaping at the structure. Two-thirds of the house was encased in a series of floor-to-ceiling windows, and the shake roof, which was interrupted by a number of skylights, rose to a point in the middle. There was a curved porch that jutted out over the massive, carved front door. The porch was supported by whole tree logs, its ceiling made up of what appeared to be bamboo poles. Cassie pressed the bell and heard the first chords of a piano concerto by Liszt.

The door swung open and Margo, aglow with a warm smile, said, "Ah, Cassandra, right on time. Welcome, welcome." She stepped aside. "Please, come in. We have been anticipating your visit with great pleasure."

Cassie looked around. We? Then she saw two Burmese cats with exquisitely gemmed collars, who were sitting side by side, so still that they could have been a matched set of sculptures.

Margo gestured to the cats. "Meet my family, To and Fro."

Cassie smiled, raising her eyebrows, "To and Fro? Really?"

Margo nodded. "They are my constants."

It was clear, Cassie thought, as she stooped to pet the sleekly beautiful animals, that she was not going to understand at least a percentage of what Margo said. As she reached toward To, his right paw rose. "My heavens, he shakes hands!"

"Yes, they both do. They have very good manners." Margo waited until the cats had duly greeted their guest, then led the way through the front hall. To and Fro followed at a polite distance.

"Your house is incredible." Cassie, eager to see the interior, followed closely behind her hostess.

"Yes, I'm extremely happy here. So many people are displeased with aspects of a house after it's built. This one turned out just as I'd pictured it. I wouldn't change a thing."

When they stepped through a curved arch Cassie gasped. Inside was one huge expanse of space that was divided into living, dining, and kitchen areas. The first impression was one of uninterrupted light. Sunlight flowed in from every angle, right, left and top. "Margo, this is unbelievable. It looks like—" Cassie laughed and shrugged, searching for an apt comparison. "I don't know, like a cozy museum."

There was an enormous marble-and-stone fireplace in the center of the rooms, with openings into all three areas. The floors were dark-stained parquet set in artful patterns, partially covered by beautiful Navaho rugs. The furniture, low-slung and modern, all but shouted "designer," and on every side table were artifacts that Cassie made a silent vow to avoid at all costs, because knocking one of them over would probably require a year of teaching to replace.

Margo, watching her go from one visual treat to the next, smiled in satisfaction. "So, you like my home?"

"Like it! It's beyond description, even for an English major." Cassie turned and looked out the stretch of windows. "Wow! You certainly took advantage of the view."

"This is God's country, but he is so very generous about sharing." Margo headed into the kitchen, which was sectioned off by curved cabinets of some exotic wood. "Would you like a drink? I have just about everything, including an excellent aperitif."

"Umm. That would be fine, thank you." Full of admiration, Cassie let her eyes slowly wander around the kitchen. All the countertops were made of ceramic tile in colorful designs that were in themselves works of art. "It must be sheer pleasure to cook in here."

"Yes, it is. I worked very closely with the architect. The kitchen is an important room for me. I love to cook, and—if I may brag a little—I'm very good at it. Let's have our drinks and then I'll show you the rest."

They took their glasses into the living room and sat at either end of the comfortable sofa, which was covered with a deep red leather so soft that Cassie found herself stroking it. There was a matching chair by the sofa, and To and Fro sat, in classic cat poses, on either arm. It was as though they had learned to place themselves in harmony with the other works of art.

"You know, I'm amazed that you managed to find land and get permission to build so quickly. You say you did so within months? I thought both steps were generally painfully difficult to accomplish."

Margo nodded. "They are. But you see, my mother came from one of the original families that settled here and donated a great amount of land to public use. So although I was raised in New York, I had connections here and was able to push along my permits. This piece of land was still owned by family members, and we worked out a deal satisfactory to all." She laughed. "Ancestry can at times be a help."

"You came from New York? What a change. Don't you feel awfully isolated sometimes?"

"Never. Just infinitely blessed to be here instead of in that jammed city so full of frantic people."

When they'd finished their aperitifs, Margo led Cassie through a doorway on the other side of the entry and down a circular hallway that opened into a guest bedroom and bath, and a mammoth master bedroom with a dressing room and bathroom complete with hot tub and two skylights.

"Sometimes," Margo explained, "after a long walk and a big dinner, my guests all end up in the hot tub. It's a wonderful place to relax and gaze up at the stars and have deep, philosophical conversations." She looked at the expression on Cassie's face and laughed. "I keep a full supply of bathing suits on hand so no one is left out."

Cassie wondered if Eric was often one of the included guests. She also wondered if he was ever there alone with

Margo, sharing that enticing hot tub in a more intimate fashion. *It's none of your business,* she told herself. But the admonition didn't put an end to the uncomfortable speculations.

Margo led her back the way they'd come. "We'll save the last room, which is my favorite, for after lunch."

Lunch was a gourmet feast, served on gold-rimmed china set on the sculptured marble table that dominated the dining area. The two cats, to Cassie's amusement, were fed a small portion of the Chicken Kiev on china plates set upon place mats on the floor. Margo nodded toward them and smiled. "You see how well they are treated, like pampered houseguests. But they afford me the same courtesy and much pleasure. They are right there when I need company and respect my privacy when I want to be alone. Cats can sense mood." She laughed. "Perhaps because they are moody creatures themselves."

The conversation was of the fact-gathering sort—two people getting to know each other. Cassie was very drawn to the woman. Although Margo had grown up amidst great wealth, she was extremely down-to-earth and warm. Cassie asked, "Is it true, what Jake said about your being a psychic?"

"To a degree. I'm not able to see the future, as some can. But I get very strong intuitions that always have a basis in fact. Sometimes it concerns the future, but more often I feel conflicts or driving forces, and know that they must be resolved."

"That sounds like predicting the future."

"No. We live in the present, and it is in the present we must work with our inner forces."

Cassie nodded, although the meaning of Margo's words were not at all clear. "So you weren't predicting some sort of trouble, as Jake said you were?"

"Ah. You see, even I don't know the answer to that. There is a disturbance all around, and I can't seem to channel its direction. It is general. Hanging over all of us."

A shudder ran through Cassie. Not that she believed in this sort of thing, but still, it made her uneasy.

As they ate dessert, a delectable strawberry tart, Margo said, "I understand you have a job in Boston? Teaching, is that right?"

"Yes. I'll be an associate professor of English Literature."

"That sounds interesting." She was watching Cassie in a strange way. "But your grandfather is not at all happy with your plans. I'm sure you know that."

"Yes. And I'm sorry about it. For myself, as well. I won't be able to spend nearly as much time out here. But I do have to make a living, and teaching is what I chose a long time ago. And I prefer the college level."

"When are you getting married?"

Cassie chewed her bite of strawberry tart slowly, bothered by the feeling of annoyance the question brought. "The date hasn't been set yet."

"What's your fiancé like?"

Cassie frowned thoughtfully, trying to picture Brian, which for some reason had become quite difficult. "Well, he's very good-looking. He's about six feet tall and has brown hair and hazel eyes. He graduated from Harvard and Harvard Business School. And he's an investment banker." She took a sip of tea. "He's intelligent and kind and good company."

"Sounds perfect."

Cassie smiled. "Well, I suppose he's not far from it, although Jake wouldn't agree."

"Jake doesn't like him?"

"Jake doesn't like anyone who will keep me firmly rooted in the East. Also, he says he has trouble with the breed. You know, Harvard lawyers and bankers and such."

Margo laughed. "But wait! Didn't Jake graduate from Harvard?"

Cassie nodded. "Uh-huh. But trying to pin down my grandfather's particular logic is seldom easy."

"Yes, I know. His logic is tied strongly to his viewpoint. He is a rare and wonderful human being. One of my favorites."

"It sounds like you have quite a large circle of friends." She couldn't just *ask* if Eric was one of them.

"Yes, that I do. I met Jake when I was applying for the building permit, and he and I hit it off immediately. He in turn introduced me to a number of his friends, and the circle grew. Of course Eric is another of my favorites. He's so like Jake in a great many ways."

Cassie almost choked on her tea. She'd been sitting there wondering how to eke out some information about E. Wagner, and here it was, being offered. "Oh? How's that?"

"They are both men of the highest principle, and both rugged individualists. There aren't really many of those left, you know."

"I suppose that's true." Cassie finished the last bite of tart to give herself time to formulate a question. "Do you know anything about a platinum mine that Eric's interested in?"

"Oh, of course." Margo had a delightful, tinkly laugh. "I'm investing in it."

For the second time Cassie had to smother a cough. "You are? Aren't you afraid it sounds a little . . . uncertain?"

"Somewhat, yes. But big returns almost always involve big risks. And Eric has a good record of wins."

"I'm beginning to wonder if Big Sur is populated by a clutch of frustrated gamblers."

"Well, my dear, I don't know about the rest of the population, but I can't term myself frustrated in any sense. And as for gambling, any form of investment carries a certain risk. Backing this sort of venture is admittedly higher up the ladder of uncertainty. But I'm lucky. I can afford to take a shot now and then without worrying too much about the outcome."

Cassie squirmed in her chair. Maybe Margo could afford it. In fact, after seeing this house, Cassie figured she must have a significant fortune, but that didn't ease her mind about Jake's participation one bit. Cassie's mind insisted on traveling back to Margo's earlier remark about not being frustrated, sending a twinge of jealousy to her heart. That same heart that was supposed to concern itself only with a very nice man who lived in Boston.

"What do you know about Eric?"

Margo's eyebrows rose and one side of her lips curled up. "The most apparent thing, of course—that he's impossibly handsome and devilishly charming. He also happens to have an extraordinary business mind. He's very successful, you know."

"No, actually I had no idea."

"Don't sell him short, Cassie. When he goes after something he usually gets it."

"Do you trust him?"

"I would trust him with my money or my life. With my heart? I'd have some reservations."

"That's funny." Cassie fiddled with her teacup for a moment while she dredged up the nerve to be unpardonably rude, then looked right at Margo. "I got the impression the other night that perhaps you already had."

Margo stared at her in puzzlement, then her eyes rounded. "You mean . . . my heart?"

"Yes."

"Oh my!" Margo began to laugh, the tinkling sound running up and down scale. "Oh my, my, my. . ." Tears formed in her eyes and ran down her cheeks. Finally, using her napkin to dry her eyes, she pulled herself together. "Oh dear, I apologize. Nothing has struck me as quite so funny for years."

Cassie had watched the display of mirth in confusion. "I don't understand. I mean, I know I could be wrong but I don't see why it would be so funny."

Margo pushed back in her chair. "Cassandra, do you have any idea how old I am?"

Cassie had to shake her head. She hadn't a clue.

"I just celebrated, or mourned, to be more accurate, my fifty-seventh birthday."

Cassie felt her mouth drop open. "I don't believe it."

"That is terribly flattering, and I do thank you from the bottom of my aging heart. I plead guilty to using every device available to preserve what is left of, if not my youth, my middle age, but even in my free flights of fantasy I wouldn't pair myself with someone Eric's age."

Cassie was sure her face must be scarlet. "I just, well, you did seem to be flirting with him."

"Of course. Flirting is harmless and ageless. And Eric is a dear, he plays right along, but it's all in fun. Were I to set my sights on anyone, it would be your grandfather."

"Jake?" Cassie's voice rose to a squeak of astonishment.

Margo reached over to pat her hand. "I know that at your age it must seem unbelievable, but Jake is a very attractive man. He has a resiliency and verve that is scarce these days, and is far more compelling than mere youth." She tipped her head and looked at her guest. "I'm sure that's what draws Jake and Eric together; they share a great many characteristics. Among which is a determination to remain unattached." She smiled. "You see, my reference to not entrusting one's heart to Eric was meant as a veiled warning to you. The currents running between the two of you were enough to short-circuit my receptors! Evidently the veil was too thick."

For a moment Cassie's thoughts were so confused that she sat mutely, staring at her fascinating hostess. Fifty-seven. Good grief! And Jake? Then the woman's last words penetrated. "You wanted to warn me? That's my second warning. Jake made it a point to caution me about Eric the day I arrived. You are evidently both forgetting I'm engaged. To be married."

Margo just smiled. "The important thing is that *you* remember." Cassie swallowed. Could the woman read minds? Or had she been stashed away in some nearby niche the day of the picnic? But Margo cut short her mental speculations by pushing her chair back and standing up. "Come. We'll go into the study and cast your runes."

Cassie followed her through the door that led out of the dining room to the part of the house Margo had reserved for after lunch. "Oh my." The room was sensational. The opposite wall was painted a dark charcoal, with the door that led to the hallway beyond blended into the color. A mammoth oil painting, alive with bright hues, dominated the wall, and there was a grouping of a couch and four chairs, all holding plump cushioned seats of a sand shade. "It's beautiful. What's the furniture made of? It looks like woven rope."

"Bingo. That's just what it is. And the cushions are covered with a divine raw silk." She waved her hand at the wall. "And don't you love the painting? I just got my hands on it and I'm so delighted. It's by Robert Goodnough."

Cassie started to admit she had never heard of him, but decided to keep her lack of art knowledge to herself. She already had to explore the mystery of the "runes." "What fun you must have had building this place and furnishing it. I've never seen anything like it outside of *Architectural Digest.*"

Margo, obviously pleased with the praise, went to a side cabinet and took out a small drawstring bag. "Now, the runes." She sat next to Cassie on the couch and set the bag on the glass-topped table. First she extracted a book, then shook the bag and held it up. "You draw three. Let your fingers touch them and select the ones that feel right."

Cassie blinked. "I have to ask. What are they?"

Margo smiled. "Of course. I should have explained. Most people don't know the runes." She reached in and took out a small white tile. On it was a marking. "The alphabet of the runes was used by the Vikings as an oracle, for guidance.

They should not be regarded as fortune-tellers, for they are meant to point out spiritual stepping stones to greater self-awareness and growth. So bear in mind that these are areas in which you might wish to look inside, to explore. Are you ready to draw?'' Cassie somewhat reluctantly picked three of the tiles. "Fine. Set them down as you draw them, blank side up, from the right to the left."

Cassie did as she was told, although she wasn't entirely enthusiastic about it. She supposed this sort of thing made her nervous because she wasn't capable of complete disbelief.

"The one to your right represents you now. In the middle is your challenge, and to the left, the outcome." Margo turned over the one to the right. "Ah. Othila. You are at a crossroads, and you must part from old attachments and end old attitudes. This is not a time to stifle your desires and thwart your instincts." The message went on, but Cassie's mind was grappling with the first information. Partings and endings? And now could any oracle worth his salt advise her to give in to her present desires? She saw Margo turn over the middle rune and gave her full attention. "Perth. Yes, you are indeed on a new course. This rune bodes flight from the known. A complete disconnection from the expected, from the past certainties, and full opening to broader vistas." As Margo turned the last rune she looked at Cassie. "They are sending the messages I read in your aura the other night." She looked at the rune and consulted the book. "Wunja. Oh my. You will exceed yourself. It is imperative that you submit, for it is time to let go old attitudes and old patterns and fully accept the newly expanded you. In so doing you may reach far beyond your present limits."

Cassie stared at her, unsure of her own reactions. "I don't know why but I'm frightened."

"Cassandra..." Margo scooped up the runes and put them back in the bag. "Growth of any significant sort includes uncertainty. Letting go of the known is more difficult for most than putting up with it, even when it's dreadful. Why do you suppose women stay with abusive husbands and men hang on to hated jobs? In your case, the knowns of your life have until now been perfectly acceptable." She put her hand on Cassie's arm. "But there is change in your future. I can feel it."

Cassie shook her head. "I just can't accept that. My future is all set. It's securely based on planning and commitments. That can't change now."

Margo just smiled. "You can't run away from your Karma, my dear. It is always there, waiting for you." She stood and returned the bag to its drawer. "Let's go in and have another cup of tea before you have to go, shall we?"

Cassie looked at the Burmese cats. Each had curled itself into a tight ball on one of the chairs. Her instinct at the moment was to follow suit. On legs that were strangely wobbly, Cassie followed Margo into the other room.

All the way back to Cliffhanger Cassie was nagged by a sense of disorientation. To sodden her mood further, the skies had clouded over and were sending down a steady drizzle. Margo and those foolish runes had raised vague feelings of... what? Discontent? If not that, surely uncertainty. She was beginning to doubt the wisdom of coming here, at least by herself. Maybe she should have asked Brian to come with her for a shorter visit. It was no time for her to allow Big Sur to work its spell, to fill her with ambivalence. And definitely not a time for thoughts of another man to keep creeping into her consciousness.

When she made the turn at the bottom of the driveway, she saw Eric's Jeep parked by the back door. She turned off the motor, sighing deeply. Hadn't her psyche been pummeled enough for one day? She sat in the car, trying to reinforce her defenses before she went in.

Suddenly the back door banged open and Eric ran out, came around to the driver's side and wrenched open the door. "Hurry! Get into some jeans and grab your slicker. We're going down to the beach."

She stared at him in amazement. "Are you crazy? It's raining. And it's cold."

He grabbed her arm and tugged. "Yes, and there's a big school of gray whales heading our way. Don't you want to see them?"

Cassie swung her legs out and made for the house. She'd never been here when the whales were migrating—this could be another first!

Very soon she was attired in jeans and a warm sweater, with her worn sneakers and full-length slicker completing the outfit. She joined Eric and Jake and the three of them started down the winding trail.

Eric cautioned, "Be careful, it's really slippery."

"It sure is. I'll take my time." She glanced out at the ocean, and in the distance saw a spurt of water come up in the air. "Look!" she shouted. "They're coming."

Eric shot her a grin over his shoulder. "Fun, huh?"

"I'll say." Her mood of dejection had vanished, replaced by sheer delight. What a wonderful thing to be doing, racing down the side of a mountain to watch the migration of whales on their way to Mexico. How many people had a spectacle like this right in their own front yards?

Jake, who was leading the way, stopped and called back. "This series of rock steps is really slick. Watch yourselves."

Eric made his way carefully down the incline, then held his hand up to Cassie. "Here, grab hold. It'll make it easier."

Cassie was grateful for the help. Being on the side of a steep hill during a rainstorm was definitely not something she'd usually choose. She reached out to him, and the moment their hands met they both stopped, just for an instant, and looked into each other's eyes. Cassie's attention was caught by that current Margo had spoken of, which was now coursing through her. Because she wasn't watching her step, her foot slid on the rock and sent her into Eric's arms.

His grip tightened and he held fast. "Whoa. It's a long way to the bottom." When Cassie looked up at him, her hood fell back and the rain pelted her face and hair. She scarcely noticed it. Eric gently pulled it back in place. "Or were you throwing yourself at me?" The teasing tone didn't match the burning gleam in his eyes.

"Hey!" Jake's voice sounded from around the bend. "What's keeping you? They're almost here."

Soon they had reached the beach, where Jake led the way up to a large rock promontory. "This is the best whale-watching spot." Cassie looked up at him, realizing that this must be a regular part of his life, bidding hello to those great mammals as they made their biannual journeys. For a moment she felt a twinge of envy.

Eric joined him and gave Cassie a hand up, carefully avoiding eye contact. The three of them huddled together, just now becoming aware of the sharply dropping temperature. Cassie stood sandwiched between them, feeling small and frail beside these two tall, muscular men. Her eyes crept up to Jake's face as she remembered Margo's surprising comments. Jake, like Eric, was bareheaded, and he stood with his neck stretched and face up, his eyes fastened on the point where the water seemed to have formed great, rolling lumps. He looked so natural with the rain flattening his gray hair and running over the ridges of his well-formed face. Cassie saw in that moment what Margo had meant. Her grandfather *was* a fine-looking man, even now. In the arrogance of youth, had she, as Eric had accused her, short-changed him, in more ways than one?

She turned her head to look at Eric, whose pose mirrored Jake's. His expression, too, was of keen excitement. She remembered sitting beside him, watching the gulls. He had been as eager as she to stay a while, to savor the unique gift of entertainment provided by a benevolent Mother Nature. She thought of Brian's "oh, that's nice" response to her description of the event and tried to imagine him standing here in a downpour to watch whales swim by. She knew there was no way he would do it. He'd watch through the plate-glass window of Cliffhanger, satisfied with as much view as could be had there. But what about her? If someone had asked her, while comfortably seated in a warm room in Boston, if she'd happily get drenched to see the migration of some gray whales, wouldn't she just laugh?

"Thar she blows!" Jake and Eric both let out whoops of glee as the sizable school of whales swam into easy view, shooting up spires of water far more substantial than the measly driblets being dropped from above. As Cassie stood rooted, taking in the entrancing sight of mammoth forms arching and dipping and spraying, like a recess of oversized children taking advantage of their freedom to play, she was filled with deep gratitude for this moment, and for the joy that filled her heart. This was something she'd never forget. And at the moment she had to admit that there were no two people in the world she'd rather share it with.

Chapter Five

Thoroughly soaked by the unremitting rain, Eric covered the short distance to his Jeep. He'd thought it was warm enough to run without his rain gear. Getting wet didn't bother him, but he could swear the temperature had dropped since he'd started jogging a little over a half hour before, and even after the exertion, the cold was seeping into his bones. He wouldn't feel too bright if he came down with a cold from running for his health. In any case, he felt better for the exercise. He was too physical a person to endure inaction for any length of time.

He climbed into the back of the Jeep and, after a quick glance around, stripped off his pants and shirt and rubbed himself down with the big towel he'd thrown in the car along with a dry change of clothes. He'd chosen the road that led down to the Fletcher place for his morning run, so he had complete privacy. Once he was dry and clothed he pulled on the heavy wool sweater he always kept in the Jeep in case he got stuck somewhere. Having emergency supplies available was a necessary precaution for someone addicted to the wilderness, as he was. Ah, that was better, the blood was warming up.

He started the motor and wheeled the car around to head back to the highway. God, this weather. Reminding himself how rare a phenomenon this damned endless rain was didn't seem to improve his mood. Instead the contrast to the usual fair conditions made it harder to bear. Besides, there'd been a fire back in the mountains that summer, and the combination of burned-out bush cover and heavy rain could make for slides.

As he waited to pull out on the highway, he saw the sheriff's car pass, then stop and back up. Ben Justin, the county sheriff, turned off his motor and ran back to Eric's car, climbing quickly into the open door on the passenger side. "Hi. Pretty crappy day, all in all, isn't it?"

"That's a fair assessment, yes."

Ben took off his rain hat and dropped it on the floor. "Just wanted to let you know I checked on the Wilsons, and they're fine." The Wilsons lived in a remote farm accessible only by the Old Coast Road. Mrs. Wilson had been sick, and there'd been some worry about them when the road was shut off.

"That's good to know. Were you able to get there in your Rover?"

"Yes. There're a couple of small slides, but nothing I couldn't get over. I tried to get them to come out and stay in the village, but you know them. Cussed independent pair."

Eric laughed. "They're used to being cut off. I'm sure they're well stocked."

"So they tell me. But the missus is still under the weather, so we'd better keep tabs. I knew you'd planned to run out there to check, so I thought I'd let you know they're okay."

"Thanks, Ben. Keep me posted. I've got my horses in the Jeffersons' barn in case we need them to get through." Eric wouldn't really mind a good hard ride, even through the rain. There was a certain aspect of "man against the elements" that appealed to him. Besides, he'd had a lot on his mind lately, and nothing cleared the mental passages like a little demanding exertion mingled with a tad of danger.

"Good idea. Never know. I wish this damned water would stop falling. I tell you, it's feast or famine. Most years we're crying for rain, this year we're drowning in it."

Eric nodded. They were all getting worried. Some of the back roads were bound to get cut off by slides, and most of the people who lived in the more remote areas were old-timers or the offspring of early settlers. A more doggedly independent lot you couldn't find, and they'd stay put in their own houses or, in many cases, cabins as long as the structure stood, no matter what was happening around them.

"So," Ben asked, "I can count on you?"

"Any time. You know that."

The other man grinned and clapped Eric on the shoulder. "Yep, I know that." He climbed out and with a backward wave ran to his parked car.

As Eric headed home his mind, despite all efforts to sidetrack it, was hell-bent on returning to the same topic that had been bedeviling him for days. Cassandra Chase. The girl was wearing holes in his defenses. Every time he got around her his responses popped up to overload. But even more troublesome, she rustled loose feelings he'd had safely battened down for years. All those dangerous thoughts that got a man in over his head, like how nice it would be to have someone to come home to, or to share your life with. He'd even found himself wondering what a child of his would be like!

Hell. Despite all his more honorable resolutions, he might just have to take her to bed and get her out of his system. The problem was, how could he do that without getting Jake riled? The other problem—the one he refused to address— was, nevertheless, significant. There was a sizable doubt, back in the part of his mind that dismissed the bull and only dealt with the facts, that going to bed with Cassie wouldn't get her out of his system at all. That it would in fact have quite the opposite effect. He'd better get the mishmash in his head straightened out before Cassie came to his house tonight, or he'd end up suggesting some damn-fool thing like that picnic. And in truth he was afraid he'd already used every reserve of self-control he had on that single occasion.

Cassie breezed into the house, juggling a load of packages, and Jake appeared just in time to grab one large bag before it slipped out of her hand. "What did you do? Bring the whole city of San Francisco home with you?"

Cassie giggled. "Just about." She went into her room, with Jake following, and dropped the parcels on the bed. "I had such a good time—don't look in that bag!"

Jake put the crammed shopping bag on top of the rest. "Thought you seemed in high good humor. What'd you and Margo do, share a bottle of wine over lunch?"

Cassie giggled again, feeling just as silly as she was acting. "As a matter of fact we did. But there were four of us drinking it, and besides, that was hours ago."

"You said you were just going in for a few things, that you'd done most of your Christmas shopping in Boston and distributed the gifts before you left."

"That's true. I was so well organized that I gave myself fifteen Brownie points. But Margo showed me such fabulous shops that I just had to get a few more things. Besides, I hadn't done all my shopping for you."

"Humph. You know I don't like you spending your hard-earned money on me."

"Oh, phooey. If Christmas morning came and there was no package from me under the tree, you'd be terribly hurt. Now admit it."

"Sassy kid. If you'd let me give you a little more help now and then..."

"Jake, how many times do I have to tell you I'm making it just fine? Between Mom and Dad's insurance and your help with tuition, I've been downright spoiled. It's past time for me to be on my own. In fact, I should start paying some of it back.''

Jake grinned. ''Wait'll old Eric finishes fleecing me, then I may need it.''

''All right, smart guy, we'll just wait and see about that one.'' Cassie was in such a good mood she couldn't even worry about bad investments. She and Margo had met a couple of Margo's friends in the city, friends who'd proved to be almost as interesting as Margo, and they'd had a real full-blown women's shopping day, something Cassie hadn't done within memory. It occurred to her that she'd become far too serious in the last couple of years. Probably the strain of being back in school and working part-time and getting herself engaged all at once.

''So...'' Jake was still surveying the pile of packages. ''Who's all the rest of it for?''

Cassie stood on her toes to kiss his cheek. ''You're such a phony. Always trying to pretend you don't give a hoot about presents, yet curious as a kid.''

''Humph. Just wondering, that's all. I'm not used to all this flutter around here. You haven't spent Christmas in Big Sur since you were...what? Twelve or thirteen?''

''I know.'' Cassie pushed aside some of the packages and sat on the edge of the bed to take off her city shoes. She'd been here less than two weeks, and her feet were already accustomed to the steady comfort of sneakers and slippers. ''I'm really looking forward to it. I wish Aunt Bertha would come out, but she's so sure the plane would crash.'' They looked at each other and laughed.

''Fine thing,'' Jake grumbled. ''She never got so all-fired concerned about *me* flying back there year after year. And it's a lot trickier flying east than the other way around.''

''I don't know—Brian says the weather back there has been clear and beautiful since that one big snowstorm, and all we've had is rain. We thought we'd drown a couple of times today, just getting from one store to another.''

"It's a pain, all right. Can't recall this long a siege. They've closed down the Old Coast Road, except to people who have to take it to get home."

"That's right, there are people who actually live back there in the hills, aren't there? I'd be scared to death to drive that right now. It's bad enough traveling Highway 1 in this weather." Cassie thought of the old road that twisted and turned through the hills inland from Highway 1. It was narrow and unpaved and prone to slides, but before the present highway had been built, it was the only access to Big Sur. "It's hard to picture even horses and carriages using that road on a regular basis." With her feet clad in snuggly slippers, she followed Jake into the living room.

"I came here on that road myself a few times before the highway was complete."

"By horse and carriage?"

"No, smarty, not by horse and carriage."

Cassie sat on one of the high-backed overstuffed chairs and draped her legs over one arm. It was mind-boggling to think of all the things Jake had seen changed in his lifetime. "How in heaven's name did they cut a road out of the side of mountains before all the big machinery?"

"The hard way. The survey was done by foot, and the work was done by convicts and Chinese laborers. One bunch started in Monterey and the other in San Simeon. Big day when they met up."

"When was that?"

"Let's see. Had to be about 1937."

"Were you here when it happened?"

"Sure. Wouldn't have missed it. Katherine and I came here for our first vacation after we were married, and every time we could manage it from then on. We used to stay with some folks in the valley then, rented a couple of rooms. We started building Cliffhanger about three years after the highway opened." He walked over to the liquor cabinet. "How about a pony of brandy to warm you up? Or are you still tipsy from lunch?"

"Yes to the first, no to the second." Cassie watched the way his face lighted up when he said his wife's name. After all these years. She wondered if she was even capable of that kind of love. She'd never thought so. Of course, just lately, she'd been surprised by the intensity of her emotions. Surprised and chagrined. At the age of twenty-six she should be able to anticipate and trust her reactions.

"Did you remember we're going to Eric's for dinner tonight?"

Cassie resented the way her heart jumped at the mere mention of that name. Such foolishness for a supposedly mature woman who was happily engaged to another man. "Yes."

"Margo probably told you she's coming, too." Cassie nodded as she accepted the small glass of brandy. "And Gus and Tom. It's to be partly a meeting about the seals. Hope you won't get too bored."

Bored? With Eric there? How she wished that was possible. At least she and Eric hadn't been alone together since the day of the picnic, so her vagrant urges hadn't had any opportunity to get out of control. She'd just make it a point to keep it that way until she went back to Boston and got herself properly reined in again. "I won't get bored. I'm interested in protecting the seals, too. I love being able to step outside and hear them barking."

"Wait till you go to Eric's. They're right below him, a big herd of them. He's got a light fixed up so you can see them at night."

"Doesn't that make them nervous?"

"Doesn't seem to faze them a bit. He only uses it now and again when he's got company. Or, so he says, when he gets lonesome."

"Eric?" She looked at him in surprise. "Lonesome? I didn't think that was possible. He seems so self-sufficient."

"The man's human, Cassie."

Oh, yes. But more than that. He seemed, well, kind of superhuman, like a character out of an adventure story.

Handsome and strong and brave... Stop! Cassie ordered herself. She was spinning daydreams around a man who was not the right target for her fantasies. "Well—" she lifted her glass "—here's to the seals."

Cassie had been anxious to see Eric's house. She didn't know what to expect—a rough-hewn cottage, sparsely furnished, or something large and professionally decorated? It was in fact a low-slung house with weathered siding. A house that appeared to be hunkering down for the onslaught of winter storms.

Jake went to the back door, opened it and yelled, "We're here!"

Cassie followed close on his heels. "Doesn't anyone around here use the front door?"

"Not in this kind of weather." She saw at once the reason for that. They'd entered a mud room, with pegs along one wall for jackets and coats and a platform for boots. Cassie took off her dripping slicker and hung it on a peg. "This looks more like a room meant for snow country than for California."

"If you love the outdoors, you're always a mess coming inside. I've been thinking of adding something like this to Cliffhanger. Come on, let's get in by the fire."

As they crossed through the spacious country kitchen they could hear the sound of talk and laughter in the other room. Cassie refused to assign a reason to the fact that her heart picked up a little speed. She glanced around the room, noting the somewhat aged appliances and the overall appearance of minimal use. A bachelor's kitchen. Just waiting for a woman. With a sigh of exasperation at her relentless imagination, she followed Jake into the living room.

It was warm and extremely cozy, with a roaring fire in the oversize stone fireplace. There was a wall of bookshelves holding a full load of volumes that looked well used, and the floor was covered by a huge Navaho rug. She wondered if Eric and Margo bought them at the same outlet. At least it was something she could now contemplate without any qualms.

Eric and the other two men stood as they entered. Margo was there, too, lounging in a chair with a wooden frame and a seat of canvas, like a vertical hammock. "Welcome, friends." Eric came toward them, a smile on his face. His eyes darted teasingly to hers as he stressed the word *friends*.

Cassie held her smile firmly in place, though she could feel her lips trembling. It was a maddening affliction that happened when she got nervous. Eric was wearing thin-wale corduroys of sandy beige, with a dark brown crewneck sweater covering a beige sport shirt. Browns were wonderful on him, emphasizing the blackness of his eyes and hair. Cassie sighed. How in the world was she supposed to have a normal reaction to a man who looked like that? She turned the diamond on her finger, trying to conjure up a reassuring picture of Brian, an image that refused to materialize.

She greeted Margo and was introduced to Gus Saunders and Tom Shea. Tom and Eric were at either end of a comfortable-looking sofa, and it was immediately apparent that the seat in the middle was meant for her. As the rest settled down, Eric took drink orders and disappeared into the kitchen. Cassie, in an effort to reinforce her emotional defenses, tried to position herself squarely in the middle of the couch. Eric returned and handed a martini to Jake, then came to give Cassie her white wine as he sat down.

She should have known. His shoulders took up more than his allotted space, and there was no way for Cassie to avoid body contact. Even worse, there seemed no way to avoid what that contact did to her blood pressure—or to avoid the accompanying spurt of guilt. "Well," she said gamely, her voice only cracking a little, "isn't this nice. I like your house, Eric. It's very cozy."

There was no plausible way to avoid meeting his eyes, and the moment she did, the chemistry that existed between them sprang into vibrant life. She could almost hear it crackle. Cassie sneaked a peek at Margo and knew from the look on her face that she could feel it in the room. For an instant Cassie was overcome by the sense of some mysterious force bent on reshaping the solid form of her life. Why was this happening? Was it a postschool, premarriage spurt of rebellion? If so, it was time for her to marshall her forces to suppress the insurrection.

Eric had a way of smiling, sort of slow and relaxed, that was unbelievably sexy. "I'm glad you approve. It's a good house for a single man. Lends itself to clutter."

Cassie nodded. Single man. Was he erecting verbal barriers as she struggled with mental ones? It was almost funny, a man and a woman frantically collaborating to build an invisible shield between them. Almost funny... not quite. Her eyes skittered around the room. It wasn't really cluttered, just fully occupied. Stacks of magazines on a side table, an opened book lying facedown on top of them. Paintings on the walls that were definitely not department store fill-ins. It was certainly enough for more than one person. She pushed her mind in another direction. "Where do you work when you're here?"

"I turned one of the bedrooms into an office. That's right, you haven't seen the rest of the house. Would you like to?" The smile had broadened, taken on a tilt of challenge.

She started to blurt out no, but stopped herself. *Come on, Cassie, you can certainly walk through a few rooms with the man without compromising yourself.* She ignored the snickering sound in the back of her head and said, "Sure. You know how curious I am. I always want to see everything."

"Okay." Eric stood and extended a hand. "Scuse us a minute, folks, we'll be right back. I'm sure the rest of you have seen all you want of this place."

Gus nodded emphatically. "Yeah. You can be sure of that."

Eric and Cassie moved out of the room to the sound of renewed conversation. He walked close beside her, his hand just touching her elbow. Cassie wondered how it would feel to be heading to his bedroom, to his bed. The jump of her heart gave an emphatic, if unacceptable, answer to the untenable question.

His office was set up for efficiency. He had a computer and a printer, as well as a small electric typewriter. There were files along one wall, cases full of what appeared to be reference books and a rack to hold newspapers. "This is obviously a serious working room."

"No doubt about that. I can take care of a good bit of my work here, which suits me fine. What traveling I have to do bothers me more and more. Even going to San Francisco takes some butt-kicking."

"You really love Big Sur, don't you?"

"What's not to love?" He gestured toward the row of large windows. "Where else could you look out of your office and get a view like mine? There isn't a day goes by without some special pleasure. Sunset over the water, the sound of waves and the barking of seals. Dolphins swimming by or a ship passing. We've got a bald eagle lives up in the hills who swoops by now and then. The whales. How could you beat something like seeing the whales?"

Cassie, full at once with that marvelous memory, shook her head. "You couldn't. I'll never forget it."

He turned her toward him. "I see what Jake means."

She stared at him in confusion. "What?"

"He said Big Sur changes you, and it does. I can see a difference just since you came."

"Oh, come on. I haven't been here very long, and you haven't seen me all that often."

"I've seen you enough to notice how much more relaxed you are, and how your face looks ready to smile instead of frown."

The warmth of his hands on her shoulders crept into her arms, spreading something even more dangerous than desire—a feeling of well-being. A feeling that this was just where she ought to be. Shaken, she stepped back out of his grasp. "Are you going to show me the rest of your house?"

His dark eyes, solemn now, held hers for long seconds, then he nodded. "Guess I am."

Cassie barely saw the two bedrooms and the bathrooms through her haze of confusion. The incessant urges that Eric aroused frightened her. Her life was neatly planned. She had secured a position that offered security and purpose. She was going to marry an extremely nice man, a man who would be considered a "catch" by any standards. She could look at the future and plot a course practically guaranteed to work out. It was the perfect situation for her. No risks, very few unknowns. Why was she reacting to Eric Wagner this way, fighting explosive passions she would have sworn she didn't have? She'd read books that used terms like "shocking awareness," "uncontrollable desires" and "overwhelming passion." Read them and laughed. Dear God, these feelings belonged with teenagers and women in mid-life crisis, not with a solid, sensible young woman like her.

When they returned to the living room, Jake and Margo watched them enter with matched expressions of concern. Both Cassie and Eric assumed a look of pleasant neutrality and sat down to finish their drinks.

Eric cooked steaks over a grill set on the covered patio and served them with baked potatoes and salad. Jake called it the perfect dinner for a red-blooded American, but Margo had some question about how appropriate it was to eat beef while discussing how to make peace between seals and fishermen.

They sat around a round oak table in the dining area, which was a good-sized alcove off the living room. The conversation ranged from world affairs to Big Sur gossip. Cassie was quickly brought into the camaraderie of these close friends. It occurred to her as she glanced around the table that it was good to see such a diverse group in so close a blend. Gus was a retired broker from Sacramento, Tom, a man about forty, a member of the highway patrol. Margo, sophisticated, immensely rich; Eric...how did one describe Eric? Age and station seemed to matter not at all. What mattered was a strong bond between people who cared passionately about nature, and particularly this stunning example of nature at its flamboyant best. They willingly put up with regular breakdowns of electricity and telephone service, exceedingly poor television reception and other missing amenities to live in one of the few remaining areas where the beauty of the terrain had not been raped by covetous developers. And they fought a constant battle to preserve it.

Eric and Tom cleared the table while Margo got mugs and the pot of coffee. When they were all seated and the coffee poured, Margo cut generous slices of the lemon cheesecake that was her contribution to the meal. "I don't want to hear one word about calories," she announced. "You can deal with those tomorrow."

There wasn't one word about anything until the delicious dessert was finished. Then Gus pushed back his chair and tackled the subject of the evening. "What's so damned maddening about this thing is that the troublemakers are a tiny minority. Most of the local fishermen would be perfectly content if they didn't have these guys kicking up the dust."

Tom nodded his agreement. "That Fletcher fellow from Monterey. Born rabble-rouser. If it wasn't this, he'd find something else to get people upset about. But it looks like we'll have to go the whole route again. Mailings, phone calls. Might have to argue it out in the legislature."

They began dividing the work, which was substantial. Cassie was just beginning to feel left out when Jake said, "We could rope Cassie in to write up the mailings. She has a fine way with words."

Tom turned to her. "How about it, Cassie?"

"Sure. I'd be glad to do anything I can as long as I'm here. I'll be leaving around the middle of January."

She could feel Eric's eyes on her but managed to keep from looking at him. It was foolishness to encourage this attraction, a game neither could win. She would leave, and she would marry Brian, and she might well never see Eric again. She tried to ignore the sick turn of her stomach at the thought.

"This thing better be well under control by that time." Gus poured himself another cup of coffee. "Tempers are heating up, and we'd sure like to avoid any unpleasantness."

Cassie asked, "Jake, do you still have that old typewriter?"

"Sure. Couldn't throw that away. You've used it to write stories every summer you've come here. I always figured one day you'd get serious and finish a book."

The subject had come up between them over and over. She'd always loved to write, and after she'd been here a week or two, the juices would start to flow and out would come the typewriter. She had drawers full of half-finished manuscripts, and a couple that were complete that she'd been too timid to let anyone read. Jake thought she should give it a good try before she settled into teaching. But after she'd been home in Boston for a while, the sensible side of her nature always reasserted itself and she put away those ambitions for later in life. Very few writers made a living at it, and the money from her parents' insurance had just about run out. She had to be practical.

Once a person had plotted a course, they should stick to it and not veer off in all directions. Brian agreed with her on that one. She looked fondly at her grandfather, and a thought struck her. This visit was in many ways a goodbye, an ending of a long-standing tradition. No longer would she be free to spend her summers here with Jake. In fact, when she did come, it was likely that Brian would be with her. The long, lazy, wonderful days with her grandfather were soon to be over. She dropped her gaze as she felt a wetness gather behind her eyes.

"Cassie?"

"What?" She looked up to see Eric looking at her with one eyebrow raised. "I was just asking if you knew how to use a word processor."

"Yes."

"Then you could work on my computer. It's the kind that does desktop publishing. You could set up the mailers and we could have them copied."

"But..." She stared at him with a rising sense of something very close to panic. "It's in your office. Where would *you* work?"

"Easy. I could move the computer to this table. We wouldn't get in each other's way at all."

She had a sensation of drowning. "But..."

Gus grinned. "Hey, now there's a terrific solution to shortening the time crunch. Looks like we're on the way." He stood up. "How about turning on that spot of yours, Eric? We can sneak a few peeks at our barking friends while we clean up the dishes."

"Good idea." Eric went over to switch on the light as the others got up and began carrying dishes to the kitchen.

As Cassie pushed herself to her feet, Margo leaned over and whispered, "I told you. Karma is Karma. There's no escaping it."

"Thanks a lot," Cassie muttered. Eric had opened the front door, and the sound of barking was loud and clear. Cassie, too curious to resist, went over to see the seals.

"Come outside, you'll get a better view." Eric opened the door and she stepped out, glad of the sturdy overhang above the front walk to shield them from the steady downpour. There was a sand beach below, dotted, in true Big Sur fashion, with large outcroppings of rock. Most of the beach was covered by seals, and others sat on the rocks while some frolicked in the waves. "There's the big honcho." Eric pointed to a huge white seal sitting atop a rock at the shoreline. "He's been the kingpin down there for years."

"He's a beauty. How do you get any work done? I should think the temptation to stand out here and watch them would be tremendous."

"Discipline, my sweet. You'll have to exercise it, too, when you come over to write."

Their eyes met and held. She tried to think of his eyes as deep black holes, bottomless and terrifying. But the darkness was softly inviting and warm tempting a willing immersion into their compelling depths. How could she do it—come here day after day and be alone in this house with him? But under the circumstances, how could she not?

She turned her attention to the seals. They were fascinating to watch, leaping and twisting and waddling up on the sand like a bunch of kids playing at the beach. The big white male stood his solitary watch like a diligent guard protecting his herd. "It's like having your own private aquarium, isn't it?"

Eric smiled down at her, nodding. "Yes. But more than that, they've become friends. I can recognize a lot of them. See the seal just coming up on the beach, over to the right?"

"Uh-huh."

"That's Arabelle."

"How do you know it's a female?"

"What else could she be? Look how small and feminine she is." He pointed. "And the big guy on that rock over there. That's Frisco Pete. He challenges King Tut every now and then, but gets whacked right back in the water."

"King Tut?"

"Yep. The white one. Absolute ruler of all he surveys."

Cassie smiled up at him. "I bet he's your favorite."

Eric grinned. "Sure. He's smart and he's tough. While you're here I'll take you down and introduce you. I stand on that ledge . . . see? That one that hangs out about thirty feet above him. I take down some fish in a bucket, and I yell 'Tut!' and throw one. He wheels around and catches it and then barks his thanks."

"Oh now, come on."

"He does! And other times, when I stand out at the edge of my lawn and holler 'good morning, Tut,' damned if he doesn't turn his head this way and let out with a great big roar." Eric looked like a pleased kid who'd just shared a special secret.

"Does he really? Are you sure he's responding to you?" Cassie couldn't hide the skepticism in her voice.

"Of course I'm sure. We've been pals for years, old Tut and I. I can't help but root for him when he's defending his role as king of the mountain. After all, think of the battles he must've gone through to gain the position. One white seal in an all-black society. Talk about a minority."

At the same time that Cassie was laughing at his descriptions, she was deeply touched by his obvious love of these creatures. Eric had described himself as tough, but he'd just exposed a decidedly tender side of his nature.

Suddenly they heard the screeching of tires on the road above. They both turned just in time to see a man jump out of the passenger side of a pickup truck. He turned to take something out of the car. A rifle! Lifting it to his eye, he took aim and fired.

They watched in horrified disbelief as the big white seal toppled into the ocean and disappeared behind the rock.

"No!" Cassie screamed in horror.

"Son of a bitch!" Before she could stop him, Eric was running toward the killer, who raised his hand in an obscene gesture before jumping back in the truck and slamming the door as it peeled out onto the highway. Eric ran all the way to the top, shaking his fist and yelling in impotent rage.

The others had joined her on the porch. None of them had seen what happened, and when Cassie told them, they all lapsed into stunned silence. Jake, his face set in angered lines, strode out into the rain and up the driveway to Eric. The two men stood, Jake talking and Eric shaking his head. Finally they turned and together started back down the hill.

"Oh, God," Cassie whispered. "How could anyone do that? That beautiful, proud seal, so very special."

Margo laid her hand on her arm. "Everyone knows how Eric feels about King Tut. He gets teased about his 'pet seal' all the time. And everyone also knows he's one of the leaders in the current fight against thinning the herds. It's pretty scary what otherwise decent folks will do to each other when they're on opposite sides of a battlefield."

"I can't believe that man with the rifle could be decent, under any circumstances."

Eric followed Jake down the hill, so full of fury that he felt on the verge of exploding into tiny pieces. King Tut. Pain corkscrewed into him. "That son of a bitch. If only I could have gotten my hands on him!"

Jake slowed down to walk alongside his friend. "I'm glad you didn't. You'd have done something rash."

"Like commit murder? You bet your life I would." He shook his head, wishing he could shake loose the picture of that princely creature of the sea toppling off his lofty perch, felled by the worst predator of all. "I think I'll go down and see if he's dead."

Jake put his hand on his arm. "Come on, Eric, be practical. What're you going to do if he isn't? Pick him up and carry him to the house?"

Jake was right, of course; there was no way he could move that massive form. In any case, by the time he got down there the strong riptide would have pulled Tut out to sea.

Jake glanced over at him, clearly suffering along with his friend. A loss like this hurt them all. "Look at it this way, Eric, at least he never got shoved off the mountain."

Eric stopped and looked at Jake. "Yeah. I suppose there's something to be said for that." His head dropped, and he knew he was treacherously close to crying—something he'd been brought up to believe no real man ever did. "But damned little. Very damned little. Getting shoved off a mountain is natural, it's the way of nature. But being shot off..." His head moved back and forth. "That bastard."

"Have any idea who it was?"

"Yes, I do."

"That's what I was afraid of."

They went in the back door, dripping all over the floor as they stood inside the mud room. The others were soon there, trying to say something comforting, not succeeding. There were times when there simply wasn't anything left to say. Eric excused himself to go in and change his clothes.

"Come on, Cass." Jake reached for their coats. "Time to go home."

"But..." She wanted to stay, to try to help.

Jake held her jacket. "He's lost a good friend, and he's got some grieving to do. Eric will need some privacy to do it in."

As Cassie obediently slid her arms into the jacket, the others nodded their agreement and all prepared to leave. Cassie wanted to go to Eric, to take him in her arms and hold him, to offer what solace she could. She could feel his pain telegraphed through her, an extension of hurt.

By the time they all had their jackets on, Eric reappeared, his face blanked of expression, his eyes dull slate. "Thanks for coming. Sorry the evening had such a bad ending."

They all gathered around to offer condolences, to share their mutual anguish and anger. Jake and Cassie were the last to leave. Before they went out the door, Jake put his hand on Eric's shoulder. "It's a goddamned shame, Eric. We'll all miss him. But not as much as you will."

Eric didn't say anything for a minute, and when he spoke his voice was dull and leaden. "The worst of it is that I helped the bastard kill him."

Jake looked astonished. "What the hell are you talking about?"

"I was the one who turned the spot on him."

"Oh, Eric, you can't—" Cassie stopped when she saw her grandfather shake his head at her.

Jake dropped his hand and stood, in the silent bond of helplessness. "You have to work that one through, Eric. Get rid of it. We're all guilty of enough without taking on what doesn't belong to us." He touched his friend on the arm and gently nudged Cassie toward the door.

She turned her head toward Eric and said, "Is it all right if I come tomorrow?"

"Sure."

Eric watched them go. He wanted to run after them, to grab Cassie and bring her back inside. He wanted to curl up next to her in bed and hold on tight all night long. He felt a deep, imbedded need. Something he hadn't felt for a very long time.

He turned and strode out to the front of the house, picking up a log from the holder by the fireplace as he went. When he reached the pole that held the spotlight, he stood silently for a minute, just looking at it. "Son of a bitch." With one powerful sweep of the log he smashed the light.

Chapter Six

Cassie slept very poorly that night, and what scattered patches of slumber she had were plagued by dream-repeats of the killing of King Tut. She was surprised at the depth of her sorrow over the incident. Sorrow and fury. The anguished sound of Eric's voice when he said "I helped the bastard kill him" haunted the wakeful hours that bisected her sleep. Another troubling memory was the ferocity of her desire to stay with Eric, to hold and comfort him. She arose the next morning more tired than when she'd gone to bed the night before.

Jake's taciturn silence during breakfast indicated that his thoughts, too, were heavy with memory. He studied her over his third cup of coffee and remarked, "You look like you slept about as well as I did."

She nodded. "I kept dreaming about it. Different versions, but even in my sleep I knew it was the white seal that was dying. Why do there have to be such mean, violent people in the world? Can they possibly fill some purpose, or are they just a mistake of nature?''

"Beats me, Cass. One problem with violence is it begets violence. I'm real worried. Eric knows who it was."

Her eyes rounded. "You don't think he'll go after him!"

Jake looked at her for a minute, his expression somber. "I don't know. If I were in his place, I think I might."

"Jake! That would just make everything worse."

"Humph. It would make everything *even*." He shook his head. "On second thought, I guess it wouldn't. One of nature's misfits wouldn't make up for that seal."

Cassie carried her cereal bowl to the sink to rinse and put in the dishwasher. "I'm going to Eric's this morning to start work." And to keep an eye on him. The thought of Eric facing that man with the rifle filled her heart with dread.

"This morning?" He paused, then added, "Cass, are you sure it's a good idea, your spending that much time over there?"

"What does that mean?"

"It means that something mighty peculiar happens to the atmosphere when you two get together."

Cassie fought a threatening rise of color and forced a flippant tone to her voice. "Oh, come now. So there's a little attraction between us. It's just surface." She gave a short laugh. "At least that's all I'm doing—admiring his surface." She brought the sponge over to wipe the table and picked up the remaining dishes.

Jake didn't crack a smile. "Very funny. And a bald-faced lie. I thought I taught you better."

"Jake—" she leaned over to kiss him on the forehead "—don't worry about it. He's obviously just as determined as I am that nothing happen. We'd be a mismatch, and we both know it. Besides, I am engaged, and I'm not likely to forget that." The last thing she heard as she went to get ready was "humph."

When Cassie pulled up outside Eric's house she had to sit in the car for a moment to steady herself before going in.

How would Eric feel this morning? Would he have forgotten she was coming? Darn. She should have called first to remind him. As she climbed out of the car she was met by the delicious odor of a fire burning in the fireplace, a most inviting scent. For although the rain had stopped, the weather was still raw and the sky heavy with clouds.

Eric heard the sound of the car coming down the driveway just as he finished transferring the computer to the dining-room table and hooking it up. She was here. The first thought in his mind when he awakened that morning had been "Cassie is coming," but the lift it gave his spirits had been quickly nullified by his second thought. King Tut was dead. It had been a dreadful night. He'd lain awake most of it, nearly drowning in sorrow and all but choking on rage. He'd heard the grandfather clock in the front hall strike three and three-thirty, and must have fallen asleep just before it struck four.

He went through the kitchen and opened the back door. "Good morning."

Her face looked wan and her smile tenuous. "Hi. I hope you remembered I was coming."

"How could I forget?" Eric held the door as she walked past him into the house and was surprised once again at the swift rise of emotion that filled him. He wished it were just lust. That he could handle. But these feelings involved more than desire. They stirred up reactions so threatening to his carefully guarded solitude that he quickly turned his mind away from them. "Like a cup of coffee?"

"Sure." Cassie hung her coat on one of the pegs, taking her time with the small chore. Why had she brushed off her grandfather's warning about coming here? It was just as Jake had noted; the atmosphere was already highly charged. Since she could only kill so much time hanging up a jacket, there was no avoiding the next step, which led her into the kitchen and into the inescapable pull of his attraction. It *is* just his surface, she told herself, the beautiful way he's packaged, that is so very compelling. She heard her own mind echoing Jake's remark about the bald-faced lie. She watched Eric fill two cups, knowing she didn't really want any coffee. What she did want, against all factions of her sensible nature, was to postpone the moment they headed to different rooms to work.

Eric handed her a mug, and she tried to concentrate on the wisps of steam rising from the dark brown liquid instead of on the tingling sensation in her fingers where they had touched his. He nodded toward the living room. "Let's go in by the fire."

The crackling flames lent an air of coziness to the large, comfortable room. Cassie saw the computer already stationed on the dining table. Would he stay cloistered in his office or wander back and forth? She couldn't avoid the hope that he was a restless worker. She stood before the leaping blaze. "Umm, that feels good."

"It does, doesn't it? A nice warm fire is one of the great pleasures of life." He was close behind her, his mere proximity doing its share in elevating the temperature of the room.

Cassie had observed dark smudges beneath his eyes and taut lines in his forehead. "Did you sleep at all last night?"

"Very little."

"Eric—" she laid her hand on his arm "—I can't tell you how sorry I am. The whole scene haunted me all night. I can imagine how terrible it must be for you. How could anyone do such a thing? You must be very angry."

"Yes." His eyes narrowed. "I'm angry."

His expression sent a shiver down her spine. "Jake says you think you know who it was."

"Uh-huh."

"He's afraid you might do something rash."

His eyes slid sideways to meet hers. "Rash? Somehow that doesn't sound like Jake."

Cassie felt herself blush. "All right, so *I'm* afraid you might. It could be dangerous."

"For him or for me?"

She avoided meeting his eyes. She was getting in deeper than she'd intended. "You. If you go after him, you'll be the one who ends up in trouble. The law doesn't excuse revenge."

"Oh, I don't know, Cassie. There're a lot of people in Big Sur who would applaud the extinction of Curt Jacobs. He's one mean bastard. He kills animals for the pleasure of seeing them die."

"But how can you be sure—"

He turned to face her. "Look, some of the fishermen really believe the seals are a threat to their livelihood, and it's our job to prove to them, with scientific facts, that they're wrong. Now a few of them might get mad enough to take a swing at me or one of the other guys involved in this, and that's fair enough. But I don't know any that would pull a trick like last night except Curt and his sidekick."

"Even so..."

"I won't go after him, because you're right. I'd be the one to end up in jail, and he isn't worth it. But if he has any brains at all, he'll stay away from me."

Relieved, she set her empty mug down on the coffee table. "It was so awful. I kept waking up, wondering if Tut was really dead, so afraid he might be suffering."

"He's dead."

She looked up at him in surprise. "How can you be sure?"

"I climbed down there last night, after you left. I took my pistol along, just in case, because I knew there'd be no way to help him."

"Oh, my God, how awful for you. Especially having to just leave him there."

"Not really. The sea will take him out, and that's where he belongs. That much of it, at least, is part of the natural cycle." He put his mug next to hers. "Now I'll show you how this computer operates and we can both get to work."

Once she got started the words flowed. She was so full of horror over the previous night's killing that heartfelt prose about protecting the seals came easily. Eric had supplied her with a stack of papers with scientific facts and figures to support the argument that seals were not decimating the schools of salmon. She was thoroughly surprised when Eric came in to tell her it was one o'clock and time to stop for lunch.

She exited from her document and turned off the computer. "Gosh, I had no idea it was so late."

"Let's fix some sandwiches and eat them out here by the fire."

Cassie hesitated. The moment she'd become aware of his presence, her equilibrium tilted and she was thrown off balance. The phenomenon was crossing from the unusual to the expected. She should go home, give herself a breather. "I should go home."

"Why?"

"Well, I'd only planned to spend the morning. And Jake might be waiting for lunch."

"Jake's been feeding himself for a long time."

Cassie stood, feeling slightly panicked. Suddenly she was acutely aware of being alone in this isolated house with Eric. She was also aware of the unreliable state of her self-control. "Just the same..."

"Come on, Cassandra. I won't eat you."

She followed him into the kitchen, unsure of the wisdom of the action. Actually, she should continue through the room and out the back door. The morning's conversation hadn't helped a bit. She'd wanted so badly to put her arms around him, to offer her sympathy, the warmth of her support, in any manner she could. And now? Now she'd like to be in his arms for any reason whatever.

More and more these feelings were troubling her conscience. At first she'd considered them a passing fancy, a reaction to the constraints that constant work and unflagging determination had inflicted on her for the last couple of years. A tiny rebellion. Also, Eric, like Big Sur, exerted a diverting magic with his exaggerated beauty. But now she had to admit that she'd seen too many intriguing glimpses of Eric, the man, to dismiss him as just another pretty face. If she was having this much trouble being properly engaged, what kind of a wife would she make? She shoved the thoughts aside. After all, she'd always been extraordinarily reliable. The moment she was back with Brian she'd return to being the steady, responsible person she usually was.

They managed to keep their conversation neutral while they made ham-and-cheese sandwiches and poured large glasses of milk, then went back to the living room and settled on the sofa, side by side. The sky, which had shown signs of brightening, turned darker, increasing the sense of being closeted together in a secluded place, sheltered against the raw weather. Remembering another drab day, Cassie smiled.

"What are you grinning about?"

"I was just remembering one of the first stories I ever wrote. I must have been about eleven or so. It was this kind of day, cloudy and ominous. I began the story with: On a dark and stormy night." She laughed. "It was quite a bit later before I learned how hackneyed that phrase was. I thought I'd cleverly invented it myself."

Eric leaned back, studying her thoughtfully. "How come you only write when you're here? Why not continue when you get back East?"

"Because I've always been on vacation out here. I don't have time for that sort of thing back home." For some reason the phrase *back home* sounded wrong. But then her loyalties always got confused when she was in Big Sur. And now, she thought, glancing at Eric, they were beyond confusion to befuddlement.

" 'That sort of thing'? You make it sound like a frivolous pastime."

"Well, that's what it is, really. At least the sort of writing I do out here. When I was young I was always working to stay on the honor roll and was enrolled in music lessons and sports, so I had little time for hobbies. And since then I've had to confine my writing efforts to serious subjects that relate to my education. After all, that's the kind I'll have to do when I'm a professor. Textbook sorts of things."

"Sounds damned dull."

"Not really." Her voice took on a defensive tone. "I mean, it isn't exactly what I'd choose, but every job has its demands, and you can't enjoy all of them."

"Do you enjoy any? Do you like to teach?"

"Yes. It's a perfectly fine way to make a living. And once I get tenure I'll be secure for life."

"Good Lord, Cassie, how can you be worrying about lifetime security at your age? This is the time to take a flier, find out if there's something you can do that you really would enjoy all the time. It sounds like you tiptoe around life instead of plunging in."

"I'm not the type to plunge. Life has enough scary possibilities without my looking for them."

"And your fiancé—is he a tiptoer, too?"

Cassie was getting irritated. What right did Eric have to criticize the way she chose to live her life? And the person with whom she chose to live it? She was also irritated at herself because she forgot—well, *almost* forgot—that person when she was with Eric. "Brian is a very solid, sensible man who will always be on firm ground. He lays out five-year objectives, just like all the planning books suggest. And now we've started doing that together."

There was a gleam of humor in Eric's eyes. "Those five-year plans never worked for Russia. What makes you think they will for you? When you're all wrapped up in five-year plans, how can you devote yourself to making the best of every single day?"

"I suppose you just stumble through your life, playing each day by ear! That's fine for you. Jake says you have no intention of ever getting married—of taking responsibility for anyone but yourself. But it's different for those of us who plan to make commitments.'' Her voice sounded angry. But why not? She was angry.

He put down his plate and shifted his position to face her more squarely. "Why were you and Jake discussing my future?"

Cassie, flustered, picked up a sandwich half, looked at it and put it back on the plate. "We weren't. I mean, it just came up."

"Oh?"

Those black eyes were relentless. She could swear they saw the printing on her mind-screen. She fidgeted in her seat. "He was . . . you know . . . concerned."

"About what?"

She put her plate next to his on the table, needing her hands free to offer each other a little support. She clasped them tightly together. "I don't know, something silly. He just, well, warned me."

"Warned you?" Eric put his arm across the back of the couch, significantly increasing her discomfort. "And was it necessary? That warning?"

Cassie doggedly kept her eyes on her hands. "No. Of course not. I—" She gulped. "No."

Eric put his finger under her chin and forced it up. Cassie's eyes met his, and they held a look of entrapment. He didn't know why he was doing this, pressing an issue that for him, too, was better left alone. But he felt instinctively that this shouldn't be ignored, that something existed between them that demanded attention. "Are you telling me the truth?"

She pulled away from his fingers. "What do you want from me? An admission that I'm attracted to you so you can add me to your list of smitten females?"

His eyebrows rose. "My list?"

"Jake said you were a walking booby trap for women." The moment the words were out, she regretted them. "I shouldn't have said that. I shouldn't repeat what he says."

"Don't worry, he's kidded me about it often enough. So what do you think I am, a lady's man? A semiprofessional gigolo?"

"I didn't say that!"

"No. But you have, from the beginning, been suspicious of me. Maybe you figure I lure women into my dubious schemes by less than straightforward means."

"Eric, listen, I—" She threw up her hands. "How did we get into this?"

"Don't dodge the issue. Do you?"

Cassie's eyes fell. "No. I don't think that. In fact—" she glanced at him, then back down at her hands "—I have a feeling most of the women who know you are probably terribly frustrated."

His mouth turned up at one corner. It gave him a devilishly rakish look that added to the unfair advantage of his visage. "How about you, Cassandra? Are you frustrated?"

"I'm engaged!"

"What does that have to do with it?"

Cassie was floundering. He had leaned forward so that his face was only inches from hers. His arm, still lying across the sofa back, had edged closer to her shoulders. She could smell the intoxicating scent of his after-shave, could feel the heat of his skin so close to hers. "It—" Her voice cracked. She cleared her throat. "It has everything to do with it. I'm going to be married. To a man."

His smile was teasing. "I should hope so."

"Eric," Cassie insisted, edging farther away, "I shouldn't be here like this. I mean . . ."

"Tell me something. Honestly."

Cassie gulped, unsure she could afford honesty. "What?"

"If you weren't engaged. If it was a clean, unencumbered decision, what would you like to be doing right now?"

She opened her mouth but nothing came out. Probably because she had no words to send on their way. She now knew the true meaning of the word *speechless*.

Eric cupped her cheeks in his hands. "No answers?"

Cassie managed to move her head back and forth.

"Me neither." One of his hands moved around to the back of her neck. "Just urges." She knew he was going to kiss her, and knew she should put a stop to it. But if he didn't, she was afraid she'd die.

When his lips met hers, Cassie's reserve, so shaky to begin with, entirely dissolved. His lips felt so good on hers, so very right. His kiss was immediately demanding, wanting her response and, she had to admit, receiving it. His arms closed around her, drawing her close, engulfing her so completely in desire that the smallest resistance, the least reluctance, deserted her. All thought of belonging to someone else vanished; in truth, no memory of any other man on earth lingered in her spinning brain.

Eric was pushed beyond rational thought. He hadn't intended this to happen today. In fact he had resolved it wouldn't. But his hunger for this woman was overwhelming. The moment she'd walked in, a fissure had opened in his usually solid discipline. He should have known after that day of the picnic... But as the kiss deepened and he felt her mouth soften beneath his, everything drained from his mind but his need for her. The memory of her body, almost nude, moving under his leapt to mind, stirring every sexual instinct in him. He ran his tongue over her lips, then pressed gently, seeking entry. Her lips opened and Eric pushed deep into her mouth. When he felt the pull of her lips, her tongue meeting his, he knew that this time there would be no turning back.

Cassie tried desperately to find some tiny reserve of resistance, but there was none available. Where had it come from, this wild, untamable passion? Had it always been there, hidden, waiting to be set loose? She put her arms around his neck, winding her fingers in his thick hair, clenching the strands in tight fists. His lips pressed harder, and his hands, moving over her back, were almost hurtful in their hold. She'd never been kissed like this, never. Never felt so strong a demand, never wanted so desperately to meet it.

His hand moved to her waist, and his impatient fingers tugged her shirt out of her jeans and slipped beneath it to touch her skin. "Cassie." He breathed her name deep into her mouth, then lifted his head to look at her. "Beautiful Cassandra." He kissed each eyelid, then bent his head to nibble at her earlobe, to tease the contours of her ear with the tip of his tongue. "I want you."

She could scarcely breathe. Every sense was focused on the shocking delight spiraling through her ear, those fingers moving across her tingling skin. The tips of her breasts hardening in anticipation of his touch.

Eric stood up and, looking down at her with hot-coal eyes, pulled her to her feet. The moment she stood she was back in his arms. He ran his hands over her back, down the curve of her waist to cup her buttocks in tight fingers that pulled her hips to his. She felt his need, hard against her, wanted him closer, closer. He kissed the spot just under her ear, then whispered, "If you want to stop, it has to be now."

Cassie's mind was a frantic last-ditch stand, sending out messages on feeble waves: run, flee, refuse, go! But the faint warnings were drowned out by the cacophonous cries of her desire. Her head fell back, and she gazed at him through eyes misted by longing. "I want..."

"To stop?"

"Oh no."

He effortlessly swept her up in his arms. Her eyes, like her needs, were prisoners of his, caught in that dark, smoldering gaze. He was taking her to his bedroom, to his bed. She had wondered last night how this would feel. The reality was far more exciting than the fantasy. The reality turned her entire body into one throb of desire. He kissed her, their eyes still locked, the closeness emphasizing a knowing between them, an irrefutable awareness. This had to be, could not be avoided. Karma? Destiny? Written in the stars? Neither of them knew. Neither cared. This was the moment they had, and nothing else could possibly fill it.

As he lowered her to his bed, they heard the sound of rain on the roof, a cloudburst pounding overhead, closing them in, the rest of the world out, isolating them in their cocoon of passion. Eric sat beside her, his fingers slow, maddening, undoing each button, the perfect contours of his face taut with yearning. He took hold of her shoulders and pulled her to a sitting position, his lips claiming hers while he slid first her sweater, then her blouse off, his fingers trailing a flaming path down her arms. Cassie's bare arms wound around his neck as his hands moved up her back, their palms titillated by the creamy smoothness of her skin. He undid the clasp of her brassiere, and felt a shudder run through her body. As he lowered her back to lie supine on the bed, he removed the bra and dropped it to the floor.

His eyes deepened, hooded, as they savored the sight of her. "You have beautiful breasts." He ran his hands gently over them, feeling the exquisite softness, recording their peaked readiness. He pulled off his velour top, noting the gleam of approbation in her eyes, then eased himself down to lie beside her, putting one leg between hers and suspending himself above her on an elbow.

Cassie stared up at him, entranced, bewitched, watching the baring of that spectacular chest, so wide, so stretched by strength, black hairs curled over the bronzed skin. Her breasts still tingled from his touch, her nipples almost painfully rigid. She should be ashamed, lying here, bosom bared, waiting with agonized anxiety for his skin to meet hers. But shame had no room, full as she was with desire, with a burning craving that consumed all reason. When his leg slid over, pushing between hers, her lower torso convulsed, her thighs tightened. She lifted her hands and ran them over his chest, her fingers tugging at the short hairs, her palms devouring the intoxicating feel of his skin.

He looked down, eyes hot, tongue wetting his lips, while his left hand cupped her breast. His thumb and finger gently squeezed her nipple, and Cassie gasped, he smiled, pleasured by her pleasure. He ran the finger back and forth across the hard nub, sending blazing darts from the tortured peak to streak down to that dampening core between her legs.

"Eric, oh—" She tucked one hand around the back of his head, her fingers tangling in his hair. His finger kept moving back and forth, his leg pushed tighter against her. Her breath was becoming jagged. "You're driving me crazy."

"Am I?" He pulled away from her.

"Don't go!"

"I want to take your pants off." He loosened the button and slid the zipper down, letting his fingers trail over her skin. "Any objections?"

Cassie searched desperately for some small core of resistance, but the only core she could find was crying for him to continue. "Uh-uh."

She lay, shamelessly anxious, while he took off her shoes and socks and removed her jeans and bikini. Every move of her garments was made almost unbearably sensuous by the brush of his hands. He stood beside the bed to discard his clothes. Cassie couldn't move her eyes from that magnificent form, and from the aggressive thrust of his passion.

He stood above her, his eyes devouring, until she whispered, "Please..."

A deafening crash of thunder shook the room as he came to her, skin to skin, one long, covetous embrace. Cassie barely heard the smashing claps of sound, or the pummeling rain. She was dissolving, her flesh mingling with his as his body moved on hers, their hungry mouths seeking sustenance. He slid down to torment her nipples with his lips and his tongue, while his hand traveled the curving lines of her waist and hips. Cassie's arms clasped him, her fingertips digging into the hard flesh of his back. A fire had started inside her, a conflagration, growing, spreading... Could she house any more of this frantic craving? Then Eric's hand moved down over her stomach, his fingers reached that aching center of her longing, and she knew, at once, that she could.

As the exquisite torture increased, a brilliant flash of lightning twisted across the black sky, filling the room with a moment's glaring brightness. She could feel the lightning streak through her, shooting sparks of hot need in every direction, uniting her with its flaming shaft of red-hot electricity.

"Eric..." His name came out in one long, hoarse groan of pleasure. She reached for him, wanting to touch him everywhere, to capture the entirety of this incomparable moment.

He slid up and his mouth covered hers. His tongue thrust deep at the same instant that he entered her, filling her with an ecstasy she could never have imagined. Flesh to flesh, flesh in flesh, they moved together in a perfect concert of giving and taking. Their breath quickened, and the tempo grew rapid. Cassie felt a scream building, her whole body bending and arching in sensations that surpassed rapture. The inner fire had ignited the wick, which burned closer and closer. The scream grew and expanded to a shriek of rapturous anguish as their climaxes teetered on the brink, then exploded, bursting in conjunction with a thunderous bang from the storm overhead.

Cassie was melting into the bed, the whole of her turned liquid, seeming to seep through the covers, infiltrating the mattress. The weight of Eric's spent body on hers was infinitely satisfying. She slowly ran her fingers through his hair, cherishing the caress of the clean, heavy strands. She had the sensation of having climbed a lofty peak, ascended to a height never before attained. Great vistas had opened to her, panoramic spreads of unimaginable beauty. Now that she'd experienced this, how could anything else ever be enough?

"Ummm..." Eric stirred. "Are we still here, or was that us blowing up?"

She rubbed her cheek on his. "Both."

He raised himself enough to see her lovely face, still flushed with happiness, her blond hair askew on the pillow. "Where have you been? Why did you wait so long to get here?"

She ran a loving finger over his bottom lip. "I've been hanging around for years. You've been avoiding me."

"I must have been out of my mind."

"I think I'm out of mine now. At least, whatever's left in my head doesn't feel like me."

"Everything that's under my body feels awfully damned good."

She giggled. "You're terrible."

"True. You should have thought of that earlier."

"I did. It didn't do any good."

He kissed her lips softly. "I'm glad. We might have missed this." His lips brushed across her cheek then settled in the curve where her neck met her shoulder. "You're delicious."

She turned her head to tickle his ear with her tongue. "So are you." She felt a resurgence of his passion. "Don't do that. My fuse has blown."

"Wanna bet?" It wasn't long before she knew she'd have lost.

They drifted off to sleep for a while, and when Cassie awoke she lifted her arm to see her watch. Dear heaven, four o'clock. "Eric, I should go."

"Okay."

Cassie frowned, in spite of herself. Did he have to be so agreeable?

"I'll pick you up about seven-thirty," he added.

"What?" She tried to look at him, but his head was buried in her neck.

"Umm. We'll go to the Ventana for dinner."

"But—"

"Don't argue. It's useless. You'll lose."

She sighed. Who wanted to argue anyway?

* * *

Cassie avoided her grandfather's questioning eyes when she went back to Cliffhanger to take a short nap, then shower and dress for dinner. When she mentioned where Eric was taking her, his eyebrows rose, but he said nothing. She was grateful for his silence because she'd have had no idea what to tell him. She wondered if it showed, this after-glow of rapture.

Eric arrived wearing a navy blazer and tie with khaki slacks and a white shirt. It was classic Easter garb, but she couldn't recall ever seeing anyone who looked this good in it. When they bid good-night to Jake, she had the uncom-fortable feeling that any unspoken questions he'd harbored had been answered.

Eric was driving a sporty silver-blue, low-slung Mercedes coupe with elegant leather upholstery. Cassie stared at it in disbelief. "How many vehicles do you own?"

"Just the three."

"Just three!"

"I need the Jeep and the truck for practical reasons. This is for pleasure." He grinned at her as he took her hand in his. "And this is certainly an evening for pleasure."

As they started up the drive she glanced around at the luxurious interior, sure that the price of the car must ex-ceed the year's earnings of an associate professor. She hadn't given much thought to Eric's financial worth. She'd been far too engrossed in his other significant points of merit. But it appeared the man not only had more than his share of looks, charm and sex appeal, but of the worldly favors, as well.

He squeezed her hand. "You look gorgeous tonight."

Cassie smiled, glad she'd had the foresight to pack this soft pink suit and the cream-colored blouse. It was the one outfit she'd really indulged herself in buying. She'd told one of those white lies to Brian, assuring him the outfit had been on sale at an unbelievable price. Since he'd started helping with her investments he'd become downright dogmatic about her expenditures. The thought of Brian made her very uncomfortable—for good reason. How could she reconcile what she'd done today with wearing his ring on her left hand?

"What's the matter?"

Surprised, she glanced at Eric. Had she been right, could he read her mind? "I was thinking about Brian."

"Oh. Feeling guilty?"

"Yes."

"I guess you would. But it's better to know how you really feel before the wedding, rather than after."

"I know." But did she? Was this crazed attraction to Eric real, or an extension of the wild lure of Big Sur? And what good would it do her even if it was real, if Jake was right about Eric being determined to make no commitments?

They soon arrived at the Ventana and turned up the curving drive that led to the parking lot. It was the only luxury inn and restaurant in Big Sur, but it made up in elegance for any lack in numbers. It sat on a towering crest of mountain, overlooking the ocean and sloping hills, and was renowned for its plush rooms and fine food. They were shown to a comfortable table next to a window that for the moment gave only a view of driving rain. For some reason the foul weather had failed to bother Cassie. Perhaps because it lent an aura of forced confinement that seemed to call for crackling fires and warm, huddling intimacy.

"Like some champagne?" Eric asked.

"Sounds perfect."

He signaled the wine steward and ordered a bottle of Shramsberg Brut. When it arrived and was opened with a festive pop, they watched the waiter fill the tulip-shaped glasses with a fine flourish. Eric raised his glass. "To now. Today. And to us."

Cassie touched her glass to his and drank, unsure of the meaning of his toast. Had she made a terrible mistake, allowing herself to give in to her cravings? Would she look back on today with pleasure or pain? It doesn't matter, she told herself. It wasn't a case of deciding, one way or the other. The events of the day had, she was sure, been etched on some unseen stone from the beginning. If only she knew what else was written there.

They ate in the manner of lovers, gazing into each other's eyes across the flickering candlelight, making teasing, suggestive remarks, touching hands on top of the table, touching knees beneath. There was nowhere else either would have preferred to be, no one else's company they would have opted to share. The food was delicious and the guitarist's soft strumming enchanting. It was, for that segment of time, paradise.

When their plates had been cleared and they were savoring the last of the excellent champagne, with senses and muscles placid from the bubbly brew, as well as from the afternoon's lovemaking, Eric reached across the table and folded his hand over hers. "I love you, Cassandra."

Her eyes flew to his. "You do?"

"Couldn't you tell?"

She stared at him, nonplussed, groping for the right words. "I hoped . . . but, well, after . . ."

"After Jake's warning?"

She nodded.

His hand tightened on hers. "Don't you remember that old quotation about the best-laid plans of mice and men?"

"Yes." She dropped her gaze, then raised it in direct inquiry. "Eric, why did he tell me that? What happened to make you distrust women?"

He withdrew his hand, and she was afraid he wouldn't answer. But after a moment of strained silence, he said, "There have really been only two women in my life. Of importance, that is. My mother and my ex-wife."

Dear God, she'd forgotten his marriage!

"My mother was wonderful as long as Dad was alive. I thought she was just about perfect."

"Did your father leave?"

"No. He worked in construction, on a backhoe. He got out one day to look under a wheel, I suppose trying to figure out what was blocking the way. The thing broke loose and rolled over him.''

"How ghastly!"

"Yeah."

"How old were you?"

"Ten." He frowned and plowed on, as though the memory was still too painful to harbor. "Anyway, his death shook my mother up pretty badly. She wasn't what you'd call a strong woman, and I'm not talking about physically. Within a year she was a drunk and a—" He stopped, his jaw setting in a hard line. "She ran around."

"Eric . . ." Cassie turned her hand over to clasp her fingers around his. "I'm sorry."

"Anyway, I didn't spend much time at home. I was too busy keeping up my grade average and hustling a buck. I figured I'd need a scholarship to go to college. But by the time I graduated from high school I was already fairly well-heeled. As I said, I had a knack for making money. I had several service businesses in place, producing profit, so I could ride on the income and spend a minimum amount of time supervising. I sent regular checks to my mother, even though I knew damn well what she spent it on. But even so, I could pay my tuition and still live as well as I wanted. Of course, my needs were simple.'' He paused to take a sip of his champagne. "I met Clare during my second semester. She was very pretty. Sparkly and outgoing and had a lot of friends. All the things I lacked. I fell pretty hard for her. It wasn't until we'd been married about a year and a half that a few things began to dawn on me."

Cassie waited, knowing this was not the time to interrupt.

"She had a lot of qualities I lacked, all right. But that didn't help the fact that we had almost nothing in common. I wanted to get better educated, to work hard and make something of myself. She just wanted to play. She'd been intrigued by my financial status and had figured we'd have a far fancier life-style than I could manage with a full load of classes, or could afford, for that matter." He pinged the champagne glass with a fingernail. "And a hell of a lot fancier than I'd want no matter what the circumstances. And—" this time the ping threatened to shatter the glass "—she had an appetite for men that rivaled my mother's."

Cassie swallowed and tightened her hold on his hand. She hadn't any notion of what to say.

"Luckily the problem solved itself. She fell for the professor of one of her classes." His smile held no humor. "I gave her no grief about separating. When we got divorced I made a very generous settlement. Far more than I'd been told was necessary. But she signed an agreement that she'd never come near me again, for any reason."

Now, in the line of his jaw and the set of his narrowed eyes, the tough man was apparent. "I can see why you don't trust women."

His black eyes rose to meet hers. "It isn't women I don't trust, Cassie, it's my own judgment where women are concerned. I thought my mother was a saint until I had the truth shoved down my throat. And I guess I repeated the same mistake with Clare."

She studied his face as her heart fell. When he had time to think about this afternoon, would he come to the conclusion that she, too, was another of the same mold...faithless and untrustworthy? She started to withdraw her hand, but he held it fast, as though hanging on to a dream. Or a fantasy.

Chapter Seven

Eric and Cassie emerged from the restaurant hand in hand. "Oh look, Eric." She snuggled against his arm. "The rain has stopped. Do you suppose it's a good omen?"

"Bound to be. There's even a little patch of light in the sky out there, over the ocean. The moon's trying to get out to smile down on the new lovers." Just then a raindrop splashed on his nose, and they both laughed. "But it isn't trying hard enough." He leaned down to kiss her lightly on the lips. "Wait here. I'll bring the car."

"Not on your life. I'm not letting you out of my sight. How do I know how many predatory females may be loitering about, just waiting for a chance to nab you?"

"In the rain?"

"You have no appreciation for the determination of predatory females."

"I see." He turned to her, standing so close that his body brushed hers. "Tell me, are you feeling predatory? I wouldn't want to discourage any of your natural instincts."

"Better be careful. Don't get me turned on. Making love could be downright dangerous in the front seat of a Mercedes coupe. And there isn't any back seat."

"I could race home for the Jeep and be back in minutes."

"No. Tonight is for elegance. A Jeep just wouldn't cut it."

He draped his arms loosely around her waist. "Guess it's too late to trade it in for a Cadillac or a Thunderbird or something with a full-size seat."

"'Fraid so."

He tightened his arms enough to pull her lower torso against his, an action that allowed Cassie to know she wasn't the only one getting turned on. "Suppose—" he rubbed against her ever so slightly, causing a major disruption of her heart's rhythm "—we whip back to my house for a little ... schnapps?"

Cassie grinned. "Is that what you call it?"

His eyebrows rose. "Or a hot toddy?"

"Now you're really tempting me."

"What will it take to put you over the edge?"

She tilted her head and frowned. "Hmm. The only requirement would be a feasible explanation to give Jake for my not showing up there tonight."

His hips pushed harder against hers. "Call and tell him we're going to a late movie."

"In Big Sur?"

"Jake has a good imagination."

"That's what I'm afraid of."

The entrance door began to open behind them, and they jumped apart, hiding their sheepish grins behind a friendly duet of "good evening" as a couple exited, bid them hello and walked toward one of the guest rooms.

"Now, there." Eric waved a hand toward their disappearing backs. "That's the answer. We rent a room. That way we can tell Jake we just left the Ventana a little late."

Cassie giggled. "My grandfather, as you know, was not born yesterday."

Eric caught her hand in his and they walked toward the car. "Why are we going through all this, anyway? We're both well beyond the age of consent. In fact, asking for consent at this point would be a bit bizarre."

"I think Jake has enough misgivings about us without, as that dainty saying goes, rubbing his nose in it."

They had reached the car and Eric opened her door. "I know. You're right. But damn, spending the night alone sounds awful."

She snapped her seat belt in place as he went around to get into the driver's seat. "You've been sleeping alone for a long time."

He closed his door and reached for her, his right arm going around her shoulders while his left hand turned her face to his. The kiss, although ardent, was hampered by the gear shift and the seat belt. The seat belt was quickly dealt with, but he stared down at the gear shift and frowned. "Hell. Who ever invented four on the floor?"

Cassie glanced down and laughed. "Five."

"Don't get clever. I'll have to take you to a secluded glen and teach you what happens to smart alecks."

"Sounds like fun."

"Up for a little rough stuff, are you? I could hold you down with one hand and have my way with you with the other."

"Oh, no you don't. I'm not settling for any one-handed lovemaking." She ran her palm over his thigh. "All or nothing at all."

"Cassandra..." He grabbed her roving hand by the wrist, his fingers closing around it like steel ropes. "You're pushing your luck."

She tried to pull her hand free, but couldn't make it budge. There was no doubt that his boast of being able to hold her down with one hand was based on fact. The thought sent shivers of desire up and down her spine. She wished for a moment that he'd drive her home and take her inside with no further conversation. That he'd carry her to his bed, as he had that afternoon, and listen to none of her protests. It took some effort to prevent her mind from carrying the scenario forward.

"Unhand me, you cad." Her voice lacked the slightest amount of timbre.

He placed his free hand on her knee. "Cad?" His hand crept under her skirt and a few inches up her leg. "Are you maligning my character?" The hand slid further, until the fingers touched a spot that caused Cassie to gasp.

"Oh, Eric, that's unfair!"

"Unfair? In what way?"

Dizzying surges of pleasure spiraled through her. "You promised there'd be no one-handed attacks," she protested raggedly. She could barely speak. How could such little effort produce such incredible results?

"I promised no such thing. Wait, this could be much better." When his fingers stopped, she was afraid she'd scream with frustration. Then she felt them tugging at the top of her panty hose.

"Eric, stop that. We're in the parking lot of a public restaurant."

"We're in a very dark corner of the parking lot, and there isn't another car in sight."

"What if someone is out for a walk?"

At that moment the heavens opened, and a solid wall of rain pummeled the car roof. "In this?"

"What did you do, cast a spell?" This was madness. She'd never even petted in a car. She'd always considered it in bad taste. What was happening to her? Now all her tastebuds were salivating for his fingers to return to their previous position.

He sat up. "Take them off. I'll demonstrate that the impossible is sometimes possible."

"I'll do no such thing. It's time for you to take me home," she said weakly. And if he did, how could she stand it?

"No way. Take them off." His eyes, darker than the night, demanded obedience.

"This is crazy. We agreed there wasn't room to do anything in a car like this."

"What's all this 'we' stuff? *I* never agreed." With one deft movement he leaned across her and pushed a lever. Her seat dropped back to a horizontal position.

"Eric." They *were* in a public place, and even though anyone would have to be nuts to be out in this rain, how could they be sure? She tried to snuggle to a sitting position, but his iron hand held her.

"Don't fight it, it's bigger than both of us."

She decided she'd better not egg him on by asking what "it" was. "Eric, we can't—" Those devilish fingers had loosened her blouse and inched their way to one of her alerted nipples.

He leaned over, his face inches from hers, his fingers gently pinching, evoking small groans from her parted lips. "Just relax, my darling, enjoy it." Without further protest she followed orders, under the spell of a quickly building passion that allowed no will to protest. "Good girl." One isolated brain cell bridled at the "girl," but could find no support for feminist causes. It soon buckled under, surrendering to the same driving need as all the other brain cells.

Cassie closed her eyes, giving in to the swiftly escalating pulsations of pleasure. Eric's fingers worked their black magic, turning her body into a finely tuned instrument that strummed an agitated rhythm of steadily increasing tempo. "Eric..." His name was a susurration of love. "Darling, darling, darling."

"Open your eyes, look at me." He leaned across the restrictive gearshift. "Tell me you want me. Here. Now."

She stared up at him, a captive of his spell. "I want you. Here. Now."

With just a few facile movements, Eric proved beyond question that making love in a Mercedes coupe was not only possible, but exquisitely satisfying.

As they drove home, looking like a matched set of Cheshire cats, Cassie wondered where the cautious, somewhat staid Cassandra Chase had gone. Never had she felt so free, so devoid of inhibitions. She was filled with the excitement of their lovemaking, the extra thrill of breaking rules, ignoring propriety. She'd been so straight all her life, so precisely *good*. Was this a late-blooming teenage fling? When she glanced over at Eric, she was struck yet again by the powerful impact of his sensual masculinity. He was the quintessential man's man—strong, rugged, independent.

She pulled her eyes away from him and stared out into the drenched night. Never had she felt so alive, so full of anticipation. Never had she experienced such heights of passion. Were there corresponding depths? If she fell from such a lofty pinnacle, would it be into a hole too deep for escape? She could hear the warnings of Aunt Bertha, doled out in a steady stream over all her youthful years: *Be careful. Don't take chances. Watch where you're going.* Cassie had built a safe, predictable life following those cautions. A life that had seemed perfectly satisfactory. Seemed. Past tense?

What greater risk could she take than giving her heart to Eric Wagner? Eric lived his life on the brink, hanging on the edge of a cliff, constantly challenging the odds. Her thoughts jumped to Cliffhanger, to the house that had represented release: from school, from regulation, from so many of the disciplines of her Eastern life. Cliffhanger and Jake, escapes from reality. Escapes into pleasure. And now there was Eric. Was he another escape, entrancing but temporary?

She glanced at him, her mind full of questions. Had he said anything, anything at all, to indicate he had something permanent in mind? He had deep misgivings about relationships with women, and she'd done nothing to uphold the honor of the female species. She was engaged to another man, but had given herself freely, eagerly to him. Wouldn't he simply conclude that she was another woman with too voracious an appetite for men? She folded her arms tightly across her chest as a shiver ran through her. For a moment she longed for the safety of Boston. Of Boston and Brian.

"Are you cold?"

Startled, she looked at Eric. "What?"

"You're hugging yourself so tightly, I wondered if you were cold. I can turn up the heat."

One glance from those eyes and her fears and misgivings vanished, overridden by a joy too massive to share inner space with pessimism. "Oh, no. I was just thinking."

"Well, knock it off." He cupped her knee with his hand. "This is a night for feeling, not thinking."

"You're right. It is." She moved over as close as the structure of the car would allow, and laid her head on his shoulder. "You did tell me you loved me, didn't you? I wasn't hallucinating?"

"No, you weren't hallucinating. I noted, however, that there was no such declaration coming from you."

Cassie gulped. He was right. Did she love him? Was this love, this wild longing, this need so gigantic it claimed not only her heart, but her reason? "I guess I haven't worked through my confusion yet." She stumbled, groping for words to explain something she couldn't really understand herself.

Eric turned down the driveway to Cliffhanger and parked by the garage, turning off the motor and the lights. "Confusion?"

"Eric, I should go in."

"Tell me first, what did you start to say?"

She knotted her fingers together. She needed a night, or a full day—maybe a week—to sort out all the patterns of her life so suddenly turned into frayed fragments with loose ends dangling. "I . . . don't know what to do about Brian."

She glanced at him and her eyes stopped, caught by the intensity of his stare.

"That's simple. You call him up and break the engagement."

"Just like that? That seems pretty cruel. Besides..."

"Besides what?"

She undid her seat belt so she could turn in his direction. "Eric, this has all happened so fast. I mean, how do I know where it's going?" His expression was closing down. Oh, God, she was saying the wrong things. But she couldn't just ask him what she needed to know, couldn't just come out and demand that he declare his intentions.

"What are you telling me, Cassie, that you want guarantees from me before you sever the safety harness? How many five-year plans must I prepare?"

"That's not fair! My life was all set before I came here. Now everything has changed, just like that." She snapped her fingers. "How can I cut off my past before I have any idea where my future is headed?" Her head, suddenly heavy, dropped.

Eric's hand shot out, his fingers grabbing her chin and turning her face to his. "Don't play games with me, Cassie. If you're that undecided, then we have nothing more to discuss. I don't want any timid, half-assed commitments. It has to be total or it's not worth the time for either of us."

"Eric, you don't understand!"

"The hell I don't." His hand dropped. "You don't want to take any chances. You want me signed, sealed and delivered before you cut the cord. Should I take my place in line while you make a few lists, weigh the pros and cons?"

"You expect too much!" She hated the sound of her voice, almost a wail.

"You're damned right I do. I expect it all. Just like you said earlier, all or nothing at all."

"How do I know you're ready to give that much back? How can I be sure?"

"You can't. You'd just have to risk it. Maybe try a little trust?"

Her chin, unsupported, fell. "I'm scared."

"Who isn't? What makes you think you should be so all-fired exempt from a little uncertainty? If you spend your life staring at the ground so you won't take a wrong step, you'll never see the sun or the stars, or the mugger about to grab your purse, for that matter."

The confusion in her mind was awhirl, a Waring blender of incoherence. "I'd better go in."

"Yes." He leaned across her to open the door. "Good night."

Cassie stumbled out of the car and into the house. Jake had to be asleep. It was quiet, dead with the stillness of night. She rushed to her room, closed the door and fell across her bed. How had it gone so wrong so fast? They'd been so happy, so full of the thrill of being in each other's arms. She'd done it. She'd done it with her damned uncertainty. Pushing herself off the bed, she forced her robotlike body through the simple preparations for bed, then crawled between the sheets, shivering, not with cold but with anguish. She didn't think she could face life without him, but could she face it with him?

She stared morosely out her window. The moon, unreliable as usual, chose this moment to peek through the clouds, twinkle a reflective hello at the sea, then duck back under cover. Cassie could feel an ocean of tears welling up inside, sloshing about in her sorrow-plagued body. She wanted him, needed him, longed for him, lusted for him. But what would a future with Eric hold? Would she, too, be a cliffhanger, digging a niche in a precarious mountainside and holding on for dear life? With a groan of pure misery, she turned over and buried her head in the pillow.

Eric drove home, doggedly commanding his foot to sit lightly on the gas pedal. He parked his car in the garage and allowed himself the luxury of slamming the door when he got out. Damn it all to hell! It served him right, letting himself get tangled up with a woman again. He slammed the door to the house behind him, too, giving way to his need for some form of violence. He stripped for bed, aware of the biting cold of the night air. He should have put the heat on before he went out. But then, he hadn't been thinking of practical matters, not with the afternoon's lovemaking jamming his mind, clogging his brain.

His anger lasted through the washing-up process. But as soon as he'd climbed into bed, turning up the dial on the electric blanket, his fury deflated like a punctured balloon. Had he been too tough on her? He'd known right from the beginning that she had a great need for security. And he couldn't, in all honesty, blame her for it. No kid could go through what she had without growing up with some significant fears. But what about him, his needs? Was it so damn much to ask that she give him her heart without a signed guarantee of safe handling? Yeah. Maybe it was too much. He could have told her he wanted to marry her, to spend the rest of his life with her, instead of losing his temper.

He flopped over on his stomach and punched the pillow a couple of extra times for good measure. Damn. Maybe Jake had reason to worry. He'd had no intention of falling in love with Cassie. Certainly no anticipation of getting so serious so fast. And he couldn't honestly say the idea of putting a ring on her finger had been uppermost in his mind until Cassie had forced it there. His mind moved swiftly over some of the stored-up pain still lodged deep in his heart from the two previous women in his life, then veered away. He'd closed off those chapters a long time ago and had no intention of dredging up the swill at this point.

He turned onto his back and stared out at the dark night. Wouldn't you know? Now the moon had decided to come out to play. Well, it could just go back inside; it was too late. When it slid behind a cloud, he grunted his satisfaction. The moon was probably female, after all. Just as fickle as the rest. He tried to recapture his anger, to fill up the space that was becoming occupied with a terrible emptiness. God, he wanted her. Wanted her here, in his bed, in his house. He should have run like a jackrabbit the first time he saw her. Pulled her off the edge of that cliff, turned his back and taken off for the city. If only he'd known.

He thought of the pleasure of having space, freedom to come and go when he wanted, being master of his own destiny. But the rush of contentment was gone. He didn't feel even a tiny surge. He wanted her, cluttering up his heart and his house and his life. He rolled back to his stomach and gave the pillow another punch. *Damn.*

Cassie spent one long, miserable day moping around the house, irritated further by the sun fighting its way through the clouds to give them the first pleasant weather in ages. It was no time for sunshine. Rain and fog would be more appropriate.

Jake sort of skirted her, casting doubtful looks of indecision her way, saying nothing. She wanted him to take her in his arms, hold her and pat her back the way he used to, assure her everything would be all right, that Grandpa would fix it. Why did she have to grow up, anyway? Life became so much more difficult. She stood at the window, staring out at the restless sea, counting the minutes as they crawled by. What was she to do? She was paralyzed by indecision.

When the phone rang about six in the evening, she almost broke a toe getting to it. "Hello?" The anxiety in her voice would have spoken volumes to Dear Abby.

"Cassie? Is that you?"

Her whole body deflated at the sound of Margo's voice. "Yes. Hi, Margo."

"Don't get too excited."

"I'm sorry, I'm in sort of a funk."

"I know."

"How would you know?"

"I did your horoscope this morning. You're waging some sort of battle. And losing."

Cassie sank down on the couch. "Thanks. Now tell me something I don't know."

"All right. You're invited to a party."

She wrapped the cord around her finger. "Oh? At your house?"

"No. At the River Inn. A bunch of us decided we should throw a bash for Jake's seventy-seventh birthday. It will be in honor of the youngest man at heart that any of us know."

"Gosh, that's really nice." Her tone lightened a little. "I hate to admit it, but I'd forgotten Jake's birthday."

"You have a lot on your mind."

"Margo, it's very disconcerting to realize that you may know what I'm thinking about. It doesn't help my mood one bit." She pulled her finger out of the cord and sucked it. She'd yanked it too tight. "When is the party?"

"Tomorrow night. Not much notice, but lots of things are spur of the moment here. Makes it more fun. Say, why don't you get in your car and come over for dinner? You need to get out of the house."

"Promise not to read my mind?"

"I'll try."

"Okay."

It was a good decision. After consuming a cocktail while sitting in the cozy study with To on her lap and Fro sitting on the back of the sofa with his paws on her shoulder, Cassie felt enormously comforted. It had taken less than an hour for Margo to pry most of the facts of her dilemma out of her. Of course she'd said nothing about making love with Eric, but she didn't for a moment assume that Margo hadn't picked up on that fact. Out of the stars or the runes or the vibrations, or the pathos in Cassie's voice.

"Oh, Margo, what am I going to do?"

Margo took her glass and refilled it. They were drinking margaritas. Cassie could envision the headache the second would give her but didn't refuse. "How would it feel to say goodbye to Eric and go back to Boston?'' She handed Cassie the refilled glass. ''How would it feel, at this point, to make love to Brian?''

Cassie gulped, almost choking on the margarita. ''God! What a question!''

''A humdinger, huh?'' Margo settled in her chair. ''What's the answer?''

Cassie held up the glass so Fro could take a sip. He loved margaritas. ''It would feel like adultery.''

''Isn't that your answer?''

Cassie squeezed her eyes shut. It felt strange, talking about such personal matters with Margo. Although Cassie had plenty of friends, she'd never had a true buddy, the kind she could confide in. She had to admit it was a wonderful release, airing out her woes like this with someone she felt sure she could trust. It made it easier to look at the situation, to try to sort it out. ''But that isn't the whole thing, Margo. It's so much more complicated than that.'' To awoke and stared up at her with round, blue saucer-eyes. Her tone of agitation had evidently alarmed him. She scratched him behind the ear, and he settled back to sleep. ''What if Eric isn't serious? He could decide he didn't want to get involved. I mean, you warned me about him yourself, as well as Jake. Why should I believe that I'm going to work a miracle and change his mind about entanglements?''

Margo's head was moving back and forth. ''I know Eric. There's no way he'd tell you he loved you if he wasn't damned serious. The man hasn't a devious bone in his body, Cassie. He's sometimes withdrawn, very private, but always, *always* honest to a fault.'' She studied the perplexed expression on Cassie's face and asked, ''Okay, what else? That's not all that's bothering you.''

Cassie sighed, expelling air that felt as though it had traveled from her toes. ''Everything. Boston, Big Sur, safety and security, living life on the brink. It seems like I'm straddling two worlds, about to fall into the abyss between.''

"Oh, Cassandra, you do have a lot to think about. What in the world makes you think life would be so precarious out here with Eric? It's the most heavenly place in the world to live, and I can't think of anyone I'd feel safer entrusting my life to than Eric, unless it was Jake. He's not the sort to make a commitment lightly. I shouldn't think an earthquake could shake him loose if he'd said he'd stay put.''

Cassie laid her head on the sofa back and closed her eyes, smiling in spite of herself when Fro licked her nose. "You're just trying to push some firm ground under my feet.''

"Yes. And you're just trying to pretend it isn't there so you can run back to the tried-and-true.''

Cassie's head snapped up and her eyes opened. "Hey, that's hitting below the belt! Besides, what's so wrong with the tried-and-true? Most people spend their lives looking for security. I'm not so different.''

"Yes, you are. You have too much potential to cut off your options so soon. Some people, Cassie, never worry about security. They're far too busy searching for new areas of themselves to open up, new horizons to discover, new things to learn. Can you imagine your grandfather settling for less than all? How do you think he stays so young? It's because he's always moving forward, eager to peek around the next corner, meet the next challenge. Eric is like that, too. What an adventure, to travel through life with someone like that!''

"But don't you see? That's a big part of the problem. I'm not very adventurous. I kind of like being hemmed in by buildings and steady routines. It makes me feel—''

"Safe?" There was just a hint of a smirk on Margo's lips.

"All right, damn it, safe! This place—'' she waved a hand toward the great outdoor expanses "—has no perimeters. No beginning, no ending. It has always seemed to be calling for more. More effort, more pleasure, more risk, more exploration. It's why I've always run back East so fast after a summer's stay. It begins to get to me, to get everything muddled. And Eric! Dear heaven, Eric is like an extension of Big Sur. No boundaries. He's too good-looking, too exciting, too challenging. The truth is," she said, her voice sinking to a whisper, "that he scares me to death."

"He's made you fall too deeply in love?"

Cassie nodded her head.

"And after you've tasted champagne, how could you possibly settle for beer?"

"You're confusing me."

"No, I'm not. You're confusing yourself. You're listening to your head instead of your heart. It's always a mistake, turning against your own instincts. Now." She stood up. "Let's go eat before the chicken dries out."

The next morning, as soon as Cassie woke up, she put in a call to Brian. She'd catch him at work, which wasn't the optimum time, but she couldn't postpone it any longer. She might chicken out, and it was far too important. Probably the most important call of her life. Luckily he was in.

"Hello? Cassie?" The joy in his voice almost broke her resolve. Brian was a truly nice man. He didn't deserve this blow.

"Hi, Brian."

"Gosh, it's good to hear your voice. Have you any idea how much I miss you?" The knife turned in her stomach. She couldn't tell him about Eric, that would be too cruel. She'd have to handle it another way.

"Brian, I have something I have to talk to you about."

"Oh? Okay, shoot."

Oh please, please, put the right words in my mouth. "I . . . we . . ." Wonderful.

"Cassie, what's wrong? You know you can tell me anything."

She felt sweat break out on her forehead. "Yes, I know that. I also know you're one of the finest men I've ever known." There was a dead silence at the other end. "I . . . that's why this is so hard." Hard? Agonizing. Brutal.

"Go on."

She took a deep breath and fought the urge to change the subject. "Brian, I've done a lot of thinking since I got here, and, well, I'm just not so sure of things anymore."

"By things, you mean us?"

Ouch. He was very bright. Obviously it wouldn't take him long to catch on. "Yes. Us and everything else. Where I really want to live, what I want to do."

"I knew you shouldn't have gone out there just now. That place always has a strange effect on you."

Yes, you're right, it does. She ran her hand over her hot forehead.

"And it looks as though this time it's worse than ever."

You have no idea. She bit her lip to keep the tears back.

"Cassie, get on a plane and get out of there before it bends your mind too far. Come back to Boston. You know this is where you belong!"

No, Brian, I don't know. I never have, really. And now? I'm almost sure I don't belong there. And I have to be sure. "I can't do that, Brian. I need to sort some things out, to make certain."

"God, Cassie, you can't just pick up the phone and scuttle my life without giving me a chance!" The tears were very close to spilling. How she hated doing this! "I'm coming out. If you won't come here, I'll come to you. We have to talk about this face-to-face."

That was about the last thing she wanted. But he was right. It was only fair. If she couldn't tell him goodbye in person, maybe it wasn't the thing to do after all. "All right. That may be a good idea. When will you come?"

"I can't get away until the weekend. I'll fly out on Saturday morning."

She stared at the floor, thoroughly tongue-tied. "I'll see you on Saturday."

"Yes."

The moment she hung up the phone, it began to ring. She just looked at it for a minute, afraid it was Brian calling back to call her all the names he had every right to call her. Finally she picked up the receiver and managed a weak hello.

"Cassie?"

Her heart flew straight to her throat and lodged there. "Eric?"

"Yes, it's Eric. Hat in hand."

"What?" Her brain was doing a double-gainer in an attempt to catch up with the turn of events.

"It's my inarticulate way of saying I'm sorry. I mouthed off at you the other night, and I shouldn't have."

It was Eric, apologizing! Her heart made a perfect dive and settled into a smooth rhythm of happiness. "I don't know what to say. I feel like I should be the one apologizing."

"Okay. I accept yours if you accept mine. Can I come over now?"

She realized her face was one big smile. "Oh yes, please do. As soon as possible."

"Is the birthday boy there?"

"Who? Oh, Jake!"

"Yes, Jake. Remember him? He lives there."

She giggled. She'd thought she'd never giggle again. "So he does. No, he's over at Margo's, pretending he doesn't know about the party tonight."

"I can imagine. I told those guys they'd never pull it off with Jake."

"He's enjoying it all immensely. He's been walking around looking like To and Fro with a canary in the belly."

"I'll be right over."

"Oh boy." She sat where she was for a long moment, staring in glazed delight at the phone. Then she jumped up and ran into the bathroom to wash her face and put on some makeup.

She was sitting at the kitchen table when she heard Eric's Jeep come down the driveway. She jumped to her feet and headed for the back door, almost colliding with Eric as he came in. They stood, both feeling awkward for a few seconds, then, with dual laughs of joy, threw their arms around each other.

"Cassie." Eric kissed her eyes and her mouth and her cheeks and behind each earlobe. "Cassie."

She held on as tightly as she could, determined not to let go again. When he'd completed his kissing course, she looked up into his face and whispered, "I love you. I love you, love you, love you!" He looked so happy it filled her heart with gratitude.

"Yeah, but how do you feel?"

With one more giggle Cassie raised her lips to his, sure, as soon as their mouths touched, that this was true love, more encompassing, more real, more uncompromising than she'd ever dreamt possible. His kiss filled her, filled and fulfilled. She was encased in his love, willingly enslaved by it. She felt something break free inside, break free and open to afford additional room for the expanse of this love.

When Eric raised his head he asked, "Will you marry me?"

"Oh, yes, I will." She frowned. "But before we can make that official, I have to get unengaged first."

"Are you ready to call Brian?"

It was so good to be able to tell him she already had. Not so good to have to tell him Brian was coming out to see her.

Eric took her hand and led her to the sofa, where they sat, the two of them barely taking up space for one. "I don't like it, but I don't blame him. I wouldn't give you up easily, either." He sat back, lost in thought until Cassie became concerned.

"Eric?"

His eyes instantly met hers, and the far-off look disappeared. "I'm sorry, I was thinking about something. I believe you're right about leaving me out of it for now. Not that I wouldn't be more than proud to tell the world, but it does seem an awful dose of salts to shove down his throat at one time. As long as you and I know we belong to each other, I guess we can put off telling everyone for a few days."

Cassie felt a surge of resistance to that idea but pushed it aside. Even though Margo had said it was wrong to ignore her instincts, plain old decency dictated these terms. "I'm sure it's the best thing to do. But I'll feel so much better when it's over with and you and I can tell the world."

Any further discussion was automatically postponed for a much more immediate necessity. They both were in dire need of a love fix, and they couldn't talk while their mouths were busy kissing.

Chapter Eight

There were at least a hundred people at the River Inn when Eric and Cassie arrived. Margo was setting up a table of food for a buffet, and everyone else was standing around with a drink in hand, gabbing with neighbors. Someone had strung up crepe paper streamers and huge bouquets of balloons. There was a mammoth poster on the wall, executed in stunning complexity by one of the local artists, that chronicled Jake's fifty-some years in Big Sur.

Gus Saunders had made arrangements to have dinner at the Inn with Jake, and they were due to arrive in about twenty minutes. Although Jake hadn't come right out and said so, Cassie was sure he was onto the surprise, but she had no idea whether he'd play along or let them know they hadn't fooled him. Margo came over the minute she saw Cassie and Eric, a big smile on her face.

"Hi."

She was wearing slacks and a loose top of a luscious beige suede. She looked beautiful. Cassie was surprised at the level of pleasure she felt in the other woman's company. In a short time Margo had become a friend and a confidante, a new and luxurious relationship for Cassie.

"I'm glad you two are here. I don't know why, but I'm getting nervous. Jake has always said he hates being fussed over, and I'm hoping it's a lie."

Cassie laughed. "Don't worry, it is. He loves it, like most men."

Eric grabbed her arm. "And just how do you know about most men? I thought you were supposed to be a bookworm."

"Well, female bookworms do run into male bookworms."

"Uh-huh."

Margo looked from one to the other and said, "Looks to me like the sun has come out in one quarter, at least."

Eric's eyebrows rose in feigned puzzlement. "And just what does that mean?"

"Nothing. Not a thing. I've got to finish putting out the food." With a knowing grin at the pair of them, she headed for the kitchen.

Eric gave Cassie a censuring look. "So. Been indulging in a little women's talk, have you?"

She tried for an innocent expression, but gave it up and laughed. "Guilty as charged. I hope you don't mind. It's kind of nice to have a pal to confide in."

He nodded. "Yes, I'm sure it is."

"Do you?"

"Do I what?"

"Have a pal to confide in?"

He touched her hand fleetingly, irritated by the strictures they'd placed on their public image. "I do now."

Cassie was sure her love must blaze from her eyes in too bright a flame to be missed by even the most nearsighted. "If I stay here with you, everyone in this room will know about us whether we tell them or not."

"That's probably true. Shall we circulate?"

"Okay." With great reluctance she left Eric to start moving through the group, saying hello to old acquaintances and making new.

The sound level was beginning to climb alarmingly when Tom Shea, who had stationed himself next to the front window, yelled, "Okay, quiet down, here they come!"

Everyone stopped talking and jammed into the kitchen and the back of the restaurant area. The silence was broken by whispers and giggles, until someone hissed, "Shh!"

Cassie heard Jake's hearty bass laugh as the door opened. Then heard him say, "Place looks pretty deserted tonight. Maybe Cal poisoned all his customers." That was followed by Tom's guffaw.

The minute they stepped inside, everyone pushed into the room to surround Jake, yelling "Happy birthday" at the top of their lungs. Cassie had to stand on the balls of her feet to see him, even though he did tower over most of the people present.

Jake looked genuinely astonished, and Cassie was just beginning to think she'd been wrong, that he didn't know after all, when he said, "What the Sam Hill is all this? I thought a few of my cronies were putting on a little dinner party."

That remark was met by a chorus of laughter and formally set off the party. A swirl of activity began—drinks were served and jokes told, with a plethora of backslapping and playful gibes. It was several minutes before someone remembered they hadn't sung "Happy Birthday."

Cassie made her way to her grandfather, who was holding court, looking pleased as a lottery winner. She reached up to give him a kiss. "So, you were a *little* surprised, after all."

"I was a lot surprised. Had no idea there were this many people in Bug Sur silly enough to go to all this bother."

"Oh, you, you're delighted by the attention."

"Humph."

Cassie laughed and left him to his swarming friends. Her eyes traveled around the room, searching for that one face more precious than all the rest combined. She found the face, so beautifully hinged to that spectacular body, surrounded by twittering females, puffing and prancing their charms before their quarry. She felt a vicious bite of jealousy and fought to control the nasty green critter. If she was silly enough to fall in love with a matinee idol of the real world, she'd have to get used to drooling women. It had become apparent that Eric viewed his magnetism with a mix of impatience and amused skepticism. Even so, Cassie longed to barge into the midst of the preening quail and claim her man. Knowing full well that it was off-limits behavior, she forced her attention to some of the young men who were strutting their stuff for her consideration.

Once Cassie made peace with her forced exile from her lover, she began to have a very good time. She'd forgotten how much fun a Big Sur party could be. These were people of different backgrounds, interests and priorities, fiercely independent, adamant in their viewpoints. But they came together like an extended family in times of trouble and times of celebration. And being alive and healthy and solvent was plenty of reason for celebration. A local jazz group had set up to play dance music, and the small floor was soon jammed with gyrating bodies. Cassie danced with one man after another, laughing and chatting at top volume.

She was just easing into a slow fox-trot with Alan Rankin, an artist who specialized in fine gold jewelry, when she heard Alan say, "Okay, okay," before relinquishing her to Eric's arms. She settled in with the pleasure of a homing pigeon at roost, snuggling into his embrace and concentrating on the deep contentment rippling through her.

"Umm," she breathed, "am I glad to be here."

"At the party?" He nuzzled her hair with his chin.

"No, silly. In your arms."

His arms tightened around her. "I bet there are a lot of empty cabins out there. I could pilfer Cal's key ring, and we could get a lot closer."

Cassie contemplated the suggestion with lustful enthusiasm. "Wouldn't that be wonderful? But no. Someone might miss us and come looking."

"We could lock the door and make love quietly. If you could refrain from moaning and tossing about, that is."

Cassie pinched his arm and tilted her head back to wrinkle her nose at him. "All right, see if I ever exhibit any overt displays of pleasure again."

That delicious rumbly laugh shook all through his body and filtered through hers. "Bet you do. Let's go find out."

"Eric!" His leg crept between hers on every turn, and he was holding her far too tightly for a show of propriety. "You are *not* behaving like a casual friend."

"I'm behaving like a man on the make, which is something no male of the right propensities would blame me for."

There was a loud whoop as all the lights blacked out. They heard Cal yell, "Damn, there goes the electricity. Where'd I put that blasted flashlight?"

The band played on, and Eric took advantage of the opportunity to run his hands over Cassie's buttocks and pull her alarmingly close against him.

She tried to push away but was powerless against the strength of his grip. "Eric, for heaven's sake! What if the lights go on?"

His face was buried in her hair and his lips touched her ear. "It'll take Cal about five minutes. I've been through this before. Five minutes is plenty of time for me to rouse a little interest . . ."

The lights flickered and held, forcing Eric to back off. "Damn, what a time for him to set a new speed record."

The band stopped playing, and Cal called, "Time to eat."

Eric gave her a squeeze before letting go. "Can't talk you into bolting for a cabin?"

"No."

"Pity." With a grin he left her and made his way to the side of the guest of honor.

Cassie filled a plate and went to sit beside Margo. "This is delicious, Margo. Did you do any of the cooking, or just the serving?"

"Some of both. Cal's chef, Andy, did most of it, but I supplied the salad and the vegetables." She gestured toward the other side of the room. "What do you think, is Jake having a good time?"

"Are you kidding? Look at that face. Did you ever see an unhappy man with that much of a glow?"

"No, can't say I have. Speaking of glow, Eric doesn't appear exactly downcast, either." She sent a teasing sideward glance at Cassie. "Is it safe to conclude that you two are back to singing the same love song?"

Cassie grinned sheepishly. "There does seem to be a certain lack of stability in this relationship, doesn't there? But yes, we made up."

"And out?"

"Margo! Behave yourself!" Bursting into combined laughter, they directed their attention back to the food.

Dinner was followed by the presentation of the birthday cake, a huge and elaborate structure with a sugar-candy replica of Cliffhanger on top. Jake, to his obvious embarrassment, actually became teary-eyed. "My God, look at this. Isn't that something! Could this be the handiwork of Janey Caldwell?" The blush on Janey's face answered the question. Jake walked over to give her a kiss of thanks, then returned to the cake, which was ablaze with more candles than Cassie could count. "Guess I'd better blow these out before they melt my house!" Amidst claps and yells of encouragement, Jake managed to vanquish the tiny flames in two huffs.

Eric, who was standing next to Jake, leaned over to examine the handsome duplicate of Cliffhanger and remarked, "That's terrific. It's perfect."

Tom Shea poked Eric on the arm and laughed. "Now, Eric, remember the commandment—thou shalt not covet thy neighbor's house."

The quip, clearly made in a spirit of fun, was met with a round of teasing laughter, to which Eric shrugged and grinned. "Now come on, don't ask too much of me."

Cassie, puzzled, turned to Margo. "What's that all about?"

"Oh, nothing, really. It's just that Eric has made no secret of the fact that he considers Cliffhanger to be the perfect house for Big Sur. He keeps saying the reason he hasn't yet built the house of his dreams is because he's still hoping to win Cliffhanger in a card game."

Cassie couldn't blame Eric. Cliffhanger had always seemed the perfect home to her, too. She and Margo joined the circle around Jake to watch him cut the cake. There were no protestations about diets that night. Everyone there had a healthy slice, heaped with ice cream.

Just as the last bites of dessert were being consumed and a few calls for the band were heard, one of the men stood up to make an announcement. "Ladies and gentlemen." That was met by a chorus of rude jeers. "Settle down now, and behave yourselves." The jeers were joined by catcalls. "Old Cal has made a special request. His stone sculptures out in the stream have fallen into disrepair, and he wondered if we'd give him a hand rebuilding them."

Cal jumped up and yelled, "Keep your hands off my stones," then dropped his head in his hands in a feigned display of horror as the group surged toward the back door.

Eric came over to claim Cassie. "Come on, pal. We'll erect a statue that'll dazzle everybody."

Cassie couldn't believe the enthusiasm with which many of the guests took off their shoes and socks, rolled up their pants and waded into the icy water. It was one of the few clear nights of the past weeks, but these people, instead of enjoying the dryness, were plunging their poor feet into cold, cold water. The stream, crystal clear and full, actively bubbled over the water-worn rocks. Years past, the previous owner had built a series of figures out of the rock of the stream, piling one on top of the other in precariously unsteady forms, creating a miniature Disneyish display of surprisingly identifiable shapes. Cal took an occasional stab at neatening the forms but just didn't seem to have the knack, so many of the stone statues had lost various parts of their anatomies.

Eric stripped off his shoes and socks and waded right in with nary a blanch as the chill water numbed his feet. "Come on, Cassie, where's your spirit?"

"It's not spirit I lack, it's the right kind of circulation, like lava instead of blood."

As she watched in astonishment, Jake, with feet and lower legs bared, joined Eric. "Okay, friend—" he bent over and picked up a round, polished rock "—where do we start?"

"Jake!" Cassie stood at the water's edge, her hands on her hips. "For heaven's sake, get out of there. You'll catch cold."

"Don't start, Cass." Jake's voice was calm but emphatic. "If you're worried, get in here and help. We'll finish faster."

"Finish what? I don't know what you think you're doing."

Eric grinned at her. "We're giving this poor scrubwoman a new head." He looked at the unlikely pile of rock. "And a few other assorted parts."

"Scrubwoman?" Cassie leaned closer. "It looks like an aborted rock wall to me."

Eric looked at Jake with an expression of pain. "A rock wall? The woman has no artistic soul."

"Sad, isn't it? And she's such a nice young thing otherwise."

"Oh, I don't know." Eric balanced the rock Jake had handed him on top of the square stack of stones and regarded it proudly. "I noticed a certain streak of intolerance the first day I met her."

"That's right, she was downright huffy with you, wasn't she?" Jake set a rectangular stone at a cross angle under the newly situated head, and nodded. "Hot damn, look at that. An arm!"

Cassie threw up her hands. "Oh, for Pete's sake. That's in entirely the wrong place." She was soon in the freezing water with them, trying to convince herself she hadn't gone soft in the head.

The three of them, taking turns placing rocks and getting out of the stream until they could feel their feet, managed to put together something that actually resembled a scrubwoman. As soon as everyone was finished, a cry went up for a panel of judges to be formed, made up from the tenderfoot group that hadn't braved the threat of frozen extremities. They were to award a first, second, third and booby prize.

Later, as Eric, Jake and Cassie prepared to leave, Jake said, "Well, look at it this way. At least we didn't get the booby prize."

"All that pain for nothing." Cassie winced as she pulled a sock over her rock-abraded foot. She glanced up and smiled as Margo came over to join them. "Here's one bright person, at least. Nobody talked her into that foolishness."

Margo hovered near them, her face displaying no sign of humor. Jake shoved his feet into his Topsiders, then stood and regarded Margo with puzzlement. "Why the long face?"

She shook her head impatiently. "I don't know, really. I feel . . . uneasy."

"Oh?" Jake put an arm around her. "Nobody's going to get mad at you for not choosing them." Margo had been one of the judges. "Well, not *too* mad." Even Jake's stab at jocularity fell flat. "Hey, you are nervous, aren't you? What's up?"

"That's just it. I don't know, but something's wrong." She glanced quickly around at them. "Are you ready? We should get out of here. We're the last ones."

Jake, still attempting to lighten Margo's mood, patted her on the arm. "My mommy always said the guest of honor shouldn't leave until all the other guests are gone."

Margo was watching Eric with fixed intensity. Cassie heard the entrance door open, but was too curious about the scenario in front of her to turn to see who was coming in. Margo frowned. "It's too late, isn't it?"

"'Fraid so." Eric's face was blank, starched. His eyes narrowed, his body tensed.

Cassie was frightened by his demeanor. This was an Eric she'd never seen. "What's the matter?" She followed Eric's gaze to the two men who had just entered. "Who are they?"

Jake's face, stiff and still, mirrored Eric's. "Curt Jacobs and his pal, Lennie Banks."

For a moment the names meant nothing to Cassie. Then she remembered Eric saying, "There are a lot of people in Big Sur who would applaud the extinction of Curt Jacobs." The man who shot King Tut. She turned anxiously to Eric. "Let's go home."

His eyes didn't move from the two men still standing just inside the door, watching Eric with unreadable expressions. "Why don't you and Margo run along? Jake, you can go, too."

"No way."

The air was thick with animosity. Cassie was beginning to panic. Somehow she must get both of her men out of here. Now. "I'd like to go home, Jake. Why don't we all go back to Cliffhanger and have a brandy? The party's over."

Margo touched her arm and shook her head. "It won't do any good, Cassie. They're bullheaded as mules, both of them. Maybe you and I should get out of the way."

Cassie's head swung back and forth. "No. We can't do that. As long as we two women are here, those men will surely behave themselves."

"You don't know them, Cassie. They don't belong here. Or anywhere else, for that matter."

The impasse was broken when Curt Jacobs, with a sneer on his face, ambled toward them. "Well, well. Understan' there was a birthday party here. Feel kinda bad me and Lennie wasn't invited." His sharp little weasel eyes focused on Jake. "How's it feel to be such an old fart, gran'pa? 'Spect they had t'give you a party this year 'cause chances are you'll be dead meat by next."

Jake shifted his weight from one foot to the other. "Well, in that case, I should think you'd want to wish me happy birthday while you have the chance."

Lennie had eased up just behind his cohort. He appeared to be a lot less sure of the wisdom of being here than Curt. "Sure. That's right. Any man lives as long as you deserves a 'happy birthday.' Must be a lotta things wearin' out, huh?" He poked Curt in the ribs as he emitted a weak guffaw. Curt didn't even smile.

"Stow it, Lennie. The old turd should spend his last days sittin' on the rocks with the seals, seein' he likes them better'n people."

Jake nodded. "They are far better company than some people I could mention."

"Why don't you, gran'pa? Tell us who you mean. You couldn' be talkin' 'bout us, now, could you? Lennie 'n' me?"

Cassie stared in fascinated horror at the man, wondering how he could swagger standing still. She stepped forward. "Look, we were just heading home. I'm sure you'll forgive us if we go along."

Curt turned his full attention on Cassie. "Well, la-di-da. Will we forgive her, Len? Pretty thing like her? 'Spect we'd forgive you about anythin', sweetie. 'Spesh'ly if you asked us real nice."

He took one step toward her, and that was as far as he got. Eric's hand shot out and grabbed him by the collar. "Don't get near her, scum. You pollute the air."

Curt was a big man, as tall as Eric and broader all the way from top to bottom. His round head, covered by an unruly patch of greasy brown hair, sat on a thick, squat neck that settled into shoulders that rivaled Eric's in width. His torso displayed years of pumping iron. His body had the look of waiting for a letup in the exercise to turn the muscle to fat. But for now he was a formidable opponent. He stared at Eric, his expression of contempt unchanged.

"Come on, patsy-boy. You gonna dirty your rich-man's hands on scum? You don' want the chick plucked, better get 'er outta here. Now." He jerked his head toward Margo. "An' the other mama an' the ol' man, too." He let loose with a wheezy chortle. "Old man takes a swing, it might topple 'im right on his ass."

Eric didn't blink. "If *that* old man takes a swing, I'd advise you to duck."

That brought forth a full blast of laughter from both Curt and Lennie. The idea that a man Jake's age could be a threat to either of them was clearly cause for humor. Cassie shuddered at the thought of her aged grandfather getting caught up in this macho-male head banging, and ending up...on his ass? She had observed Curt's scornful attitude about Eric's chances of defending himself and wondered if it was founded on knowledge or ignorance.

She turned a pleading look on Eric. "Please, let's go home."

His eyes moved to her for just a moment. "I told you to leave. You and Margo."

Lennie, buoyed by his partner's bravado, added his voice to the unsocial patter. "How about the old fart? He better go, too." He curled his lip. "Spesh'ly if he don't like the sight of blood."

"Eric! Jake!" Cassie stepped forward, wanting to *will* them out of the door.

Eric dropped his hand from Curt's collar. "Cassie—" a steel girder ran through his tone "—get going."

Curt's lips curled in an evil grin. "'Less you'd ruther come with me, chick. Give you a chance t'find out what a real man does in bed." He put out a hand in her direction, but it didn't reach its goal before Eric's fist connected with his jaw.

Cassie screamed and jumped back, followed closely by Margo, as all hell broke loose. All four men were embroiled in a brawl, fists flying along with curses.

Margo touched Cassie's elbow, causing her to jump with alarm. "Sorry. I'm going to call the police."

Just as she headed for the other room, Cal came running in from the back, where he'd been cleaning up. "What the hell's going on here?" He took in the situation at a glance. "Oh, damn."

Cassie ran to him. "Can't you do something?"

"Me? You kidding? I'd crumple with a look from any one of those bozos, let alone a punch." He reached into his pocket and extracted his wallet. "I'll put ten on Eric and Jake. How about you, want to get in?" Cassie's astonished look was enough. "Okay, okay." With that he settled down to watch.

Cassie's heart was beating so hard she was afraid it would crack her ribs. She stared in disbelief at the scene in front of her. She'd never in her life actually seen a fight—out of the ring, at least. It was terrifying. Eric and Curt had paired off for the bout, and Jake and Lennie. The ferocity of their blows sent tremors through her body. How could they be hit so hard and just keep going?

Curt had a cut on his lip, and Eric had one above his right eye. The pounding they were giving each other was ferocious. Curt had a stunned look on his face, as though he'd had no idea how tough the competition would be. And Lennie wore an expression of disbelief as Jake, with expert footwork and well-placed solid jabs, forced him to retreat.

Cassie watched with mounting awe as her seventy-seven-year-old grandfather forced the younger man against the wall and, with one final punch, sent him sliding to the floor. She had no chance for the tiniest surge of pride, because Curt Jacobs had pulled a knife. He circled Eric with the blade held toward the floor. It brought a terrifying memory to Cassie's mind of a film she'd seen where the policeman had warned his partner, "Watch the position of the knife if he has one. If he intends to do real damage, he'll have it down in chopping position."

By this time Jake had turned to watch warily, obviously ready to charge in at any opportunity to disarm Curt. Lennie sat against the wall where he'd been felled, rubbing his chin. He looked decidedly unready to rejoin the fray. Cassie, her eyes held by the glint of the blade, felt her stomach turn over. "My God, Cal. He could kill Eric."

Cal stood up, his enjoyment of the fight clearly gone. "Damn. If any of us try to interfere, we'll all get cut up." He glanced around the room. "Where's Margo?"

"Gone to call the police."

"Good. Wish they'd hurry."

Eric watched every move of the other man, keeping his weight on the balls of his feet, circling as Curt circled, in a grim dance of survival. Back to the streets, he thought, where the real beasts live. How the hell could something like this be happening in a place like Big Sur? The knife jabbed toward him and he dodged nimbly. Curt must have grown up in the same kind of neighborhood he had, with worse results. His fighting skills were excellent, but his motivations stunk.

"What kinda burial you want, seal-man? Wanna be hacked up in bite-size pieces and fed to your slimy wet pals?"

Eric took advantage of the moment to lunge and chop the edge of his hand on Curt's wrist. Curt almost lost his grip on the knife, but managed to retain it. Eric smiled. "Better keep your mind on the business at hand. It's too small to cover two things at once."

Curt growled and cut the air inches in front of Eric's face. "I'm gonna enjoy watching you bleed, Wagner."

Eric heard the squeal of brakes out front. His opponent's attention was distracted for a mere split second, but that was enough to give Eric a shot at him. Putting all his power into the strike, he slammed the side of his hand on Curt's arm, sending the knife clattering to the ground. Eric stepped in and swung, landing a punch that sent Curt reeling over backward, slamming into a table and chairs, and folding to the floor just as two patrolmen lunged through the door, guns drawn.

Cassie, her legs turned to jelly, sank into a chair. Margo, who had been standing by the kitchen door, went to Jake to check his wounds. The policemen stopped, took in the situation, and holstered their guns.

"Well." The younger man in uniform, Buster Adams, stood over Curt, his body poised and tense as though fighting the urge to deliver a good swift kick. "It appears there's been a little party crashing going on here."

Lennie struggled to his feet. "Listen, Mac..."

The cop barely glanced at him. "Buster."

Lennie had a moment's indecision, evidently trying to figure out if he'd been corrected or called down. "Yeah? Well listen, all we did, me 'n' Curt here, was come in for a drink, and these two guys started baiting us."

The older cop, Boyd, stood watching Lennie with undisguised contempt. "Ahh. Poor baby."

Curt had staggered to his feet. His lower lip was bleeding profusely, and his shirt was torn. His eyes skittered around the room, searching for his knife, which was clearly in view under Boyd's foot. He pointed at Eric. "That bastard pulled a knife on me."

Boyd leaned over and picked up the sharp, metal-handled blade. "This your knife, Eric?"

"Hell, no."

"The bastard in question denies ownership. Guess we'll have to see whose prints are on it." He glanced around the room. "Or maybe ask the witnesses?"

Cal stepped forward. "It was Curt here who pulled it. Damned shame, too. It was one hell of a good fight until then."

"Hell." Curt grabbed a napkin off the nearest table to staunch the flow of blood. "They're all friends of his. They'll lie in their teeth. Every damn one of 'em was eggin' him on."

Buster walked over with a handkerchief in his hand to take the knife from his partner. "I don't know, Boyd, it seems to me that on accounta it's Jake's birthday and all, we shouldn't mess it up for him. Maybe just let him and his friends go on home while we take these two in to make a statement."

"Sounds good." The two cops, with a wink and a grin in Jake and Eric's direction, ushered the profanely protesting pair out to the cruiser, with Cal close behind, giving a running commentary on the scrap.

Cassie, who'd been mesmerized, first by fear, then by the peculiar interaction of the police and the fighters, ran over to check on the two men. "Jake, Eric? Are you all right?"

Jake, who'd been muttering protestations to Margo's ministrations, waved them both away. "I'm fine. He never laid a glove on me."

Margo, her voice heavy with sarcasm, asked, "Then what are all those scrapes, and how come your eye is swelling?"

"I bumped into the wall."

"Oh, Jake, what a crock!" By this time Margo was laughing, and so was Eric.

Eric grinned at his cogladiator. "That was some punch you threw, grandpa. The one that set Lennie on his ear. Not bad for an old fart." All three of them laughed aloud.

Cassie, who was standing with her mouth agape, stamped her foot in maddened confusion. "What's with you people? You've just been in a terrible fight, where you both could have been seriously hurt, and you're laughing!"

Jake came to her side and patted her arm. "Cass, honey. It's over and we're fine. You wouldn't have wanted us to walk away from those jerks, would you?"

"Of course I would. Fighting is silly and infantile. You didn't have to lower yourselves to their level."

Eric looked at her, his eyes full of humor. "We couldn't get that far down if we tried. You don't understand men like that, Cassie, and why would you? If Jake and I had backed down tonight, they'd never have let up on us."

"And what about now? You think they'll just forget this? You humiliated them in front of witnesses—they'll really be after you for that."

Eric shook his head. "You've been watching too many crime movies on TV." He held his voice steady, laced with a coating of amusement, but his eyes had gone serious. Cassie was filled with dread about the consequences of tonight.

She waved her hands around in agitation. "I had no idea this sort of thing went on in Big Sur."

"It doesn't." Eric stretched, feeling the tug of tight muscles. "This is the first fight I've been in or seen here. This place can't hold a candle to Boston for mayhem." He had to wonder, like Cassie, if it would be his last fight. If Curt came after him again, it would be with something more serious than fists.

Margo, who had stood by silently during the interchange, said, "Well, enough is enough. Let's go home. Jake, could you drop me? I got a ride over with Janey."

"Sure thing." Jake looked at Eric. "You'll take Cassie home?"

"Glad to." His eyes swung to hers in readable anticipation.

Cassie was too upset to think about love or sex or anything but the paralyzing fear she'd felt while watching the two men she loved being pummeled and threatened by a knife. She said good-night to Margo and followed Eric mutely to his car. They traveled the first mile in silence, which Eric finally broke. "Pretty upset, aren't you?"

"Eric, I was terrified. What do you expect? You and Jake could have been badly hurt or even—" she choked on the word *killed*.

"Cassie, we didn't go looking for it."

"But you weren't sorry when it came to you." She turned in her seat to face him. "Come on, the truth."

"No. I wasn't sorry. It felt good to hit that bastard."

"Eric, revenge always backfires. Now he'll really be mad."

Eric pulled to the side of the road and stopped, so he could look at her while he spoke. "Cassie, what did you expect me to do? Did you really think, for one minute, that I could crawl away from that encounter?"

She dropped her eyes, uncertain what to reply. Part of her understood, the other part just felt alarmed. "I don't know. It seems to me that sometimes it takes more of a man to walk away from a fight."

"Only if there's a good reason for doing it."

Her head came up and she stared at him, eyes round with earnestness. "What about to protect Jake? You must have known he would stand by you. Eric, he's an old man. He shouldn't be involved in a fight at his age."

"Good God, Cassie, how can you keep on about that 'old man' stuff after watching him tonight? He's about as frail as an aged grizzly." He looked at her intently, his expression serious. "Do you really think a man should back away from a confrontation instead of standing up for what he believes?"

"This wasn't a question of beliefs. It was just settling grudges."

"You're wrong. Dead wrong. He came there to start a fight, and it wasn't about personalities, it was about the right of other species to share the planet with man."

"If that's true, maybe you should have given him the benefit of the doubt. Maybe his viewpoints deserve consideration."

"He shot Tut, and I didn't kill him. That's all the consideration he deserves."

She heaved a sigh, too weary to continue the argument and too unsure of her position to take a definite stand. It was entirely possible she was confusing the awful fear she'd felt for Eric when that dreadful man went after him with a knife with cool reason. The truth, probably, was that she had just wanted him safe and out of there, without counting any side issues. She laid her hand on his arm and said, in a tone changed from semistrident to warm, "I do appreciate the way you leaped in to protect me. It made me feel so...cared for."

"You are cared for."

She didn't tell him how much of an inner struggle she'd gone through to make that admission. All her city-girl independence blanched at the tableau of strong man protecting weak woman. But fair was fair. He had stepped in when she needed him, and it had filled her with a brand-new emotional experience. Being the maiden in distress rescued by the strong, handsome prince had a lot going for it. There was something rather thrilling in that aspect of the male-female chemistry that she'd never before encountered. Of course, she would never in her whole life admit that to any of her female friends in Boston.

She was content to let the subject at hand rest as they completed the trip home. More than satisfied to forget everything else when he took her in his arms to kiss her good-night. She touched the cut above his eye with tender fingers. Man had gone out to fight the marauders for centuries, and women had tended their wounds when they returned. Maybe certain things didn't change as much as a lot of people thought they did. Without lying to herself, she couldn't deny the distinct sense of pride she'd felt when she'd watched her man besting his enemy.

Chapter Nine

All during breakfast the next morning, Cassie couldn't stop looking at Jake. Her fixed attention made him so nervous that he humphed off to his room with his second cup of coffee. She had really tried to stop staring, but the sight of her grandfather with a black eye and a number of facial abrasions was too incongruous to ignore.

She ate an orange and had a piece of toast with her coffee, chewing the food absently, her mind miles away. Brian would arrive day after tomorrow. This weekend promised to be unendurably difficult. She wished she'd suggested going to Boston for their talk so she could control the length of stay. She went into the living room and looked out the window, buoyed by the sight of a dramatic ray of sunshine breaking through the clouds and dancing across the ocean. The water was brilliantly blue this morning, with none of the shadings of green or turquoise that often dominated. For that matter it was nice to see color in the water instead of the gray blacks that had accompanied the rain. She heaved a sigh. If she could decide to settle in Big Sur after this spate of terrible weather, the choice should seem inspired in sunny conditions.

Cassie was going to spend the day at Eric's, continuing her writing assignment, but unfortunately Eric wouldn't be there. He had to go to San Francisco to settle the business he'd postponed before. She would have loved to accept his invitation to go with him, but the text for the mailings was due if they were to go out on time. She thought about the adversaries of the seal-protection issue and shuddered. The pictures of violence of the past week were engraved on her brain, vivid and frightening. She thought about what she and Eric had discussed concerning the choice of walking away from confrontation or standing up for one's beliefs. What would she do if threatened by physical danger? The question was embarrassingly difficult to answer.

Once at Eric's, Cassie worked steadily through the morning, trying to avoid lapses of attention. Even the smallest segment of mental vacuity brought rushes of longing for the man of the house. Just as her stomach was signaling a need for lunch, the phone rang, forcing a welcome halt to the typing. When she lifted the receiver and said hello, the voice that replied brought a big smile to her face.

"Hi, darling. Did I catch you during lunch break?"

"Let's say you called just in time to rescue my stomach. It's so good to hear your voice. Isn't it amazing? You've only been away for a few hours and it seems like days."

"Maybe you're in love."

"No maybe about it. When are you coming home?"

"About three. I have an idea. Why don't we pack up a bottle of wine and some crackers and cheese and have our cocktail hour at the picnic place? The weather's supposed to hold."

"Oh, Eric, that would be lovely. So, I'm to watch the sunset from your viewing spot after all."

"Well, times have changed. There's no reason for me to control myself anymore."

A delicious shiver ran through her. "You're absolutely right, there's no reason at all. You can just let yourself go. In fact, it's practically obligatory that you let yourself go."

"Cassandra, don't tease me while I'm so far away. It's cruel."

"Ahh. Poor baby." They both laughed and said good-bye, comforted by the bright promise of later delights. Cassie replaced the receiver, now filled with two distinctly different kinds of hunger.

As though Providence had decided to give the lovers a present, the sky cleared entirely as the day wore on, and by late afternoon there were only enough long strings of clouds to guarantee a dramatic sunset. Cassie went home in time to dress for their excursion and pack the wine and cheese. She remembered to take extra provisions for their friends, the sea gulls.

It was with a spirit of holiday that Cassie and Eric parked the car and set out on the trail to their rocky sanctuary. The late afternoon sun hovered in the sky, waiting for them to reach their destination before starting its descent. The air was crisp and alive with vitality, scrubbed as it had been for days on end. They had dressed warmly, for this sunshine didn't carry the heat of that other picnic day.

When they reached their haven Eric spread the cotton blanket he'd brought for them to sit on, and Cassie laid out the Sterling's Chardonnay and the glasses. She smiled at Eric's surprise at the gleaming crystal. "No substitutes. Only the best. This is a first . . . of something I hope we do often."

He pulled her into his arms. "Only the best. You fit that description perfectly. I love you, Cassie."

"And I love you."

"Sure?"

"Absolutely."

He kissed her. Deeply, passionately. A kiss of promise, of commitment. Its tenderness held a message of feelings too deep to fathom or explain.

Eric glanced up and stepped back. "Look, the sun is making its exit. Time to uncork the wine." He set about that task while Cassie spread out the cheese and crackers.

She couldn't recall ever being quite so happy, or nearly so full of anticipation. The future stretched ahead, rosy with promise. That unique sense of limitless expectation that Big Sur often brought was multiplied in leapfrog numbers by the additional equation of Eric. Nothing seemed unobtainable, nothing impossible. She felt she could stretch out her hand and singe her fingers on the setting sun.

They sat, side by side, sipping wine and watching the incredible show of light and shadow and spectacular color produced by nature. Just as the giant flaming ball sank into the ocean, a fishing boat crossed the horizon, adding the perfect finishing touch.

Eric put down his glass and turned to her. "Will you be happy here, Cassie?"

She cuddled closer, hugging his arm, her head resting on his shoulder. "As long as you're here I will."

"I would never leave you. Never of my own accord."

Eric took Cassie's chin in his fingers and raised it to touch lips to lips. He still had trouble believing in this miracle. He'd thought for years that true love had passed him by. That for some reason there simply wasn't that one special person made only for him. But he'd been wrong. Here she was, in his arms, in his heart.

They made love slowly, quietly, almost reverently, matching the beauty of their caring to the natural wonder that surrounded them. Eric had brought an extra blanket, and they took off their clothes and pressed together beneath its cover. Eric ran his hands over her silky skin, cherishing the feel of her. He kissed her lips and her shoulder and the rosy tips of her breasts, sucking in the wonder of her beauty. Her low groans of pleasure escalated his own, filling him with an excitement unique in his life. This was what love added to sex, this engulfment of joy, this candy coating of supreme contentment, this all-encompassing yearning that so surpassed mere lust.

He tasted all of her, his lips and tongue greedily going from one feast to the next, his body reacting to the steadily building passion. It was wonderful to feel her response, to know the happiness of bringing pleasure to this one most special person in his life. When he entered her he felt a cascade of rejoicing flow through his body, an exultation of pure ecstasy. They climaxed together, the force of their orgasm threatening to shatter the sill of stone upon which they lay. He stayed in her for a while, sure of only one thing—that there could be no other place on earth as perfect as this.

They had to take great care in climbing back up to the trail in the darkness. Eric led, holding Cassie by the hand, guiding her steps from rock to rock until they reached the safety of even ground. "Wow, look up there. Real honest-to-God stars. I was afraid we'd never see them again. Maybe the rain is over, and wouldn't that be a relief."

Cassie's gaze followed his, and she was rewarded by the sight of a great blue-black canopy spattered with an infinite number of flashing stars clustered around the moon, a sliver of gold holding center stage amid gleaming diamonds.

The rain did not reappear the following day. Sunshine flooded Big Sur with its benevolence. Everything was at its most beautiful, a washed-clean green paradise. Since Eric had an all-day business meeting going on at his house, Cassie spent the morning cleaning closets and doing chores around Cliffhanger that the cleaning woman didn't tackle. It was kind of fun, really, playing mistress of the house, especially of this particular house. She remembered the comments about Eric's love of it and smiled. Maybe someday this house would be theirs. It was certainly Jake's fondest dream, that this granddaughter would inhabit his beloved home when he was no longer around.

She spent the afternoon pounding on the old typewriter, finishing a short story she'd started about four years before. When she'd taken it out of the drawer to reread, she was surprised by how much she liked it. Perhaps she should take her own writing ability more seriously. It gave her a marvelous feeling to type the last page, fully satisfied with what she'd done.

She was in a fine mood when Jake came home late in the afternoon, looking as pleased with himself as she was with herself. He came in just as she was putting away the typewriter. Cassie gave him a welcoming hug and asked, "How come the satisfied glow? Have you been out showing off your black eye?"

"Now, Cassandra, don't be snide. I have been at Eric's house, and the others there weren't at all impressed with my black eye. They probably thought I'd run into the door trying to find my way to the bathroom, and I didn't choose to elucidate."

"At Eric's? How come? I thought he was having an all-day business meeting."

"He was. Part of it concerned the platinum partnership." He glanced at Cassie, as though awaiting an outburst. When it didn't come he continued. "And then he had a cattle man there explaining a scheme to freeze the embryos that are the product of two prize animals, and place them in host—" he grinned "—or *hostess* cows to develop."

"Why?"

"So a much greater number of prize calves could be conceived by the one pair of champions and brought to a healthy term. The idea is to introduce the Simmental breed to this country. They're the prevalent cattle in Switzerland. Huge animals that carry a lot more meat than our native breeds. Lean meat, the kind the fast-food places want, and the kind more and more Americans look for when they do eat beef. It's an intriguing idea."

Cassie frowned. "You didn't buy into that one, too, did you?"

Jake's jaw set. "Yes, as a matter of fact I did."

"Jake! How can you let yourself be sucked into these things?" The angry words were out before she could think them through.

"I'm not 'sucked in' to anything. The project is interesting, and I like to invest in things that I can follow. Besides, the investment isn't terribly high."

"I thought you told Aunt Bertha you were short on cash."

His eyebrows rose. "Bertha's got a big mouth sometimes." He frowned. "I can't even remember why the subject came up. Anyway, it doesn't mean anything—it just happens sometimes, when too much gets tied up in nonliquid assets. It's nothing to worry about."

"So you don't have to put up any cash for this?"

"Yes. But Eric's advancing it until I get a few things shifted around."

Cassie felt a sickness of suspicion sprout to life inside. "Did you sign a note?"

"Sure. Has to be done legally. Look, I'm going in to take a shower. I'm taking Margo out to dinner tonight. Thought it was the least I could do after all the work she put into my party."

He set off down the hall, whistling happily, leaving his granddaughter behind, grinding her teeth. Apprehension and distrust built for the next few hours, clouding her reason and setting her teeth on edge. She was due at Eric's house at seven. They planned to barbecue steaks on the grill and eat in front of the fire. She wished she could stop her mind from thinking, from conjuring up scenarios that filled her with a dreadful distrust. Suddenly the innocence of Eric's desire for Cliffhanger vanished, and in its stead a plot unfolded, a clever plot to separate a man from his coveted home.

Cassie pushed the heels of her hands against her temples, hoping to force the awful thoughts from her brain, but her mind, activated by doubt, churned on. What better way to get a man's house than by holding unpayable notes? Had

Jake put up collateral? And if so, what? She was afraid to ask, afraid her suspicions would be confirmed. Then another thought squirreled into place. She'd been contemplating, just a while ago, the possibility that she and Eric might someday live here. Had the same idea occurred to him? It was surefire, wasn't it? If the first plan failed, there was a dandy backup.

She went to her room, closed the door and threw herself across the bed. Dear God, how could she even entertain such grim ideas? She loved Eric. He was the man of her dreams, the man of any woman's dreams, beyond the hope of most, too good to be true. She flopped over on her back and stared at the ceiling as wave after wave of mistrust washed over her. Oh, God, please let me be wrong! But how could she know for sure? If she asked Jake, he'd probably tell her to mind her own business, and he'd already shown a total unwillingness to entertain the smallest smidgeon of suspicion where Eric was concerned.

Cassie stopped, her mind screeching to a sudden stop. And how about her? She was about to terminate an engagement, to pledge her life and love to this man, so how could she even consider the possibility that he wasn't honest? The question swung back and forth in her mind like a baited hook. This sort of thought shouldn't even occur to her, and if it did, she should have brushed it aside without a second's hesitation. Confusion whirled in her head, making a logical sequence of deductions impossible. Maybe Eric was, as she'd suspected, too good to be true. Otherwise, how could he have escaped capture this long? He'd been divorced for years. It seemed highly unlikely that this man, more handsome, intelligent, successful—etc., etc., etc.—than any she'd ever met, should fall in love with her after passing up hordes of eligible women.

All of her natural built-in apprehensions, all those fears and doubts she'd so blithely banished, snapped back into place. Perhaps, as Aunt Bertha maintained, this was the price of too much trust, of allowing yourself to forget that every step was a potential pitfall, every dream a possible ruse. She'd always been so very careful, and nothing like this had ever happened before. Before she had come back to Big Sur and fallen in love with Eric Wagner.

Somehow she got herself dressed, propelled her reluctant body to the car and drove to Eric's house. What was she going to do? She couldn't just barge in and barrage him with questions. But how would she get her answers subtly? "Oh, darling, by the way..." Damn.

When she got to his door, accepted his kiss of welcome and went in to the suddenly claustrophobic living room, overheated by the blazing flames in the fireplace, she was accompanied by her shadow of suspicion, tripping over it every time she turned around. Eric had chilled a bottle of Shramsberg champagne, which he ceremoniously uncorked and poured into two gleaming tulip glasses. He held up his glass and said, "To us in marital bliss. Together, always." Cassie clinked and drank, surprised the liquid went down her throat without choking her.

Eric watched Cassie, puzzled. She seemed to have withdrawn, shrunk away from him somehow. Perhaps she was worried about telling Brian. He couldn't blame her; it would be tough. Sorry, Brian, old chap, he thought, but your loss is my gain. Cassie belongs with me, I can feel it. She had come to him at just the right time, filling a void he'd come to consider permanent. But as time passed and her tension remained, he grew concerned.

"Hey. Are you in there? You seem to be miles away."

She tried a smile, not very successfully. "Oh, sure, I'm here, all right." She took another gulp of her champagne. It was her second glass, and a bit of welcome numbness had crept into her limbs and, more importantly, her mind.

"Is anything wrong, honey? You don't seem yourself."

She smiled grimly. "Maybe I'm more myself than I've been for some time." Oh dear. As her mind grew numb, her tongue grew overactive.

"And what does that mean?"

She sat up straighter and waved her fingers in a dismissive gesture. "Nothing much. Shouldn't we put on the steaks?"

Eric studied her face, searching for a clue to her behavior. Wasn't it just last evening they'd been so happy? Hadn't he held her in his arms, felt her response to his lovemaking? Why this frosty demeanor? "Cassie, something's wrong. What is it?"

She felt trapped. Trapped if she told him and trapped if she didn't. Once in his presence, all will to question had left her. She wanted only to lose herself in his arms, to surrender her will into his. If he was a dream too wonderful to be real, what was the harm of staying in this fantasy paradise? "I don't think we should talk about it right now." Her fingers turned the tulip glass around and around.

"I'd say if there's any problem at all, we'd better talk about it now. Your ex-fiancé is showing up tomorrow. You'll want to have all your ducks in a row."

And when she got them all in a row, would Eric shoot them down? All the ugly suspicions of the day were piling up, crowding her brain with an unwieldy mess of accumulated doubt. *Just ask him, Cassie. Ask him and get it over with.*

"Jake mentioned that he'd been here today."

Eric's eyes narrowed slightly. "That's right."

"You didn't tell me the meeting was about the partnerships."

"You didn't ask. Besides, what else would it be about? That's what I do for a living."

Cassie recalled Curt Jacob's gibe about Eric's rich-man's hands. Evidently he made a very good living out of it. Who else invested in these partnerships? Little old ladies? "I...understand Jake invested in something to do with cows."

Eric's eyes slid away, evading hers. "Yes, he did."

"Why would you let him do that?" The tone of the question left no doubt about her anger.

"I advised him against it, Cassie. It is riskier than some of the other ventures. But Jake was fascinated by the concept and figured he'd get his money out of enjoyment, if no other way."

"Enjoyment! They're not going to rear the cows on his land, are they?"

This brought a smile to Eric's lips. "No, hardly. But Jake's been invited to Minneapolis to tour the facilities, and he can observe the whole process. Removing the embryo, freezing it, placing it in the host cow. So..." Eric held up his hands in a "what can I do?" gesture. "He bit."

"Bit! That's how you describe a so-called investment?"

"Cassie, for crying out loud. It's like betting on a high-odds horse. If you win, it's big bucks, but you have to be prepared to lose."

"And if he loses, he's in debt to you?"

Eric frowned. "He told you that?"

"Yes." Cassie could see he was surprised. So, she wasn't supposed to know.

"It's no big deal. He didn't have the cash handy, so I loaned it to him. He's good for it; I know that."

"Did he give you any collateral?"

"What are you getting at?"

She was on a roll and couldn't seem to stop. "Like Cliffhanger, for instance? I understand you'd hoped to win it in a card game. Maybe this would be easier." Her words rolled out, muddying the air, making everything look dirty.

Eric's face had closed down, shutting him in and her out. He looked furious. Furious, sick and deeply hurt. "You think this is a scheme to take Jake's house away from him?"

"Well..." Cassie's stomach was tying itself in knots. What if she was totally off base? Was there any retreat? "It just looked kind of suspicious—Jake getting into these deals when he's short on cash. And from what everyone says, you've openly admitted wanting Cliffhanger. Then you make love to me..." She stopped. Oh God, she hadn't intended to say that.

He just sat for a few seconds, obviously unable to believe what he'd heard. Cassie watched his face blank out completely, his eyes retreat. He sat back against the cushions of the couch, too stunned to react. The silence was deafening.

Finally Cassie blurted, "Eric, I'm sorry. I shouldn't have said that. I shouldn't have said any of it."

"Why not? It's what you believe, isn't it? We agreed to be open with each other about our feelings." He gave a short, angry bark of a laugh. "Boy. You do a more thorough job with words than Curt Jacobs could do with fists and a knife."

Cassie's knotted stomach turned rancid, sending sickening waves through her body. Some small brain cell in the back of her head was screaming "Error! Error!" "Eric..."

Eric stood up and walked over to stand in front of his large picture window and gaze outside. Such a spectacular night. A night for romance. All the ingredients were in place; the moon, the stars, the rippling water. There was champagne to drink and steaks to eat and a roaring fire in the fireplace. And a man who'd made a terrible mistake. Had laid his heart on the line and had it smashed to bits. Without turning he said, "I think it's time for the evening to end."

Cassie got up and walked over, putting her hand tentatively on his arm. "Can't we talk about this?"

He swiveled so suddenly that she jumped back. "Talk about what? If you really believe I'm slimy enough to con my best friend out of his house and make love to his granddaughter for...what? You figure it's all part of the scheme?" He held up a hand before she could speak. "I don't think we have anything left to say to each other. Unless it's salt-in-the-wound time."

Cassie was drowning. Drowning in her own sea of suspicion and mistrust. What had she done? Eric's entire demeanor, the look on his face, the set of his shoulders, the stiffness of his body, said No Trespassing. He had fenced her out, and there was no gate.

Cassie spun and ran, grabbing her jacket off its peg as she went. She didn't remember, when she got home, how she'd managed to get there. She went into her room and yanked off her clothes, then put on a long flannel nightgown and a heavy chenille robe. She was freezing. She found a pair of wool socks and pulled them on, then crawled into her bed, tucking the covers tightly under her chin. And there she lay, shivering, for a very long time, not really thinking about much of anything, because thinking was beyond her. She'd done enough thinking for one day, and the product had been the murder of her love affair. She had killed it dead with her own sharp tongue, driven by her own stupidity. She wished she could cry, but even her tear ducts had dried up.

She just lay, staring at the ceiling, muttering, "Stupid. Stupid, stupid, stupid."

The next day was one long stretch of misery for Eric. He tried to fill his time and his head with work, but stray thoughts kept creeping in, sliding needles under the fingernails of his mind. He was still numb from the shock of the night before. How? How in God's name could Cassie, who said she loved him, accuse him of being so low?

He was sitting at his desk, where he'd been staring blankly at a document for half an hour, still unaware of what it said. He opened a drawer, took out a pen, made a notation about a phone call he must make, turned to put the note on top of his briefcase and banged his knee into the drawer. "Damn it to hell!" He slammed the drawer shut, feeling a split-second's pleasure at the loud bang.

She'd been suspicious of him right from the start—so damned sure he was some sleazy con man out to bilk her grandfather. But to think she could still have such doubts about him after getting to know him....

He got up, too restless to sit still. All right, so she didn't really know him, so their love affair had been too brief for that. How could she make love with him, make plans to spend her life with him, and still not trust him? It was a good thing it had come out when it did so they could call a halt before she broke up with that Boston dude. They could take up where they'd left off. Get married. Invest in safe, triple A stock and government bonds. Dig their ruts and live in them. Just the right thing for Cassie. She could trust old Brian, because he'd never do anything out of the ordinary. It would all work out fine.

He sat down and put his head in his hands. If only it didn't hurt so damned much.

Cassie was taking a trip through misery. She'd gotten no answers, but that didn't keep her from feeling awful about asking the questions, because she knew instinctively she'd been wrong. So where had all that great instinct been when she needed it? Buried. Buried in the muck of her own built-in fears. Everything had been going too well. She had begun to yield to the magic of Big Sur, begun to expand, to reach out, to dare. She'd even dared to believe that someone as wonderful as Eric could really love her. That he could choose her above all other women. He really seemed to, didn't he? Love her and want her. In marriage. He'd mentioned marriage, even though she'd been told he would never get tied down to anyone. Ergo, something had to be wrong with him. He must have a fatal flaw. Otherwise, dreams came true. Fantasies could become reality. The wildest wish could be granted! But things like that didn't happen, not really. She'd been taught that all her life. Taught to be skeptical, taught to doubt. Taught that dreams turned to nightmares with great regularity. So, good little schoolteacher that she was, she'd set about to prove her beliefs were right.

She wished she could die. Curl up in a little ball and roll herself into a corner, where she'd quickly evaporate. She just couldn't stand the pain, so much worse because she'd brought it on herself. She glanced at her watch. Dear God, Brian would be here in a few hours.

Cassie moved her head back and forth, physically denying the reality implanted in her mind: everything was over between her and Eric. What did she do now?

She got up and began to pace. Maybe it was all for the better. A scaredy-cat like her didn't belong in a place like Big Sur with a man like Eric Wagner. It was all too much for her. The spectacular sweep of the scenery, the spectacular specimen of manhood. Both demanded more than she had to give.

She stopped in front of the window, gazing out at the endless stretch of glistening ocean, watching the sea gulls and the pelicans swoop and soar. Too much. She'd go back to Boston, marry Brian. Settle. Settle for what she could handle.

Brian was due to arrive at five-thirty. Jake had come home from a day of hiking with one of his buddies in time to wash and "make himself presentable" for the Boston banker. He kept eyeing Cassie as they waited, clearly wondering what had happened since the previous afternoon to so radically alter her mood. At one point he came up beside her at the front window where she'd been for five or ten minutes, just staring out, to ask, "Cassie, what's wrong? Are you this upset with me because I invested in those damned cows?"

She fought an instantaneous impulse to shout, "Yes! If you hadn't made that investment I'd still be waiting to tell Brian I wasn't going back to Boston. I'd still be happy. I'd still be alive!" But of course she didn't. No matter how much she might want to, she couldn't shift the blame for her own actions onto someone else, especially Jake.

"No. That bothered me, as you know. But that isn't what's wrong."

"Then what?" He looked at his watch. "Come on, it's only four-forty-five. Time to tell me why you're so sad." He turned her to him. "Cassie, you and I have always been straight with each other. I've tried to keep my curiosity to myself, even though it's been pretty damned plain there's something going on with you and Eric. But I think maybe it's time for me to butt in."

Cassie took one look at his kind face, its forehead furrowed with concern, and burst into tears. She cried too hard to talk for long moments while Jake held her, murmuring comforting words, running his hand over her hair, just as he used to when she fell down and hurt herself as a child. It felt so good, to slip back to a pattern of her youth that gave her such a feeling of safety, that she had to force herself back into an adult mode.

"Oh, Jake, I've been so stupid."

"I see. And what have you done to qualify for that deduction?"

She pulled back and turned away from him. "If I tell you, you'll be furious with me, too. Pretty soon there'll be no one left to love me!" It was the pitiful wail of a child seeking solace, which matched exactly the way she felt.

"Cassandra, there's nothing in the world you could do to make me stop loving you."

She stared up at him with tear-stained eyes. "Do you mean that?"

"Of course I do. Now, I can't promise not to get mad, but that's different. That's temporary, and you can handle it."

She turned back to him and rested her forehead against his wide chest, her fists balling up handfuls of his soft blue sweater. She wasn't entirely ready to relinquish her temporary retreat to childhood, but she knew she couldn't stretch it much farther. Taking a deep breath, she stepped away and stood up straight.

"I'm in love with him, Jake."

"I assume we're talking about Eric."

"Yes."

"So, what happened? Did he tell you he didn't want to get tied down?"

She shook her head. "No. Quite the contrary. He told me he loved me, too. He said he wanted to marry me."

Jake's face lit up like his birthday cake. "Hot damn! That's wonderful! Always knew that man had good sense. So you're worried about what to say to Brian?" He watched her face crumple and laid a comforting hand on her shoulder. "It is one hell of a time for him to show up, isn't it?"

Cassie walked over to sit on the sofa, her legs too weary to hold up her body any longer. "Jake, that's the reason Brian's coming out. I told him I wasn't going back to Boston. That I had a lot of thinking to do, but I was pretty sure I would stay here."

Jake, obviously puzzled, said. "Okay. So what's the next chapter?"

Cassie knotted her fingers together. "I talked to Eric about your investment in the cows."

"Now, damn it all, Cassie, why'd you do that? Anyone would think I was a child, the way you worry. I've been making my own decisions since I hit puberty, and I've done pretty damned well."

"I know, Jake. I'm sorry."

"Yeah, the picture's beginning to focus. Bet Eric got pretty sore, huh?" Just the hint of a smile played around his lips. "That what this is all about? He maybe told you to mind your own business?"

Cassie looked at him with pleading eyes. "I have to say this right out all at once, or I won't be able to."

"Okay." Jake sat down beside her, giving her his full attention. "Shoot."

"I went over there last night. He had champagne and steaks and a fire. It should have been wonderful. But after you'd told me about the cows, and about signing a note to Eric ... well, all my suspicions began to kick up. Then I remembered the thing at your party, when your friends were teasing Eric about coveting Cliffhanger ..."

"Oh, no. Cassie, you didn't."

"Oh, yes I did. I laid it all out there in a sticky pile. I even threw in the possibility that he wanted to marry me as a backup."

Jake looked too stunned to reply. It took several seconds for him to find enough breath to spurt, "Sweet Jerusalem! Of all the screwy ideas. Eric?" He got to his feet and paced back and forth in front of her, making a couple of loops before continuing. As for Cassie, she'd shot her bolt. She couldn't say anything else. Finally he stopped and stared at her. "How in the good Lord's name did you come up with that one?"

"Well, it was the fact that you'd already said you were short of cash. And that was before you made the first investment, in the platinum mine. Then when you said you'd signed a note. To Eric . . ."

"My God, Cassie." He plunked down heavily on the overstuffed chair across from her. "I had no idea you had any such thoughts in your head or I'd have straightened you out in the first place." He ran his palm over his eyes. "Hell. I'm afraid this is partly my fault." He wagged a finger at her. "Only partly, mind you. You should have better sense, if not better manners, than to run around poking your nose in my finances." He shook his head, as though to forestall her saying anything. "Now, you listen up, young lady, before that half-baked banker gets here and convinces you he's right and I'm not playing with a full deck." He leaned forward, his eyes pinning hers. "I've never told you much about my financial situation because I believe every young person should grow up with every expectation of having to take care of himself. Or herself. In your case, it's always been a possibility, because I've been a financial gambler all my life. The blue-chip stocks never interested me any more than the blue bloods did. I wasn't foolish, but I was rash more often than not. But—" his gaze sharpened "—that was my right."

Cassie shrank into the cushions. "I know."

The finger wagged again. "Luckily, I've done mighty damned well. You are looking at a well-fixed man. A damned well-fixed man. I was short of cash for exactly the reason I gave you. It was tied up in nonliquid assets. I bought one of the last stretches of California coastline to be had, and I got one hell of a buy on it because I paid cash. It was one of the best deals I ever landed, and Eric helped me cinch it. And, I might add, without there being one damn thing in it for him. That was like buying a great big hunk of gold dust instead of soil, and it'll undoubtedly be yours someday.

Cassie blinked. The picture being painted before her was swiftly verifying her assessment of herself: stupid, stupid, stupid!

"I could've got the money from any bank, but Eric didn't see any reason for me to bother. Being two of a kind, we've made short-term loans to each other several times, when there's a cash crunch. And no, of course there wasn't any collateral. I'd be willing to bet Eric would loan me anything he had if I just told him I needed it." Jake got up again to resume his pacing. "Oh, Cassandra. Do you know what you had? He's one of the finest men I've ever known. I'd take his word above any collateral offered. If he said he loved you, wanted to marry you, he was giving you all he had."

Cassie sat, dumb with pain, her heart cracking into tiny segments. At just that moment the back door opened and a voice called, "Hello, anyone here?"

"Oh, God," she murmured.

With a heavy sigh Jake started toward the kitchen, calling, "Come on in, Brian, you're right on time."

Chapter Ten

Reluctantly, Cassie followed Jake into the kitchen. She was surprised that Brian, with his Boston Brahman manners, had used the back door. Perhaps, at this late date, he was trying to seem like one of the family. It was an awkward moment. Brian stood just inside the door, decidedly ill at ease. He had on his usual attire, a gray suit with a white shirt and rep tie. After a second's hesitation Cassie went to him and gave him a hello kiss.

He smiled at her, a tentative signal of hope. Brian was a very nice-looking man. About five-foot-eleven, with a lean, well-exercised frame, sandy-brown hair and hazel eyes. His features were pleasantly arranged on his face in genial, symmetrical lines. He had, overall, a neat, compact appearance, pleasing to the eye.

She returned his smile as best she could. It was, after all, nice to see Brian. His presence reminded her of the old Cassie, the one who had lived in this body before. Before Eric. When she looked at Brian, there were no fireworks, no rushes of adrenaline, no stabbing currents of desire. Just a welcome feeling of everyday peace. Peace without a price. Cassie cringed as one of Jake's old clichés came to mind. *Most things that cost nothing are worth just what you paid for them.* She pushed the admonition aside. Right now a free ride sounded pretty good.

"Well, Brian, welcome." Jake seemed almost as rattled as she was.

For the first time it occurred to Cassie that their earlier conversation must have hit him pretty hard. He hadn't thought Brian was the man for her since the two men had first met a year ago. It wasn't really, he'd assured her, that he disliked Brian, he disliked the way Cassie was when she was with him. "Prim, proper and staid" was his assessment. In other words, dull. She was sure Eric was everything her grandfather could wish for her. And to be told in one breath that she had won him and lost him must be terribly disappointing.

Cassie said, "It's nice to see you. How was your trip?" The question sounded prim, proper and staid. She glanced at Jake and saw the judgment confirmed in his eyes.

"It was fine. Nothing out of the ordinary, which is what a plane trip should be." He shook Jake's proffered hand. "Nice to see you, sir."

Cassie blanched. Jake hated being called sir. It made him feel old and stuffy, two of his least favorite things. She hurriedly stepped in. "Why don't you bring your bag? You may as well get settled in your room."

"Good idea."

Jake stayed behind while she led Brian down the hall to the guest room. She felt starched. Too stiff to bend with the wind, way too stiff to survive the hurricane raging inside. "I don't think anything has changed since your last visit. Jake hasn't done any redecorating for a long time. Things could use a little sprucing up."

"Looks fine to me." He put his valise on the bed and hung up his jacket, taking more time than necessary with the simple chore. Cassie felt a wave of sympathy for him. The ups and downs of volatile emotions threw him. He'd been raised in a home where quiet, soft-spoken control was the working order of the household. He was unfamiliar with dramatic highs and lows; his world tended to stay pretty stable. It certainly wasn't a bad way to function; in fact, more desirable than many. Why did it no longer seem as satisfactory to her as it once had?

When he turned around he met her gaze solidly, once more in control. "We need to talk."

"Yes." But what in heaven's name was she to say? I'm in love with another man, but I've messed it up beyond hope? I've had the best time of my whole life, and the worst, what do I do now? "Why don't you change into something more casual and we can walk down to the beach."

"Fine. I'll be with you in a minute."

Cassie went back to the kitchen, where Jake sat at the round table, lost in thought. She pulled out a chair and sat down. "Brian's changing, then we're going to take a walk."

"Does he know about Eric?"

"No." She gave a mirthless laugh. "As it turns out, he doesn't need to."

Jake covered her hand with his. "Cass, don't close the door on Eric. You may be able to iron it out."

"He's already closed the door, Jake. And I don't blame him." She looked down at their two hands. Comforter and comforted. It had been like that for such a long time. Most of a lifetime. Usually, nothing seemed as bad when Jake was there, but this time it was a heart that was broken, and even Jake couldn't fix that.

Before anything else could be said, Brian appeared, and she got up, gave Jake a kiss on the cheek and joined Brian for their walk. The sun was peeking through the clouds, filtering sunlight over the hills and the ocean. The green was cushiony lush, displaying its gratitude for the plentitude of rain. They picked their way down the mountain path, not talking until they reached the sand below. Brian was very careful on the way down. He was uneasy with heights, and Big Sur set his nerves on edge.

They sat side by side on a large flat rock. He picked up a handful of sand and let it run through his fingers. "So. Where are we, Cassie?"

She stared out at the shimmering water. "I don't know." Now he would say, "If you don't, who does?"

"If you don't, then who does?"

Cassie stifled a perverse urge to laugh. Funny, Brian's very predictability had been one of the things she'd liked about him. Why did it now irritate her? She was growing increasingly out of patience with herself. Such a silly will-o'-the-wisp she'd become, blowing this way and that. A flibbertigibbet. She would have to make a decision and stick with it. She wished she felt more capable of making the right one.

"You're right, Brian. I'm the one who's zigzagging around." She shrugged her shoulders helplessly. "Something in me has changed, and I don't know what to do about it. I was so sure, when I called you, that I wanted to stay here in Big Sur. That I wanted my life to be far different from the one I'd planned. Now..."

"Now you're not so sure?"

"No."

"There's someone else involved, isn't there?"

She stared at him, surprised. "How did you know?"

"Just a guess. The way you sounded, like you weren't telling me everything." He looked down at his hands, folded in front of him. "It seems awfully sudden. I mean, you haven't been out here long enough to get to know anyone that well. Is it someone you'd known before?"

"No." Funny, it hadn't even occurred to her that it was a short amount of time. She felt as if she'd known Eric forever. As if they'd fused a relationship in some other time that immediately renewed itself when they came together. "He's a friend of Jake's." At Brian's amazed expression, she hastened to explain, "A much younger friend."

"He must have swept you off your feet."

Off my feet. Off the earth. Straight to heaven. "It...was pretty intense."

"Are you going to marry him?"

"No."

"Then what?"

She turned her gaze on Brian. Damn, this was terribly unfair to him. He deserved straight answers. Yes or no instead of maybe. She straightened up, hoping the motion would affect the inside of the backbone as well as the outside. "Brian, I feel very badly about putting you through this. You don't deserve it. It's not that I'm trying to avoid telling you the truth, it's that I'm so confused. I've never felt like this in my life. I'm well aware of how wrong it was for me to get involved with someone else while we were engaged. It was certainly the last thing in the world I expected, or wanted. It just—" she waved her hands helplessly "—happened." She dropped her eyes to cover the quivering of her lip. God, she couldn't cry. That would be too much.

"Cassie, I'd like to say something."

She nodded. He always introduced a subject of substance by that statement. Brian's preamble.

"As I said on the phone, this place always has a strange effect on you. When you come back from a visit, you seem..." It was clear that the first word that came to mind didn't pass muster. "Not wild, you could never be wild."

Oh, yes I could. I could indeed.

"But some of your, well, your good sense seems to desert you. It's never been too much of a problem before, because a short time back in Boston, where you belong, straightens you right out. Honey, this isn't your kind of place. Look at it." He made an all-encompassing sweep of his arm. "It's too...primitive."

Cassie bridled at the description, wondering how some of the natives would react to it. All their conservation work to protect this wonder of nature. Primitive.

He was continuing, "I wish you'd come home, Cassie. Come home and pull yourself together, then take another look at things. You and I belong together. We're two of a kind. We're civilized people who need the challenge and the activity of a city. Gosh, Cass, we had it all so well planned. Our future so perfectly laid out. You can't just throw it over for some... fluke of nature."

Eric. A fluke of nature?

"I'm sure your grandfather would be disappointed if you left before Christmas, but you could come right after the holiday." He took another sweeping look around. "You should get out of this place."

What he said was true: she *did* change when she was here. Her grandfather thought it was for the better and Brian for the worse, and Cassie was too befuddled to have a clear opinion. She was overwhelmed by the question, as she was by all the circumstances that led up to it, and as she was by the massive, elaborate scenery and the power of the love she'd found here. Maybe Boston *was* where she belonged. That was certainly part of what she needed to settle. She had to take stock, to find and steady that core of herself that seemed to shimmy back and forth like a boneless wonder, before she could possibly make a solid commitment to anyone else.

She touched his hand with her fingertips. "I have to be honest with you, Brian. The relationship got very... personal."

"You slept with him."

"Yes."

His head hung for a moment, then he lifted his eyes to look at her. "I assumed that. Something as fast and as intense as you're describing is usually based on... physical attraction."

Physical attraction. Oh, yes. And mental and emotional and spiritual. All encompassing. Too much.

"And you still want me to come back?"

"Yes."

Cassie looked at him, struck by what a decent man he was, a man any woman in her right mind would latch on to without a second thought. But had she ever really loved him? Not in the definition of the word she'd found here.

She sat for a moment, staring out at the ever-moving sea, remembering the excitement of seeing the whales, the glory of those two times she and Eric had come together on the rock ledge, the crazy fun of making love in the Mercedes coupe, experiencing heights of passion beyond imagination. She thought of King Tut and the campaign to protect the seals. She thought of the surges of creative energy she got when she was here. She thought of Margo and some of the other friends she'd miss terribly. She thought of Jake, and felt like crying. Most of all, she thought of Eric, and felt her heart break. The questions she must answer and the decisions she must make were awesome, but absolutely necessary.

"All right. I'll come right after Christmas. As for anything else, I have to be honest and say I just don't know."

In the ensuing days the requirements of a swiftly approaching Christmas were the only things that kept Cassie going. Because Jake usually flew East to spend the holidays with Cassie and his sister, Bertha, he had taken the opportunity this year of including some of his closest friends in his preparations. Jake was hosting an open house on Christmas Eve, and he and Cassie were to have Christmas dinner at Margo's house. For Cassie, the devastating ingredient in both instances was the inclusion of Eric in the guest list.

She rolled whole conversations over and over in her mind. What she'd say and what he'd answer, her apology and his acceptance, always leading to a happy conclusion that included their mutual declarations of love. But even in the midst of her daydreaming, she recognized the unlikelihood of such a happy resolution. Her halcyon days had ended. Time to return to reality.

She threw herself into the Christmas preparations with determination, in a vain attempt to block out the pain that was her constant companion. After a brief discussion following Brian's departure, she and Jake had avoided the subject of her future. His disapproval of her decision to leave right after Christmas permeated the air around them and introduced a forced amicability upon their relationship that had never been there before.

She and Jake went out together to select the tree, and settled, by mutual agreement, on a magnificent giant that fit the dimensions of Cliffhanger's living room. Margo came over to help decorate it, and her presence helped reduce the uneasiness between Cassie and her grandfather. When all the ornaments were on and the crystal star had been added to the treetop, Jake stood back and smiled. "Okay, here goes!" He plugged in the lights and the three of them gasped in unison. It was beautiful.

While Jake went to the kitchen to pour them each a glass of eggnog, Margo turned her attention to Cassie. "Now all we need is someone to turn on *your* lights."

Cassie sighed. She might have known there was no way to disguise her mood from her friend. "That," she said, "is impossible."

"Well, the cause is no secret. I've seen Eric several times in the last few days, and he looks like walking death." She arched her brows at Cassie. "Must be contagious, whatever it is."

"Margo, to make a sorry story simple, our Karma has been canceled."

Margo shook her head. "Karmas aren't canceled, they're interfered with. You couldn't handle it, could you, Cassie? Being that much in love."

Cassie started to make an angry retort to Margo's automatic assumption that it was her fault. But one look in the other woman's eyes stopped her. Margo's intuition, as usual, was correct. "No, I don't suppose I could."

"Are you still in love with him?"

Cassie hesitated only a second before remembering there was little chance of concealing anything from Margo. "Yes. I suppose, to some degree, I'll always love him. There's something in all of us that insists on clinging to fantasy."

"What bull! What you and Eric had together was not fantasy. It was the rare sort of supreme reality that few of us are fortunate enough to experience."

Cassie held up her hand. "Margo, please stop. I can't keep up with your psychic insights right now. It's finished, and I am returning to Boston, probably to marry Brian. And that's that. Nothing can change it."

"Never attempt to forestall fate, Cassie. It's impossible."

"What does that mean?"

Their conversation was interrupted by Jake's return. He set the small round tray on a side table and handed them each a full glass before taking his own. Lifting it, he said, "Here's to a Christmas full of the Lord's blessings." His eyes swung to Cassie. "And maybe a little heavenly interference."

Though Cassie was sure her problems were not about to be solved by a messenger from above, she raised her glass and drank.

The Christmas Eve party was, blessedly, too crowded to force much contact between Cassie and Eric. But that didn't keep her eyes from following him or her heart from lurching painfully every time he talked to another woman or glanced at Cassie then quickly looked away. The longing that accompanied each glimpse of him was immense, and no amount of mental gymnastics could convince her heart that there was any logic or advantage to this estrangement. As she moved through the groups, stopping to chat and wish everyone a happy holiday, another realization added weight to her heavy heart. Because she had, on this visit, opened up to these people as never before, many of them had staked a claim on her affections, and leaving them was going to be very difficult. Dear heaven, how in the world had she managed to foul up every aspect of her life so thoroughly?

Eric tried to keep his eyes away from Cassie, but it was a futile exercise. He wanted, above all else, to cross the room and pull her into his arms, to push aside the doubts and the misunderstandings and return to the happiness they'd known for such a brief time. But the anger and hurt caused by her accusations were still imbedded in his mind. Better to let it go. Fate was clearly against him in matters of the heart. Three strikes and you're out. Life's umpire had called it, and arguing with an umpire fell in the same category as head beating on a brick wall.

He stayed only half an hour, then made some lame excuse to Jake about other social obligations. It was clear from Jake's expression that he wasn't fooled, but there was no censure in the older man's eyes, just a deep sorrow. Eric shook his hand as he said goodbye, wrestling with the question of whether to broach the subject. He decided he couldn't just let it lie. "I suppose you know that Cassie and I got beyond friendship." Hell. What a clumsy way to put it.

"Yes, I know. I also know the balloon has been punctured."

Eric looked down, rather surprised to see that his feet stood just as solidly on the ground as before. He'd have sworn every part of him was shaky. "I don't know what to say, except I'm sorry it didn't work out, and I hope it doesn't damage our friendship."

"I'm sorry, too, and of course it won't. Cassie made it clear that she's the one who messed it up."

Eric's eyebrows rose in surprise. "She did?"

Jake nodded. "Yes. Believe me, she's well aware of how wrong she was about you. I'm afraid part of the blame was mine, Eric. A few things I said led her to believe I was in rocky shape financially, so her imagination concocted some weird scenarios."

For a moment Jake's words formed a lifeline of hope that Eric was sorely tempted to grab. But the hurt had cut too deep for instant cures. There was a fundamental flaw in the relationship between him and Cassie, and it would take more than a few words to remove it. After a brief hesitation he repeated his goodbye and turned to leave.

The following morning, Christmas dawned bright and cheery, lit by welcome streaks of sunlight cutting through the clouds. Cassie and Jake had an indulgent breakfast of orange juice, coffee and sticky cinnamon buns, then tackled the surprisingly big stack of gifts, oohing and ahhing over each and every one, as might be expected. Unfortunately no amount of sunshine could disperse the gloom of unhappy conditions and impending separation that clouded their world.

When it came time to leave for Margo's, Cassie got dressed, followed Jake as far as the car, then stopped and said, "I don't think I can do this, Jake."

He turned and looked at her sympathetically. "I know it's hard, honey, but it would be unpardonably rude to back out now."

She took a deep breath and blew it out audibly, then nodded. "You're right. Let's go."

Margo's house looked beautiful. Her Christmas tree was perfectly formed and trimmed with a collection of miniature handmade dolls she'd collected on her travels around the world. To and Fro met them at the door, resplendent in fancy new jeweled collars. Although Fro wore his proudly, To kept stretching her neck in a vain attempt to bite the new addition.

"Come in, come in. Merry Christmas." Margo was all smiles, and Cassie barely heard any of the friendly exchanges as they were ushered in and introduced to Margo's parents from Dallas, a handsome couple who wore their age well, and Barry and Joan Lindsay, old friends of Margo's from her youth.

Eric stood back, his dark eyes studying Cassie, relentlessly passing their view of the young woman to his guarded brain: beautiful, appealing, sexy, sad. He yearned to stamp across the room, grab her by the hand and pull her outside where they could have a good healthy fight and clear the air. But every defensive habit accumulated from years of dealing with his mother's unpredictability, followed by the awful erosion of trust in his ex-wife, had been snapped firmly in place by the airing of Cassie's suspicions.

The afternoon passed, somehow, with both Cassie and Eric expelling most of their energies avoiding each other's eyes and searching their blocked brains for suitable snagends of conversation. The atmosphere was also charged with Margo's restless energy. She was clearly disturbed, and when questioned by Jake, simply brushed it off. "It's probably nothing. You know how I've had a sense of impending calamity for some time. Just my overactive imagination, I'm sure."

At long last the afternoon melded into evening, and the time for departure arrived.

Jake and Cassie left, followed closely by Eric. They walked in strained silence toward their cars. Jake purposely accelerated his stride to leave Eric and his granddaughter together. They trudged along, trapped in painful quiet, until Eric said, "I hear you're going back to Boston."

Cassie didn't look at him. She couldn't. "Yes. Tomorrow."

He stopped, his hands jammed in the pockets of his slacks, his head lowered. "I suppose it's for the best."

Cassie had thought her heart was too shattered for further damage, but she must have been wrong, because his words caused a definite cracking in the left region of her chest. "I suppose."

They looked at each other for a long moment, two prisoners of reticence. Then, with a hurried goodbye, they went their separate ways.

As Cassie got ready for bed that night, her mind kept replaying the scene with Eric. The brief confrontation had forced one decision among the many that must be made. She was still unsure of much that lay ahead, but there was little doubt about her relationship with Brian. It was over. She had found a depth of feeling she'd had no idea was hers, a depth she couldn't share with Brian, and there was no way she could, or would, turn it off.

Cassie struggled to wake up, her sleep-drugged mind fighting through the veiled cocoon of slumber. "What...what's the matter?"

Jake was standing over her, shaking her awake. "I'm sorry, Cass. I have to go out for a while, and I didn't want to chance your waking up and finding me gone."

She rubbed her eyes. It was still black outside. "Why? I mean, what's happening?"

Jake sat on the edge of her bed. "There's been a slide on the Old Coast Road. A couple of the rangers need some help getting the residents out."

"But why do you have to go?"

"Don't worry, I won't be doing anything dangerous. I'm more familiar with the back land than just about anyone. I make a good guide. A couple of the rangers were already out on calls, so they need extra manpower. I should be back in plenty of time to say goodbye." He leaned over to give her a quick kiss on the forehead, then hurriedly left. She lay awake for some time, worrying about Jake, fighting a general sense of uneasiness. A strange aura of peril hung in the air. Probably a result of Jake's departure added to Margo's disturbed mood of the day before, piled on the dreary circumstances in which she'd been trapped. It was no help to hear the pinging of the rain on the roof once again. Although, on second thought, it would be easier to bid goodbye to Big Sur in bad weather than in good. Eventually she drifted back to welcome sleep.

* * *

Cassie jerked awake, her eyes wide open and her heart pounding. She lay staring into early-morning shadows as her breath came in gasps and her pulse beat erratically in her throat. She was terrified. Why? Her ears strained, listening for something, a clue to whatever had jarred her awake. She sat up, clutching the covers under her chin, moving her eyes slowly around the room, wondering what had frightened her. Maybe Jake was back and had made some noise on his way to his room. Shivering, she climbed out of bed and struggled into her robe and pushed her feet in her slippers. With nagging fear slowing her steps, she made her way down the hall to Jake's room. The door was open and the bed empty.

That discovery did nothing to ease her mind. What was taking him so long? And what had she heard? The awakening dawn sent dim shafts of light through windows and doors and small apertures, lending a ghostly pall to the threatening ambience. Cassie, wearing her heart in her throat, tiptoed down the hall, half expecting a burglar to leap out of one of the shadows. Her timid tour of the house turned up nothing suspicious, so Cassie went back to bed, irritated at having been so rudely awakened. It must have been one heck of a dream to bring on such a reaction. Once she was snuggled in her still-cozy bed, it didn't take her long to start to drift off.

But sleep was forestalled. An ominous noise, distant but massive, rumbled a warning, then her bed shuddered, as though struck by its own personal terror. She sat bolt upright just as something banged loudly on the roof. In reflex action Cassie ducked, folding her hands over her head. Huddled in that position, she waited. Silence. By this time fear had moved in to stay. There was no question of trying to get back to sleep. She had been shaken to full wakefulness.

She climbed gingerly out of bed, alert to any new sounds, and rapidly dressed. Jeans and a sweater and sneakers with socks. She brushed her teeth, washed her face and combed her hair. Filled as she was with watchful apprehension, she wanted to be ready to move at a moment's notice. Damn. Of all times, why did Jake have to be gone now? She headed instinctively for the phone, stopping just as her hand reached for the receiver. For crying out loud, she certainly couldn't call Eric. He'd be sure to think she was trying some last-minute ruse to get him back.

Gathering up her scant store of courage, she put on a jacket and, pausing at the back door to take a deep breath and offer herself a little encouragement, she pulled the door open and stepped outside. The rain had stopped, but the sky was covered by low-hanging, dingy gray clouds that gave the whole area an aspect of apprehension, as though cowering before an expected blow. God, she was really letting her imagination run rampant. The noise had probably been thunder, and the movement of the bed her jangled imagination. As for the thump on the roof, undoubtedly a broken branch pushed by the wind. She stepped a few feet farther from the house. Except there wasn't any wind. Not even a breeze.

She stood, rooted to the ground by an overwhelming sense of oppression. Something felt terribly wrong. To hell with stiff upper lips—she'd call the ranger station and ask if they'd heard from Jake. She hurried back inside and picked up the receiver. There was no dial tone. Swallowing hard, she rattled the lever and listened again. Dead. Don't panic, she ordered herself. The phone connections do come down occasionally. It means nothing.

She'd have a cup of hot tea to steady her nerves before trying to make any decisions. After filling the pot with water, she placed it on the front burner and turned on the heat. It was still dark enough to be gloomy, so Cassie crossed to the overhead light switch and flicked it on. Nothing. Oh, no, not the electricity, too. But a check of the burner, still cold, and a couple more switches that produced no light confirmed her suspicions. What in the world was going on? Instead of hanging around here alone getting the willies, she'd go to River Inn where many of the early-rising workmen ate breakfast. They were the most avid harbingers of news as, well as gossip; they should know what was happening. She might even be able to get word about Jake.

She turned off the burner in case the power came back on and wrote a note to Jake, which she left on the kitchen table. After getting her purse and car keys and putting her jacket back on, she went out to the garage. She disconnected the automatic opener and lifted the door manually, glad to have a purpose that involved a little exertion. It helped hold her jumpiness at bay. She wondered if she should just leave the door open for Jake, but decided against it. There was a lot of accumulated debris from Christmas in the bins, waiting for the trash collector, and there was an occasional scavenging dog or raccoon. After carefully backing out she put the car in neutral and set the brake while she climbed out to lower the door.

As she reached for the door handle it moved to the right, just out of grasp. Cassie stared up at it in disbelief. She blinked her eyes and tried again, but this time the earth shook beneath her, and she stumbled back toward the car. Dear God. An earthquake! She put out her hand to steady herself on the fender, her mind whirling. She'd never been in an earthquake, not in all the years she'd been coming West. She didn't think they had earthquakes in Big Sur! But a slight tremor under her feet stabilized her terror. What should she do? Go inside? Stay out here? Oh, Jake! Where was he?

The car radio! She'd drive back into the garage, then sit inside and listen. Surely she'd hear some news. She hurried to the driver's side and lifted her foot to get in; but she was startled to a halt by a tremendous roar, a booming monolith of sound that shattered the air and shook the ground. Grabbing hold of the car for support, she froze in fear, her eyes darting about, her heart leaping in a frenzied pattern of alarm. Then her heart stopped for a moment, suspended by horror. Down the road, not more than a half mile away, what looked like all the dirt in the world was careening down the mountainside, with huge boulders and rocks of all sizes flying in every direction. Cassie stood, mouth open, eyes round, blood pounding through her veins, watching the awful spectacle. Landslide! Just then, a flurry of small stones with some loose dirt fell on the roof of the house, shocking her back into action.

She slammed the car door and raced for the cover of the garage, where she flattened herself against the inner wall, next to the mountain. She could barely think through the dense matting of fear that encased her brain. Should she shut the garage door? No. An instant picture of being trapped in there, buried under deep piles of dirt and rock, snapped into her mind. She wanted to see outside as long as she could. The dreadful thunder of plunging earth seemed to go on forever. Cassie hunkered down, sitting on her heels, her head in her hands, her eyes closed, as though shutting out the sight could cancel the action. At last the ground ceased to shudder and the ghastly noise died out. Still she huddled against the wall, too scared to move, her mind whipping from one anxiety to the next. Where was Jake? Was he all right? And Eric? Oh God, the landslide was in the direction of Eric's house. What if—

Her hands dropped from her eyes, and she got quickly to her feet. Eric. She must get to him—make sure he was safe. As she headed out of the garage her eyes fell on a shovel leaning against the wall. Yes. She'd better take it. In case.

She ran out of the garage, wedged the shovel in the back seat, got behind the wheel and drove up the driveway. She made a right turn and stopped cold. It wasn't necessary to go any farther to see that up ahead where the landslide had been a good part of the highway was missing, and the section that was left was cluttered with rocks and debris. Overcome by the enormity of the disaster and the terrible possibilities it held, she slumped forward, laying her head on the steering wheel.

"Cassie!"

Her head jerked up and she looked out the window. She couldn't believe it. It was a miracle! Eric stood there, hair askew and face smeared with dirt. His jeans were stained and his shirt torn. He looked wonderful. "Eric? Oh, God. Eric!" As he pulled the door open, Cassie jumped out of the car and into his arms. "I was so scared! I thought..." She gulped for air. "I was trying to get to your house."

Eric pulled back from the embrace, his eyes taking in the car and the shovel. "You were coming to rescue me?"

Cassie nodded, too choked up to say anything else.

"Cassie." He tightened his embrace. "My darling, brave Cassie."

Brave? Her?

A wobble beneath their feet shook them both to attention. "Come on." He turned her toward the car, where she slid under the wheel to the other side, with Eric right behind her. He jammed the gearshift into reverse and backed up enough to head the nose of the car down the driveway and into the garage. As they headed into the house, he asked, "Where's Jake?"

"He left in the middle of the night. There was a slide on the Old Coast Road, and Jake went to help one of the rangers get to someone. I don't know any more than that."

Eric pushed his fingers through his hair. "Damn. He could be stuck back there. That must have been the first slide. There's been another on that road, as well as on Highway 1."

She stared at him. "Another on Highway 1? You mean before this?"

"Yes. At the other end of the valley. Big Sur is cut off at both ends." He looked at her, one brow rising. "Guess you'll miss your plane."

She held her gaze steady, so happy to have him here that guarding her silly pride had fallen right off her list of priorities. "It looks like it." She smiled, ever so slightly. "What a shame."

He shook his head. "God, what a woman. It takes an earthquake and a landslide to keep you where you belong. Next time you try to leave we may be hit with our first typhoon."

She laid her hand on his arm. "I'm so glad you're here. You can't possibly know how terrified I was when I thought you might be injured."

He slid his hand behind the nape of her neck and pulled her to him. "Oh, yes, I can." When his lips touched hers the whole world seemed to sort itself out and come back together, with all the pieces in the right place.

She slid her arms around his neck, holding on in near-desperate tightness. The kiss, deep and demanding, shut out the terror of the morning, the worry about Jake, the sadness of the days just past, for that little, welcome space of time.

Then Eric raised his head, his eyes full of love. "How did we get so fouled up?"

She shook her head helplessly. "It was my fault. I—"

"Shh." He put his finger on her lips. "Let's not assign blame. We both let go of something we should have been ready to fight for. I wish we could stay here, just the two of us, so we could get a lot of things settled. Let the rest of the world fall into the ocean, if that's what it has in mind."

She could read the *but* in his eyes. "But..."

"Yes, but. There are people out there who need our help. And I want to know how Jake is doing. I'm afraid our personal affairs will have to wait." He took her face in his hands. "Ready to go to work?"

Cassie felt, and dismissed, a wave of fear. She was scared to venture out, but she wanted to be with Eric, wherever he went. "Yes."

Eric gave her a kiss on the nose, then took her hand and headed for the unpredictable outdoors. As he closed the door behind him, he turned and gave it a pat. "Hang in there, old friend. Time to live up to your name." He put his arm around Cassie's shoulders. "We may be about to do a little cliffhanging ourselves."

Chapter Eleven

When they were outside, Cassie cast an uneasy glance up at the mountain that towered above them on the other side of Highway 1, checking it for stability. She was so intent in her examination that she failed to notice, for a moment, that they were headed up the driveway instead of to the garage. "Aren't we taking my car?"

"No. We'll need the Jeep. I parked it up the road. Couldn't get past a couple of boulders that had fallen."

They walked hurriedly, Cassie keeping a wary eye on the hills. "Eric, I haven't had a chance to ask, is your house okay?"

"I don't know. I've been in town since the middle of the night, helping out. A few people are already homeless, and there'll be more. As you saw, access to my place has been cut off. All I can do for the moment is hope."

"What a mess."

"What a mess, indeed."

The "couple of boulders" turned out to be a mass of huge and not so huge rocks that had slid down to rest in the middle of the highway, making passage by motorized vehicle impossible. As they walked around the obstruction, the full measure of the disaster, along with a realization of what might have happened, hit Cassie, and she felt her whole body begin to shudder.

Eric stopped and pulled her into his arms. "Honey, take it easy. You're shaking so hard you may get the mountain started again." When he saw the terror in her eyes, he said, "I'm sorry. It's no time for corny jokes."

She huddled in his arms, grasping him tightly around the waist. "Oh, Eric, I was so scared."

"So was I."

"You?" She stared up at him in surprise. "I didn't think anything frightened you."

Eric's dark eyes were tender as he gently pushed a strand of hair off her cheek. "Anyone who isn't scared by an earthquake and a landslide has got to be a little soft in the head."

She hugged him ever harder. "That makes me feel so much better."

Eric looked up. "For two people concerned about landslides, we've picked a hell of a place to stand."

Once they were in the Jeep and on their way, Cassie began to relax a little. There was something about being on the move, having something to do, that erased the feeling of being a victim-in-waiting.

It was amazing how normal this part of the highway looked. Here and there a stray rock or two sat in the road, but nothing that hinted of the devastation behind them. Eric drove straight to the small grammar school, where cots had been set up and men and women were busily engaged in preparing the facilities to house a number of people.

Cassie was delighted to see Margo there, and she hurried across the room to give her a hug. "Gosh, am I glad to see you! Is your house all right? How about To and Fro?"

Margo, who looked uncharacteristically rattled, answered, "The garage was damaged but the rest of the house is fine. To and Fro are nervous wrecks, but they're unhurt." She gave Cassie a visual inspection. "You appear to be in one piece."

"Yes. Cliffhanger wasn't in the line of fire, thank God."

"Then Jake's okay?"

Cassie frowned. "I don't know. I'm awfully worried about him." She told Margo about his middle of the night departure and Eric's concern about another slide.

Margo glanced over at Eric, who was deep in conversation with Ben Justin, the sheriff. "How did you two hook up?"

"He came to check on us. He's worried about Jake, too."

At that point Eric left the sheriff and came to join them. "Jake and Bill Coogan should have been back hours ago, and nobody's heard from them. The road's impassable."

Cassie's hand flew to her mouth. "Oh my God! What if Jake's hurt?"

"Let's not jump to conclusions. He may be fine. If they had to abandon the Rover, obviously they'd have no way to make radio contact. They could be at one of the houses out there."

Margo looked skeptical. "But if they had to leave their car, why wouldn't they have called in to let someone know?"

Eric had thought of the same thing and had no answer. "Ben thinks I could drive as far as the Goodhue farm. I'm going to borrow one of their horses and go take a look."

Cassie said, "I want to come with you. Do they have two horses?"

"Cassie, this could be dangerous."

"He's my grandfather, Eric! And I'm an excellent rider. I've ridden all my life."

Margo put a staying hand on Cassie's arm. "Can't one of the other men go with you, Eric?"

"Not right now. Everyone who's capable is up to his neck, and helicopters will be a while coming. I don't want to wait."

Cassie nodded emphatically. "Neither do I. Let's go."

Eric looked at her, eyebrows raised, wondering how this self-proclaimed city girl would hold up in a crisis. Better than she thinks, he decided. "Okay. Let's hit the road."

They said goodbye to Margo, gathered up a pack full of emergency supplies and headed back to the Jeep.

They started out at what seemed to Cassie like a terribly fast clip, considering the conditions. She had impulsively dealt herself into the rescue mission, and although she wasn't sorry, she *was* scared. How had she of all people ended up in such a precarious situation? Her tolerance for danger was very slight, and she preferred it meted out in controllable portions from a movie or TV screen. She glanced over at Eric, whose attention was focused entirely on the road ahead. His jaw was set, his brow furrowed with lines of concentration. He exuded competence and strength, and just looking at him increased her tiny, wavering store of courage. Would she follow him anywhere? Yes. At this moment, she would. She could trust him to do everything in his power to ensure her safety. Hers or Jake's. And in the present circumstances she must be prepared to do no less.

The road was slippery and, in spots, cluttered with rocks. She and Eric had to get out several times to clear the way, but they were able to reach the Goodhue farm. She followed Eric to the door, where he banged impatiently.

Barney Goodhue pulled back the curtain of the adjacent window, peered out, smiled and opened the door. "Hot damn, Eric, what're you doing here?"

"Heading out to check the damage, Barney. I'm hoping we can borrow a couple of horses. The road's out."

"Yep, I know. Tried to drive that way myself to see how Myra's doing, but didn't get very far. You're welcome to the horses, they're all wanting some exercise, anyhow. Tell me, did Jake and that ranger fellow get back okay?"

Cassie asked. "You saw them?"

"Yep. Long time ago, though. Must've been three, four in the morning. They stopped to see if we were all right, and I gave them a cup of coffee." He took another look at her. "You Jake's granddaughter?"

"Yes."

"Uh-huh. Good man, Jake."

Eric looked more worried than before. "No one's heard from them, Barney."

Barney looked from Eric to Cassie and back to Eric. "I see. Guess you'd like to get saddled up and on your way."

"Please."

They followed him out to the barn as he continued to fill them in. "Talked to the Blacks just before the phone went out. They're okay. And the Cases, too. Bess and Jim Craigie should be in a pretty safe spot." There were six horses in the barn, all watching with apparent interest as they entered. "See there? Every one of them hoping to get a gallop. Poor things. Since I pulled my back out they haven't been ridden as much as they'd like. Have to rely on neighbors to take them out." He patted two of the handsome animals on the nose as he passed. "Better take Jericho and Casper. Neither of them is skittish."

Cassie led the animals out of the stalls while Barney and Jake readied the saddles and bridles. Her heart was accelerating, spurred by the uncertainty of what lay ahead. She was a good rider, but she certainly wasn't used to going out on slippery mountains where the footing was bound to be hazardous.

It didn't take long for them to be on the way. Barney had thrown a couple of blankets behind the saddles, in case they were needed, and assured them he and his wife would have food ready and extra beds made.

Jericho and Casper strained at the reins, eager to be turned loose to run. Eric and Cassie cantered side by side for a way while the road allowed it. Even here, where the damage was slight, the road had deep tire ruts and potholes filled with water. They hadn't gone far before they ran into the first obstruction and had to go single file. Eric led the way, keeping his eyes sharp, his body ready for instant reflex. The twisting road offered only short spans of forward vision, and soon even the spirited horses began to pick their way more carefully.

Eric pulled Jericho in, slowing him to a walk, and just in time. They rounded a corner and were instantly faced with a totally washed-out roadway. Jericho whinnied and stopped, tossing his head in disgust.

"Eric, look!"

He followed Cassie's pointing finger. "God almighty."

Down the face of the hill, about a hundred yards, was the Rover, lying on its side. Jake was leaning his back against it, his eyes closed. Beside him lay Bill Coogan, with his legs trapped under the vehicle.

"Oh my God." Cassie slid down off the horse. "Jake!"

Eric quickly dismounted and, grabbing the pack full of gear, started down the mountain, with Cassie close behind.

It was slippery going, but when they reached the Rover Jake's eyes were open and he had a relieved smile on his face. "Well, look who's here. Eric's back on the rescue squad." His tired eyes moved to Cassie. "And he brought his beautiful woman with him, 'cause there sure aren't any here." He held up his hand. "Hi, honey. How'd this guy manage to get you out on the trail?"

Eric squatted beside him. "She wouldn't stay behind. That's the trouble with women today, too damn pushy." He looked from Jake to Bill. "What's the damage?"

Jake hadn't moved his right hand from the trapped man's shoulder. "Bill passed out about an hour ago. Good thing; he was in a lot of pain." He gestured at his left foot. "I think I've got a broken ankle. I was no damn use trying to get this thing off him."

"Don't know why. Couldn't weigh more than a couple of tons."

Cassie knelt down by Jake, ignoring the way her knees sank into the mud. Her eyes were full of tears. "Are you all right? Are you sure?"

Jake patted her hand. "Fine, honey, just fine. It's Bill here I'm worried about."

Eric moved over to examine Bill's situation more closely. "Damn. Looks like both legs could be broken. He needs to be in a hospital, and I sure don't know how we're going to get him to one." He leaned down to see the position of the Rover. "At least it's resting on a big rock on one side of him."

"Yeah, I know." Jake eased himself away from the vehicle. "I tried scooping out some dirt under him, to see if I could pull him out, but it was obviously not going to work. On top of the other handicaps, I'm afraid I don't have much strength left. Seems to have been pretty thoroughly jarred."

"I should imagine."

"Jake—" Cassie stood up "—we've got some blankets. Are you cold?"

Jake shook his head. "Save them for Bill here. Did you bring any pain medication? He'll need it if he comes around."

"Eric? Is there any in the pack?"

"Yes." He turned back to Jake. "Are you sure you don't need anything?"

"Hell no. What's a broken ankle? A mere twinge."

"Jake, come on. Maybe you should take something."

He shook his head. "No, Cass. It's not that bad. And it's better for me to stay alert."

"Do you have a jack in the car?" Eric got up, ready to go to work.

"Yes. In the back."

"Cassie, we should've brought your shovel."

"Got one of those in there, too."

Eric looked at him in surprise. "Been digging a few holes?"

"Never got over the habit of carrying one after leaving Boston. Even without snow, it comes in handy more often than you'd think."

"Well, flex your muscles, Cassie. I'm going to need all the help I can get." Eric went to the back of the Rover and managed to get the rear door open. He located the jack and the small fold-up shovel. "Cassie, see how many good-sized rocks you can find. They'll need to be as flat as possible and as big as you can carry."

Together they searched the area and found a good number of rocks that Eric deemed usable. And between them they pulled a fallen tree trunk over to the car. After a couple of unsuccessful attempts to stand, Jake was persuaded to sit still and watch. "Now, let's see if this works."

By wedging the jack under the Rover and setting it on the big rock, Eric was able to slowly hoist the car while Cassie pushed stones into place with each slight movement, to hold it in place. It was laborious and frustrating work, but little by little they began to open up a bit of space.

"Okay. Cassie, let's see how hard you can lean against this while I try to shove the tree trunk under the other side. I'll have to dig some, so I'll need as much time as you can give me."

Jake held up a hand. "Get me on my feet, Eric. I can at least add my weight to the leaning." Neither Eric nor Cassie tried to discourage him. They needed all the help they could get.

After almost two hours of meticulous, painstaking work, Eric had the car elevated just enough to leave a tiny space between Bill and the auto. With both Cassie and Jake leaning on the jack, he managed to dig under the trapped man's shoulders enough to get a fair grasp on him. Bill groaned and moved his head.

"Don't come to now, friend," Eric mumbled. "This would probably just knock you out again." Sliding his hands and forearms as far under Bill's back as possible, he started to slowly, slowly pull. Sweat stood out on all three foreheads from the exertion, and they were all breathing in hard gulps of air. But there was no pausing and complaining.

Just as Cassie was sure her arms would shake loose from the strain, Eric gave a whoop of victory. "He's out!"

Jake cautioned her, "Let go slowly, Cass, so we don't jar anything loose." They eased up, and both sank to the ground exhausted.

After they'd all had time to regain their breath, Eric asked, "Think you could ride a horse, Jake? If we get you in the saddle? Just as far as the Goodhue farm."

"Sure I can. But what about Bill?"

Cassie looked at the two men, and her overworked heart crept up to her throat. It was quite clear what they needed her to do. "I'll stay here with him."

Eric cast an uneasy eye up at the fractious hill, then looked at her with a troubled expression. He didn't want to leave her in the path of the slide, but he'd have to drag Bill a long way to get them to safer ground, and he wasn't sure the man could stand any more trauma. "Guess we'll have to take you up on it." He knelt beside her. "I'll need to ride behind Jake to hold him. He's just about ready to collapse."

She glanced at her grandfather and nodded. "I know. I'll be all right. But shouldn't we wrap Bill in the blankets?"

"Yes. In fact..." Within minutes, Eric had taken the carpeting out of the rear of the Rover and gently moved Bill on top of it. Then he went up to the horses to get the blankets. As he and Cassie wrapped them around the injured man, he gave her instructions. "If he comes to, you'll want to give him some morphine." He dug a small bottle out of the pack. "Not more than two of these. And see if he'll drink some water. Talk to him, too. He may be in shock, and the more you can put him at ease, the better."

Cassie kept nodding her head, even as her mind rejected the notion of such calm, capable ministrations. She was fighting wave after wave of fear as the time for the men's departure got nearer.

When Bill was as well protected as they could make him, Eric stood up and surveyed the terrain. Cassie stood as close as she could get, huddling in the comforting curve of his arm. She glanced over at her grandfather, whose head was nodding. Eric was right, he had just about reached his limit. It was the first time she had ever thought he looked old. It made her stomach tighten.

"You'd better get going, Eric. I don't think Jake can take much more."

Eric followed her gaze and nodded. "Yeah." He held her by her shoulders and looked at her like a stern schoolmaster. "Now, listen. I'm going to lead the horses down here and tie Casper to the Rover. You watch the path Jake and I take back up to the road and remember it. If you hear any rumblings or feel the ground shake an inch, you get on that horse and get out of here as fast as you can move. Hear?"

Her mouth was dry halfway down her esophagus. "Yes." It was a mighty weak little reply.

"Promise?"

"I promise."

Eric drew her close and held her for a moment, his face buried in her hair. "You know, for a city girl, you sure come through in a pinch." Before he could lose his resolve and refuse to leave her, he stepped away and started up the steep slope to the horses.

It took some effort to get Jake in the saddle. He'd used up his reserve of energy and endurance and was very near passing out. But that indomitable spirit asserted itself, and with considerable help from his friend he climbed on the horse's back. Eric swung up behind him and reached around to take the reins. "Hold on, pardner."

"I'm holding." His voice betrayed the measure of his weakness.

Eric gazed down at Cassie, who looked so fragile and frightened that it took every ounce of his resolve to leave her. He didn't dare wait. Bill was in bad shape, and there was no way to get him moved without help. He reached down to touch Cassie's upheld hand. "I love you."

"I love you, too." She blinked, determined not to let the tears fall until after they'd left. "Better hurry."

"Yes." With one last, reluctant look, Eric nudged the horse into motion. All too soon they were completely out of sight, and Cassie was left alone with an an unsteady mountain and an unconscious man.

She went to Casper and checked his reins to make sure they could be quickly untied. Then she spotted a couple of old towels Jake had left in the back of the Rover. She pulled them out and placed them next to Bill's inert form. She'd never felt so entirely exhausted in her life. She was sure it was less the physical exertion than the mental trauma. After taking a close look at Bill she stretched out on the towels to rest. She'd have sworn there was no chance of her falling asleep in such a precarious position, but she did.

Eric badly wanted to spur Jericho to a gallop so he could get Jake to the farm, radio for help and get back to Cassie, but it was out of the question. Jake was very wobbly, and it took all of Eric's strength to keep him upright in the saddle. Although they made it to Goodhue's in less than an hour, it seemed like days to him.

Barney had put a stiff brace on his injured back so he could offer some help if it was needed. Emma Goodhue had started their generator so they could heat up some soup and coffee. Jake managed to slide down off the saddle and land on his good leg without incident. Between Barney and Eric, they got him to one of the spare beds, where Eric left him to Barney and Emma, who, despite Jake's protestations, cut off his trousers and wrapped the swollen ankle in cold cloths.

Eric ran out to his Jeep and radioed the location of the wrecked Rover and the condition of Bill to the sheriff, who promised to get some EMTs out there as quickly as possible. Taking a few minutes to look in on Jake, who was now being ministered to by a no-nonsense Emma, he told them he'd sent for help, bid them goodbye and raced for his horse.

This time he let Jericho have his head, and the sure-footed animal spurted forward in a fast gallop, keeping to the un-rutted outside segment of the narrow road. Eric knew he'd soon have to slow his pace, but he was desperate to get back to Cassie. He had a bad feeling in his gut. And his gut was seldom wrong.

Cassie, for the third time that day, was shaken out of her slumber. By the time she was fully awake she was sitting upright with her heart pounding. The earth was moving. Not much—a tiny shudder—but enough to put the fear of death into Cassie, to cause Casper to toss his head and whinny and to send a few rocks tumbling down the mountain, none of which, happily, came near them.

Cassie, terrified, leapt up and ran to the horse. Her hands flew to the reins, ready to loosen them so she could, as instructed, ride to safety. As she started to untie Casper, her eyes fell on Bill, lying there so still, so vulnerable. She'd never met the man before, and her instinct for survival was sending out steady alarms, but she knew at that moment that there was no way she could leave him there alone, in the path of another slide.

Even as she stood, uncertain of her next move, a section of muddy earth broke loose above the partly demolished road and tumbled down, barely missing Bill. Casper jerked back, shaking his head in fear. Cassie, absolutely certain she was far too scared to move, was miraculously galvanized into action. She took the looped rope Barney had attached to the saddle and ran to Bill. How could she move him without too much damage? She tried to calm herself, so her mind would work with some degree of clarity. What would Eric do? Just the thought of Eric gave her a needed rush of courage. He'd find a way. And so would she. With a fearful glance at the hill, she got to work on the only solution that came to mind.

With a great deal of pushing and tugging, she managed to get the rope under both the man and the auto rug. She looped it tightly and tied it around his waist. Digging through the pack, she found an army knife, which she used to pierce holes through both top corners of the carpet. After threading the two ends of the rope through the holes, she hurried back to the horse.

"Come on, Casper. Easy, boy. We have to work together now." Talking in as soothing a voice as she could muster, she untied him and led him to a spot just beyond Bill's head. What if the horse bolted? Oh God, she couldn't even think of that. She had to let go of the reins in order to finish her task. Talking softly, persuasively, she secured the ends of the rope around the saddle horn. Giving it a couple of tugs to test its holding power, she went to Casper's head and took the reins. She looked up in the direction that Eric had taken.

Too steep. Then where? She settled on the only course that looked possible.

"Okay, fella, it's up to you now. Slow and easy, that's the way." Giving Cassie a look she could only term doubtful, Casper started forward and the improvised sled-bed began to move. She needed to be two people, one to guide the horse and the other to walk beside Bill, to steady his passage. But she could only do so much. Just as they were getting underway, she heard something and stopped to listen. It was a muffled rumble that sounded as though it came from the bowels of the earth, and it was followed by a rolling movement beneath her feet. "Oh, dear God, not now!" Shutting out the terror that threatened as best she could, she urged the horse forward.

Eric, too, heard the earth's angry roar. He reined Jericho in and listened for the direction of the sound. God almighty. Straight ahead. He dug in his heels and they bolted forward, dodging rocks and bypassing washouts. Jericho seemed to sense his panic and responded expertly to each pull of the reins.

The Rover should be just ahead now, not too much farther. He pulled the horse in, anticipating the tricky curves ahead. After rounding the first, they were stopped in their tracks by a stream of small rocks that hurtled down the steep grade above. Eric tensed, afraid Jericho might buck. But the horse lived up to his billing. He wasn't skittish. Eric leaned forward and patted his neck. "Good boy. Now, let's go."

With surprisingly little urging, Jericho moved forward, lifting his feet over the rocks and dirt that hampered his stride. "I'm coming, Cassie, honey. Hold on." But just as they reached the last turn before the scene of the wreck, there was an ominous grinding sound, and the path began to rock. "Cassie!"

Eric dug in his heels, and after a protesting toss of his head Jericho went forward. The moment they rounded the bend, Eric saw Cassie, down the hill. She was walking in front of Casper, hanging on to his reins for dear life, dragging Bill behind them. He yelled, "Cassie!" and directed Jericho's nose straight down the muddy slope. The game horse followed orders and half walked, half slid down the steep terrain.

Cassie's head snapped up, and she cried, "Eric! Oh, thank God!" Never in her whole life had she been so happy to see someone. She stopped for a minute, but then the rumbling became louder, and the entire mountain appeared to shimmy. At its summit a portion of the dirt detached and started down the slope. Cassie screamed and pulled on the bridle, and Casper, straining against his encumbrance, surged forward.

Eric, without a second thought, kicked Jericho to a sliding careening gallop. They raced against the fall of the loosened mud, darting through flying rocks and stray clumps of earth. The moment he reached them he leaped down from the saddle and grabbed Casper's reins. "Get on Jericho and ride!" he shouted at her.

"I don't want to leave you!"

"Cassie—damn it!—do as you're told for once." He gave her a swat on her behind, which propelled her toward the horse. Without further hesitation she mounted.

The moment she was in the saddle, Jericho removed any need for decision by bolting for safety. She was hit on the head by a small rock, but although it hurt, it didn't stop her. When she got beyond the slide area, she managed to rein in the frightened horse and turn to watch Eric. He was running alongside Casper, urging on the gallant horse through falling rocks and mud and tree limbs. She looked up at the mountain and saw that the main slide was perilously close. She wanted to ride back to him, to help him pull, but knew there wasn't time to tie part of the rope to Jericho's saddle.

She dismounted and, dropping Jericho's reins, ran toward Eric, who yelled, "Cassie, stay back!"

"No!" She reached the carpet sled and twirled around, grabbing a section of the rope. Running and pulling, she managed to help steer Bill around some of the major bumps while she curled her body over him to ward off any of the flying rocks with her back.

They cleared the area seconds before the mass of earth, which had gathered bulk as it fell, crashed down just behind them and buried the Rover.

Cassie glanced behind her at the plummeting mud and whispered, "Oh my God." Her legs turned to butter and she folded to the ground next to the unconscious ranger.

Eric quickly took stock of their situation and ran back to pull Cassie to her feet. "Sorry, love. We're not quite out of the woods yet." He saw that she was very close to a state of shock, so he took hold of her arm firmly and placed her next to Casper's head. "Lead." He went back to help push and steer the precious cargo. As they moved he made a visual search for Jericho, who had understandably run from the frightening slide. After a few minutes he located the horse, standing uneasily under a tree up ahead, lifting his feet in a strange little dance, probably ready to sprint at the least provocation.

When they'd gone far enough to enter a more level area, where the hills dipped down to more gentle curves, Eric called, "Okay, we can stop here." He went to Cassie, took her in his arms and simply held her, so full of gratitude for her safety that he could find no words to express his feelings.

She leaned against him, her arms hanging at her sides, too heavy to move. "Oh, Eric." Her voice was a mere murmur. "I thought we were going to die."

His arms tightened around her. "I wouldn't have bet against it for a few minutes there." He turned his face into her hair, breathing in the scent of her, so full of love that he could barely house it. Reluctantly he lifted his head to look at her. "Honey, will you be all right for a minute? I'd better go after Jericho."

She nodded. "I'm okay. I'll check on Bill."

She watched him for a moment as he took off at a trot toward the horse, calling, "Jericho, good boy, atta baby, stay there," in a singsong tone of reassurance. When Cassie began to walk she realized how numb every part of her was. When she reached the ranger's side, he was moaning. She knelt down beside him and gently ran her hand over his forehead.

"Bill? Can you hear me?"

"Uhh..." His arm rose a couple of inches, then dropped heavily.

"You've been hurt. Lie still." His eyelids fluttered, then lifted partway. He looked at her with no appearance of focus. His head turned to one side and he groaned. "Oh, Lord, the pack!" She looked around, sure it must be buried deep under the newly transferred ground. Then her eyes lit on a small patch of blue. "Oh boy...maybe." Getting to her feet was a bit of a chore, and walking back in the direction of the slide took every ounce of gumption she could muster. But the effort was well worth it. It was the pack, partly hidden beneath fallen dirt. She pulled it loose and hurried away, back to Bill's side.

Eric, who had turned back with his captured steed just in time to see her heading toward the area of danger, had broken into a run. He got to her at the same time she returned to the sled. "What the hell are you doing? You could still get hurt!"

With a wisp of a smile, which was the best she could do, she held up the pack. "It must have stayed on top of the carpet most of the way. It was sticking out just enough to see." She gestured toward Bill. "He's coming around. He'll need the morphine."

"Lord Almighty, Cassie, I've come so close to losing you twice now. Don't round it out to three, please."

She looked up at him. "Yes, sir. I'll try to stay alive." They both managed weak but happy smiles. Her gaze moved over him. "You're a mess." He was. His hair was rumpled and full of small particles of debris. His shirt was torn and dirty, and he had nicks and scrapes on his face and arms, with trickles of blood running from them. "You look absolutely wonderful."

This time his mouth curved into a full-fledged grin. "I could say the same for you, lady, on both counts." He picked a twig out of her hair and tossed it to the ground. "I'm so damn proud of you. Aren't you proud of you?"

Cassie nodded as, for some reason, tears began to flow down her cheeks. "Oh, for crying out loud. Why would I start to bawl *now*?"

"Relief, honey. Sheer relief. You're entitled."

After one more stolen moment for a quick kiss, they went back to minister to Bill and to wait for help.

Chapter Twelve

Bill was conscious and, in spite of the morphine, terribly uncomfortable when the helicopter finally arrived almost two hours later. When they heard the motor, Eric mounted Jericho and rode to the level landing pad he'd located earlier, where he waved the pilot in. It took the expert EMTs little time to put Bill on a stretcher and hoist him into the copter. After assurances from both Eric and Cassie that they were in good enough shape to ride, the copter lifted off and soon disappeared over the hills.

By the time Eric and Cassie returned to the farm, they were both so tired they were tempted to accept the Good-hues' offer of a bath and a bed. But the urge to get home was too strong. They were told that Jake, protesting all the way, had been airlifted to a hospital in Monterey, where he would be kept at least overnight.

They got a couple of apples from Barney and returned to the barn to give the two gallant horses a treat, and to try to convey some of their gratitude for performances above and beyond the duty of horsehood. Cassie gave Casper a last rub on the nose, then joined Eric to walk to the Jeep. "I started to quote the line, 'You're a better man than I am, Gunga Din,' but since neither of us is a man, I figured it didn't fit."

Eric grinned. "That's okay. It's the thought that counts." He put his arm around her. "But I disagree, in any case. Casper is a stalwart steed, but you turned into a real bona fide heroine out there. The medal for bravery definitely goes to you."

"Oh, I don't know. You were the picture of heroism. Brave, handsome, fearless, riding to the maiden's rescue like a modern Galahad."

"Sorry I didn't have time to don my armor. Come to think of it, armor would have come in very handy." He touched a scrape on her head that was oozing drops of blood. "Lucky we were both only hit by *small* flying rocks."

"Funny how things turn out. I always figured I'd wilt like a week-old daylily in an emergency."

"So, you found out you underrated yourself. Gives you something to think about, doesn't it?"

Cassie glanced up at him, about to ask what he meant, but decided whatever it was, she'd have to think about it later. Her brain, like the rest of her, was worn out.

When they got back to the highway Eric parked his Jeep in the same place it had been that morning. Hand in hand, they walked down the sharply slanted driveway, too bushed to talk, too aware of the fragility of their reconciliation to let go of each other. Both of them felt the need for discussion, the urge to sort out feelings, find solutions; both recognized the absence of the energy necessary to do so.

The moment they were inside Cassie gave a sigh of relief. "Gosh, it's good to be here. There's something about this house that makes me feel safe." She gave a rueful smile as the irony of her statement hit her. "Great. Here I am, the survivor of a landslide—no, two landslides—feeling safe in a house that's named for the fact that it hangs on the edge of a cliff.''

"There's some logic there. Learning that you can survive catastrophe gives you an increased sense of strength and safety.''

Cassie looked at him skeptically. "You, maybe. Me? I'm not at all sure. It gives me more of a sense that I should improve my defensive planning. Stay away from potential hazards.''

Eric gently pulled her to him, holding her close, relishing the feel of her in his arms. "And how do you accomplish that? Life is full of potential hazards, many of which are unavoidable.''

Cassie leaned her head against his chest. "I know.'' This subject was right at the core of their conflict. But she couldn't possibly deal with it right now. She looked up at him, a teasing gleam in her eye. "That's what Aunt Bertha always told me.''

"Aunt Bertha. Dear God. Aunt Bertha's teachings should be banned in Boston.''

It was time to change the subject. Her mind was too numb to cope with this one. "Do you by any chance know how to start the generator?''

He nodded. "Yes. Why don't I work on that while you find us something to eat? I'm famished.''

"That's a good idea. So am I.''

They sat at the big round kitchen table to eat the sandwiches Cassie had made. The steady drone of the generator gave promise of hot showers. It powered electricity for the stove, the water pump and heater, the refrigerator and the lights in the kitchen.

Eric took a sip from his can of beer. "I have to check on my house.''

"How? The road's still blocked.''

"Ever heard of feet?''

She laughed. "Good point. You're not going right away, are you?" He mustn't leave. Not yet. She couldn't bear it.

"No. I can't pass up a hot shower."

"And a nap?"

He looked at her for a long moment. "I imagine sleep is about the extent of what we're capable of right about now."

She looked down at her hands, holding the thick ham-and-cheese sandwich. Everything was so complicated. She was supposed to be back in Boston today. Poor Brian would be frantic. He'd surely hear of the problems in Big Sur and try to call, with no success. She was sure there was no hope of getting word to him for a while. Any spliced-together phone connections would be busy with emergency communications.

Meanwhile because she felt she owed Brian the courtesy of making her final break with him in person, she was still sort of engaged, still sort of committed to returning East, still dangling somewhere in the middle of a lot of loose ends. She thought back to her first day here, in late November, hanging on to the side of a mountain for dear life. Maybe she should have recognized it as a portent of things to come. One of these days she'd have to get a firm grip on something. But not now. Now was a segment cut out of time. Somewhere to the east of reality and the west of fantasy, where she could tarry in limbo, devoid of resolutions, for an unspecified duration.

She looked across the table at Eric. Such a beautiful man—inside as well as out. Every instinct, impulse and intuition within her reached out to him. She felt somehow whole with him. Complete. Assembled. So why did she have any reservations? She couldn't sort it out, couldn't make sense of it. Not now. Now she needed to get clean and get some sleep. In Eric's arms.

She stood up and reached out her hand. "Let's take a shower."

Eric's eyebrows raised just a little. "Good idea."

When they got to the bathroom they stripped off the dirty, torn clothes and dropped them in a corner. Eric watched Cassie as she pulled off her garments. Her lovely cameo skin was nicked and scraped by the flying debris she'd run through. The memory leapt to mind of coming around that bend in the road, of seeing Cassie tugging at the horse's reins, placing herself in terrible jeopardy to drag Bill Coogan out of danger. He'd known true terror at that moment, watching part of a mountain tumbling toward her. His instant emotion had been fury. How dare she place herself in such danger? Later, when they were all safe, anger had been quickly replaced by respect and admiration. She had more guts than he'd imagined. Far more, he was sure, than she'd given herself credit for. Would she still want to leave? And if so, how in God's name could he let her go? Damn. He'd been so successful at closing off his heart, guarding it from injury, until Cassie came into his life. Now it was too late. If she left him the pain would be awesome.

Cassie stuck her hand in to test the water. "Thank heavens, it's nice and hot." She stepped into the stall and reached for the soap.

As Eric joined her he was amazed to feel himself becoming aroused. He'd have sworn he was too tired to react to anything. Obviously he was wrong. He took the soap Cassie offered him and lathered up his body, then soaped Cassie's back, running his other hand down to curve her waist and spread the foam over her buttocks. "Umm. That feels good."

She glanced at him over her shoulder. "The water or the soap?"

"You."

She leaned against him, rubbing the soapsuds on his chest, then moving her hips back to distribute the lather further. He lowered his head to kiss the nape of her neck. "If you're as tired as you said, you'd better stop that. Your sleep is about to be postponed."

"Sleep?" She nuzzled into his kiss. "Who needs sleep?" Lazily, provocatively, she turned and reached behind him to the ceramic shelf to get the shampoo, deliberately brushing her nipples against his chest. Standing far closer than even the cramped quarters demanded, she lifted her arms to pour some of the liquid onto her head, then tipped the bottle over Eric's, squeezing a few drops into his black, tousled hair.

With a guttural laugh Eric wove his fingers into her hair to work up thick suds, while Cassie reached up to return the favor. Their bodies slid together, lubricated by the slick of soap. Cassie's exhaustion seemed to flow down the drain, washed away with the soil of the hills, and the tiredness was instantly replaced by desire. Each tiny sector of her body yearned toward him, this man of her heart. She didn't bother to fight the flood of feelings engulfing her. She'd lose the battle. His chest, so wide and muscular, pressed against her breasts, causing the tips to harden and throb their need. She pushed forward to hug the jut of his passion with her thighs.

They let the hot water run over their heads while their mouths met in a hungry kiss. Their tongues thrust and parried, escalating the mutual arousal that was heating their bodies far faster than the warmth of the shower was. Cassie pulled back and looked up at Eric through cascading water. "I think I'm drowning."

His dark eyes smoldered. "Me, too. But it has nothing to do with water." He reached around her to turn off the faucets, then led her out of the shower stall. They dried each other, concentrating on the parts of the body that took more pleasure in the rubbing than others. With hair still dripping they headed without discussion to Cassie's bed. Eric turned her to him. "I was going to ask if you were absolutely sure you wanted to do this. But now—" his smoky gaze ran over her "—I don't think you have a choice."

She wound her arms around his neck, her head dropped back provocatively. "You mean you'd use force?"

"I mean—" He ran his hands down her back and held her tightly at the waist. "I hope there's no reason to answer that." He kissed her then, savoring the sweet taste of her, amazed anew at the way everything in him responded to her touch. He'd never felt this way about anyone before, and he marveled at the totality of yearning that consumed him. "I love you," he whispered.

Cassie's arms tightened around him. "And I love you." About that there was no question, none whatever. She wanted to fold herself into him, become part of him, so they could never be separated, even if her own lack of courage dictated division. Each time they came together the passion that she'd have sworn had reached its zenith before attained new heights. Every tiny, distinct molecule became electrified, fired by its own ignited energy. Desire ran rampant, flowing through her like a flood-filled stream.

Eric reached behind her and pulled back the covers, then, with his lips still covering hers, gently eased her to the bed, blending into the movement as though joined to her by more than love. "Cassandra." He loved the sound of her name, the feel of it on his tongue. He stretched out on top of her, his body cushioned by soft, smooth flesh. As his tongue dipped deep into her mouth, each thrust mimicked by a surge below, he slipped to one side of her so his hand could travel over the silky skin, touch the proud peaks that tipped her beautiful breasts.

Cassie sucked in her breath and held it, loath to disrupt in even the smallest way the thrilling shocks rocketing through her. His fingers teased her heated nipples to aching tautness, then moved down to slide between her legs. This monumental pleasure seemed almost indecent, a surplus of riches.

She moved her palms over his massive chest, closing her fingers tightly to tug lightly on his chest hair, then she slid them down to circle and hold him, giving back some of the sensual delight with which he was so generous. She squeezed and caressed him until he lifted his head. "Stop that," he whispered raggedly. "You'll make it happen too soon."

With that he pulled free of her maddening fingers and made a slow descent, traversing her body with infinite care, maintaining a constant contact of lips and hands. Those hard tender lips took her nipple in their grasp, kissing and pulling until Cassie's entire body quivered with gratification. When his tormenting mouth moved lower to send need pulsing through her, she moaned her plea. "Come to me, Eric, please. Now. Oh, honey, now."

With one fluid movement Eric's lips met hers at the same moment that he entered her. She pushed her hips upward, desperate to be closer, even nearer than it was possible to be. His deep thrusts sent torrid shafts of ecstasy shooting into every part of her, the intensity of her passion frightening in its fierce demand. Undulating waves of pleasure ran through her, whipping her senses to a madness of excitement, excelling the bounds of endurance until, in a shattering explosion of emotion, her body lunged and buckled in supreme climax.

Eric slid his hands under Cassie, his fingers pressing into the soft flesh, urging the compliance of her body to the rhythm of his. He'd held back as long as he could, to prolong her pleasure, but now he could wait no longer. With a deep growl, he let the hot gush of fiery delight spiral through him, bathing him in immeasurable pleasure.

His body relaxed into hers then, the dampness of spent passion still melding them together. They heaved one great, contiguous sigh, then both slipped quickly into blissful slumber.

They slept until early the next morning and awoke together, as though a silent alarm signaled a dual alert. The alert extended itself, and they made love again with a near-savage desperation that revealed their lingering fear that this paradise might soon be lost.

It wasn't long before the realities of the mess that surrounded them took hold of their lives. For the next week, both of them labored ceaselessly to help the people who had suffered the most damage. Many were homeless. An unlucky few had lost their houses entirely, and some were forbidden to return home until the authorities were sure the emergency was over. Jake came home in two days, his ankle encased in a cast, an encumbrance that he refused to allow to slow him down. He and Cassie set up bunks in the spare rooms and took in two of the local families who needed shelter.

Cassie managed to get word to Brian and Aunt Bertha that she and Jake were all right and that she'd call as soon as possible. Then she pitched in to do what she could in the process of cleaning up Big Sur.

Two weeks after the slide Jake and Cassie were sitting at the table, finishing up a large breakfast of bacon and eggs. All the members of their "adopted" families had eaten early and gone to work on the reconstruction of their houses.

Jake leaned back and heaved a big sigh. "It's going to be a while before things are back to normal, but at least the worst is over. I think."

"Don't sound so uncertain. I'm not at all sure I could survive another catastrophe."

Jake patted her hand. "It sounds to me like you can deal with anything that comes your way. Anyhow, this sort of thing should be a once-in-a-lifetime occurrence. It takes a special series of events that's pretty rare, luckily. That big forest fire in the mountains last spring burned off a lot of the vegetation that usually catches water, followed by more rain than we've seen in decades. Then, even though that earthquake didn't amount to much, it was enough to jiggle the mud loose."

"Didn't amount to much! I thought it was terrifying."

Jake laughed. "That's because you've never been in a real, big-time quake."

"And I hope I never am, thank you."

"They're very rare here."

"Jake, I have to admit to you, all this makes the East seem more attractive."

"I don't know why. You're in far more danger of having your car skid on the ice and wrap around a tree. That's not even addressing the hurricanes that blow through with fair regularity."

Cassie grinned. "So, what you're saying is that Aunt Bertha is right. There are hazards awaiting us everywhere."

"Bertha. Humph."

"It's a good thing she wasn't here. She'd have had a heart attack."

"Don't kid yourself about Bertha. She's good Yankee stock, just like you. She'd've been behind that horse, kicking him in the butt to hurry him along. It would've been afterward that all the gnashing of teeth started."

"Well, maybe Aunt Bertha and I are two of a kind, after all."

"Cassie, you come into the world with a certain set of tendencies. An important part of the journey through life consists of strengthening those you're happy with, and controlling those you aren't. Nobody needs to be ruled by fear. It's just harder for some to overcome it than for others."

"I sense a message in that."

"You always were a bright girl."

It wasn't until the real crisis was past, about a week later, that Cassie began to suffer aftershocks of her own. Whatever it was that sustained her through the slides and the rescue and the period just past—a time when every pair of hands was needed and there existed the spirit of a community come together in mutual effort—it started to fade, and all the postponed fear squiggled into place, jarring her nerves and pushing her into a state of massive confusion.

She and Eric had managed little time alone. They were both kept very busy, and chances to sneak off together were few. Finally they got a little breathing space, and Cassie walked to Eric's house, which had been undamaged, to have a cozy private dinner.

Eric had started the charcoal grill and wrapped potatoes in foil to cook in the coals. Cassie had observed that, whenever the choice was his, he was still a meat-and-potatoes man. It was impossible to look at Eric and see any bad effects from the diet. Every once in awhile, when she caught sight of him across a room, it struck her again how extraordinary he was. He was the picture of heroism, the sort of man every writer of romance must try to capture in words. Dark, brooding, handsome. And oh, so sexy. Maybe that's why she'd had such a hard time accepting the fact that he was a thoroughly decent person. It seemed too much largess of nature to be housed in one man.

When she arrived Eric took her by the hand and led her out the front door. "I want to show you something." They walked to the fence that ran around the front of the property and looked down at the seal colony. Eric pointed to the big rock that King Tut had ruled for such a long time. There, in splendid superiority, stood a majestic, glistening bull seal. "The king is dead. Long live the king. Some things seem to cut right across the species."

"He's magnificent, but . . ."

"He isn't Tut."

"Right. It still seems so sad that such a beautiful, un-usual animal had to die." She glanced at Eric's face and added, "Well, not had to . . . but did."

"Yeah. Well, at a certain point you quit beating your breast and accept what is. They have a new ruler, and I wish him a long, happy reign."

"Are you sure that Curt Jacobs won't come after him?"

Eric looked at her in surprise. "I guess you haven't heard."

"Heard what?"

"Jacobs was one of the three casualties of the slide."

Cassie faced him, her eyes wide. "Really?" She looked down at the big seal, presiding with dignity on his stone throne. "That seems almost . . ."

"Providential?"

"Yes."

Eric nodded. "The same thought occurred to me—that perhaps the man upstairs has pretty good aim."

"Eric . . ."

"I know. Thoughts like that won't get me into heaven. Hopefully I'll have time to make amends." He put his arm around her shoulders and they headed back to the house.

They had a lovely dinner, complete with crackling fire and candlelight. Afterward they took their mugs of coffee over to the sofa and sat close together, watching the leaping flames. Eric said, "This may be our last fire for a while. They're predicting temperatures in the eighties by the weekend."

"That will be quite a change. It hasn't been really warm since that day we took the picnic out to the rocks."

He smiled. "That was quite a day, wasn't it? I think we both knew we were caught by something that wouldn't let go."

"You make it sound like a large critter with claws."

"That's just what it felt like to me at first. Before I got used to the idea."

She leaned her head against his shoulder, staring at the profusion of colors that danced through the fire. "Are you used to it? You were so dedicated to staying uninvolved."

"I know. But it began to penetrate my thick skull that it was pretty stupid to transfer all the suspicion and mistrust I'd been left with by my mother and my ex-wife to you. You're an entirely different kind of person." He tilted her chin up with his fingers. "I love you, Cassie. I'd like to marry you."

Cassie pulled in her breath, caught in a moment she wasn't prepared for, even though this possibility had turned over and over in her head. "I love you, too, Eric. More than I thought I could ever love anyone."

"It sounds like there's a 'but' at the end of that sentence."

She closed her eyes and dropped her forehead to his shoulder. "You're right, there is. I've thought so much about this the last few days, and I can't make any sense out of it. So I don't know how in the world to explain it."

"I think you'll have to try." She could hear his voice flattening out the way it did when he withdrew into that secret guarded place to which he retreated.

"Eric, I've felt so overwhelmed lately. It's like the aftermath of a close miss on the highway, only much stronger. Suddenly I'm full of so much fear, sort of like I'd locked it all away, and it's finally broken out."

Eric rubbed his palm over his eyes, then stood abruptly. "Are you trying to tell me you're going back to Boston?"

She sat silently for a moment, staring at her hands that lay clenched in her lap. "Yes."

"Damn it, Cassie." He leaned over to grab her by the shoulders and yanked her to her feet. "What the hell are you doing? You and I belong together. What we have is magical. How can you even think of just walking away?"

"Eric, I have to be sure."

"Sure?" He pulled her roughly to him. "How sure?" He kissed her, and the kiss was close to an assault. When he lifted his head, he demanded, "That sure?" His hands moved around to her hips to press her into him, and their bodies wedged together as his lips once again took command of hers.

Cassie was melting into the savage embrace, her whole being crying for surrender to this engrossing passion. But doubt had taken too strong a stand, and she couldn't rid herself of it, not even in Eric's arms. She tried to keep her body from stiffening, but failed. He drew away angrily and strode across the room, where he stood with his back to her, staring out the window. "Damn it. I thought we'd come past all this. I really believed our love was real and very special."

Cassie went over to stand beside him. She hated to see him so upset, hated being the cause of his pain. When she spoke, her voice was low and shaky. "Eric, please believe me. This has nothing to do with the way I love you. There isn't the faintest question in my mind that I could never feel like this for anyone else."

He turned to her. "Then why?"

"We're talking about a total, all-encompassing change in my life. The shift would be monumental. When I came out here, really such a short time ago, my life was all planned, neatly laid out for the foreseeable future. I was engaged, I had a job all lined up, I knew where I was going to live for the rest of my life. Boston makes me feel safe, kind of . . . fenced in. I've never experienced the exhilaration and excitement and . . . I don't know, *expansion* there that I've felt here, but that was a plus, in a strange sort of way." She swallowed hard and ventured a direct look at his face. It was no longer glowering, and he was giving her his full attention. "Big Sur has always been a tremendous challenge to me. It demands something that I've never been sure I can give. It's like you can't just live here, you have to be so in tune with your environment that you sort of blend into it."

"And you don't like that?"

"It's not a question of like or dislike, it's can or can't. I never thought I could make such a total commitment to anything." She looked up at him, her eyes pleading for understanding. "Or anyone. It frightens me, Eric. I know that's far from heroic, but there it is."

Eric took her elbow. "Let's sit down." They walked back to the couch and sat. "Crazy, isn't it? We both seem to have the same problem with commitment for different reasons. I guess you can't get away from your past, even when you want to."

Cassie laid her hand on his arm. "I want to, Eric. I do. Part of me is absolutely ready to say yes to all of it. Another part of me is more and more terrified at the mere thought."

"Is it just the place, Cassie? We'd live about half the time in San Francisco, you know." He frowned. "But I can't say I'm ready to buy a three-piece suit and move to Boston." He gave her a look that bordered on hopelessness. "So I guess that squashes my right to get mad at you for not being able to just pack up your life and move it out here."

Cassie managed a slight smile. She didn't manage to keep the sadness out of it. "I can't picture you in Boston. It's hard enough to think of you in San Francisco. You seem so much a part of Big Sur. You've made the connection. I wish I could. I don't know why I'm such a damned scaredy-cat."

"Cassie . . ." He took her hand in his. "Don't punish yourself. How could you possibly have lost your parents in such a horrible manner and grown up under the tutelage of good old Aunt Bertha without having significant fears? I can understand why security is so important to you. I just disagree with what security means. I don't think it comes from external circumstances. I think you have to find it someplace inside yourself."

Cassie's eyes filled, and the tears began to roll down her cheeks. "Eric, could you give me some time? I need to go back, to experience Boston again, before I can even begin to be sure." She glanced down at their hands, interlocked. Her hand felt so good tucked into his. "And . . . I need to talk to Brian, and to get that settled."

Eric's jaw set, then with visible effort he relaxed it. "I hate the very idea, but I couldn't ask you not to go. You're right, you need to be sure, for both our sakes. Of course, the thought of your being with Brian tears me up, but I'm sure it hasn't been easy for him, either."

"I can't begin to tell you how much I appreciate your being so understanding."

"It's a royal pain in the prat, all this understanding. I'd rather throw you over my shoulder and take you to my bedroom and seduce you, and then lock you in until you came to your senses."

"I have to admit, under all these layers of feminist independence there's a part of me that would welcome that."

He took hold of both her hands and shifted his position to face her. "Cassie, I love you with all my heart. I want to marry you and spend the rest of my life with you. But I only want that if it's mutual. I've had a one-sided marriage, and I sure as hell don't want another. Go East and make your decision. But don't take too long."

She went gratefully into his arms, where he held her tightly. His message was quite clear. He was doing his best to give her a large quotient of that famous commodity, space, but he wasn't about to put his life on indefinite hold so she could procrastinate. It was more than fair. It was more than she'd expected, and probably more than she deserved.

Chapter Thirteen

Eric walked around his house, making a last inspection. The house, like him, had suffered only minor injuries, more annoying than serious. The problem was, it was impossible to get any help from the local tradesmen unless you had major troubles. For that reason Eric had abandoned his regular work so he could replace damaged boards and re-wire broken connections and rebuild a smashed tool shed. He was too impatient to put any of it off.

He sat on the front step and took a few minutes to just gaze out to sea. The weather had cleared and was putting on a dazzling display, as though to make amends to the residents for its blatant misbehavior and to convince them, once again, that this was a magic land, and a little trouble now and then was a small price to pay for the privilege of living in it.

Eric thought back to the first day he'd come to Big Sur. He had been stunned by its beauty, and he still was. He gazed around, trying to understand at a gut level what intimidated Cassie. She used the word overwhelming a lot when she talked about it. It was true that everything was on a massive scale: mountains, shoreline, view of the ocean. But to Eric it seemed like a chunk of heaven dropped onto earth as a teaser. Not being able to live here, at least part of the year, would be like being banished from paradise.

He propped his chin on his fist and let his mind wander, a freedom his mind seldom got. He had contentedly settled into his life-style, which he considered pretty darn special. He had total flexibility to come and go as he pleased, and it had been a long time since he'd had to worry about the cost of anything, at least any material thing. He had a more elaborate condo than he probably needed in San Francisco, considering the amount of time he spent in it, but he liked the layout and the location, high on Nob Hill, and he enjoyed San Francisco as much as he could enjoy any city in the world. He seemed to have the Midas touch; his successful ventures far outnumbered the few failures he'd suffered, and the same investors stuck with him, eager to have a piece of his new enterprises. He never had any trouble finding female companionship. He had lots of buddies and a few close friends, which was as much as he could find time for. And just stepping outside his own front door provided him with the most beautiful scenery anywhere.

His only problem was that Cassie had knocked all that complacent contentment into a cocked hat. She stayed wedged in his consciousness every minute. He had to think around her, a sort of mental hurdle that made plain thought an achievement and concentration next to impossible. She'd been gone almost a month now, and he hadn't heard a word from her. They had agreed the separation should be complete, with no communication, but a month was longer than he'd anticipated for her to make up her mind, and one hell of a long time for her to choose not to call. He'd picked up the phone a dozen times and set it back in its cradle before placing the call. After all, it had been her decision to leave.

It should also be hers to get in touch. The silence had become ominous; an unspoken goodbye.

He got up and went to the rail fence to check on the seal colony with its new leader. They all looked perfectly happy, and the new bull in town had settled right in and appeared to be very much in control. He felt a sharp stab of sorrow as he looked down on King Tut's replacement. Well, nobody lived forever; the question wasn't if, just when. He leaned on the top rail, watching a sea gull catch an updraft and soar overhead.

Falling in love, King Tut's death and the hazards during the mudslide had conspired to make him more aware of his own mortality. Time would run out for him, too. He found he no longer felt satisfied with the prospect of living the rest of his life as a bachelor. He wanted companionship and love. He wanted Cassie. No matter how much he fought it, her silent absence rankled. His ability to be reasonable was growing thinner by the day. Certainly her background gave her plenty of reason to want to hang on to the knowns and to fear drastic change, but damn it all, she had no corner on those feelings. His childhood hadn't exactly been a bucket of laughs, either. He was probably being a damned fool, hanging around like a lovesick schoolboy, waiting for the phone to ring. He'd postponed several business trips lately. This was probably the perfect time to take off for a while. He had to do something to get rid of this feeling of being dangled on a string like some limp-jointed puppet.

He straightened up and whacked the railing with the palm of his hand in a gesture of frustration. It wasn't at all satisfying.

Cassie sat in a stiff Chippendale chair, watching her Aunt Bertha's nimble fingers busily employed with an intricate needlepoint patter. Bertha never just sat. One of her favorite quotations was, "For Satan finds some mischief still for idle hands to do." She was an ample woman who filled the straight-backed armchair to the straining point, and her busyness sometimes wore Cassie out.

She pulled the needle through the fabric and peered at Cassie over her half glasses. "Believe me, Cassandra, coming home was the smartest move you could make."

Cassie was surprised to find that the word *home* brought instant thoughts of Big Sur. And Eric.

"A born-and-raised New Englander should never move West. It's too drastic a change for the nervous system."

Jake had been Boston born, Cassie thought rebelliously, and was as happy in his western home as a California sea otter.

"That place," Bertha continued, her tone almost pompous, "will never be truly civilized, and the people have different values from ours."

Now what did that mean? Were they different because they treasured the unspoiled beauty of nature and had soft spots in their hearts for seals and otters and mountain lions? Because they felt other creatures had an equal right to live out their lives in peace?

"Besides, you'd become terribly bored, dear. What on earth would you have found to do?"

Cassie thought of making love with Eric, of taking picnics, of watching the whales...of making love with Eric...of working for conservation causes that fired her fervent interest; of long, relaxed breakfasts with Jake, of writing her stories, of that special sense of one-for-all closeness she'd had with the inhabitants when she'd pitched in to help after the slides...and, of course, of making love with Eric...

"And Brian is such a nice young man. Absolutely perfect for you. So entirely civilized."

Cassie had tried, several times since her return, to explain that her relationship with Brian was over, but Bertha, with dogged stubbornness, had refused to process the information.

All Cassie had wanted every minute since her return was to pack up everything and head West, but she'd promised herself she'd be careful and wait long enough to separate the reality of Boston from what she still thought of as the fantasy of Big Sur and the dream-come-true that was Eric. A little over a month had passed, and her impulses hadn't changed. Her caution had begun to feel excessive, and her wisdom in taking so long to make the decision, flawed.

She shifted on the hard seat. "Aunt Bertha, did you love Uncle Leonard a lot?"

Bertha looked at her as though she'd asked the amount of her bank balance. "Why on earth do you ask that?"

"I just wondered. You never talk about him."

"That part of my life has been over for a very long time, Cassandra, and it isn't healthy to dwell on the past."

Cassie subdued a smile. Aunt Bertha had endless lists of things that were good or bad, healthy or unhealthy, dangerous or safe. The safe column was very short. "I've just wondered whether you were happy with him."

The tempo of Bertha's stitching accelerated markedly. "It was a satisfactory marriage. Leonard and I came from similar backgrounds, so we moved easily into wedded life." This question was obviously not to be rewarded with yes or no.

"Did you ever love someone else?"

The fingers stopped and stayed frozen for several long seconds. "Well, there was a man..." She squared her shoulders and put the fingers back to work, double time. "But he would have been completely unsuitable. He was an *Irishman*."

The sides of Cassie's lips twitched. "Oh my, no wonder you didn't marry him! What was he, a politician?"

In Bertha's family that would be a combination sure to inspire the kiss of death to any budding romantic relationship. Had she mentioned Eric was part Indian? No, she didn't think so. That, in league with his Californian ties, would fit the same category.

"Heavens, no. He was a lawyer. And a very good one. He has established quite a reputation in the legal field." The fingers took another short break, as Bertha, for the first time in Cassie's memory, gazed off into space.

"Is he still alive?"

"Yes."

"Where does he live, do you know?"

"Right here in Boston."

Cassie immediately grew more interested. "Really? What's his name?"

Bertha pinched her lips and got back to her needlepoint. "I see no advantage to mentioning names."

"Did you ever wish you'd made a different decision?"

This time Bertha's hands rested in her lap as she looked past Cassie with a thoughtful frown. She had a look on her face that Cassie had never seen before, sort of soft and sad and vulnerable. "Every day of my life." She glanced around quickly, as though just remembering where she was, then resumed her stitching with a solid "Humph! Enough of that nonsense. Now, where were we?"

Cassie barely managed to respond to Bertha's comments for the rest of the visit. Her mind was off on a tack of its own, mulling over the last four weeks. She'd spent hours walking through the streets of Boston, looking at everything with a mind bent on pulling in and analyzing what she saw and felt. Dirty snow lined the sidewalks, and a cold wind cut through her heavy coat. But it wasn't the weather she concentrated on. It was the strange switch in perception that had taken place. Instead of making her feel safely enclosed, the city felt claustrophobic, hemming her in on all sides. Instead of towering mountain slopes, there were tall, grey, concrete buildings, shooting straight up, cutting into the view of the sky. Instead of sweeping vistas, there were jammed streets with backed-up, honking cars and hastily moving pedestrians, oblivious to all but their own destination.

Every wakeful minute had been filled with thoughts of Eric, overlayed on impressions of Big Sur. She missed Jake, and Margo, and lots of the other people who had come to mean so much to her. It was time to admit to herself that she'd hoped to come back to Boston and settle happily into her old life. She'd hoped to recapture that safe, tame, stability, free of volatile emotions. But it hadn't worked. Not at all. The Cassie Chase who had left for Big Sur in November had vanished and couldn't be found. Someone else had taken her place. Someone who wanted to see beyond the end of a block, who needed challenge and stimulation, who wanted to seek new horizons. And, most of all, someone who was madly, irrationally, totally in love.

Cassie excused herself as quickly as possible and drove to her apartment on Chestnut Street. When she closed the door behind her, she hurried across the room and sat on the edge of the chair next to the telephone table. She reached for the receiver, then stopped. She wanted to call Eric, to ask him if he still loved her and wanted her. But what if he said no? Or was hesitant? How could she stand it? She had taken far too long and been too rigid about not talking to him. Her painstaking adherence to slow, careful deliberation now seemed the height of folly. How would she feel if Eric had done the same thing? Abandoned. Unwanted. Oh, God.

She snatched up the phone and hastily punched a number. It rang and rang. Just as she was about to hang up in frustration, a deep voice answered. "Hello?"

"Jake! I was afraid you weren't at home."

"Well, hello there, Cassandra. And how is my granddaughter, aside from being out of her mind?"

"Come on, Jake, give me a break. This decision required a little time."

"Phooey. If ever I saw two people meant for each other, it's you and Eric."

"That's quite a change from the warning you gave me when the subject first came up."

"That was before."

"Before? Before what?"

"Before I saw you together and before I knew you could snare him."

"Humph! Fine thing. Didn't it ever enter your mind that I might not want to snare him?"

"No. I figured you were smarter than that. Do you realize you just said 'humph'?"

"Oh, Jake, don't tease me!" She twisted the cord around her finger. "Have you...seen Eric recently?" A terrible fear was mounting that she might have waited too long. She'd taken too much for granted in coming back East and not so much as calling for a whole month. How could she have been so stupid?

"No, I haven't. I think he may be away on a business trip. He's grown progressively more taciturn and he's been wearing his black-eyed Indian look lately. I don't know, Cass, you may have waited too long." There was a long enough pause for her to hear the frantic hammering of her heart. "So. How's Boston? And Bertha, and that young whippersnapper? Everything hunky-dory?"

"Jake, please don't try to aggravate me!" Her voice sounded shrill, and why not? She was riddled with worry. "Jake, I want to come home."

His voice, when he answered, was guarded. "Oh? I thought that's where you were." He was obviously not going to make this easy for her.

"I was wrong, Jake. About everything. Listen..." Her mind raced, trying to figure out how to take care of things here in the most expeditious manner. "Look, I think I'll come on out. If—" Her voice broke. "If everything works out okay, I can come back later to close my apartment and all."

"Well then, get a move on. You'd better leave a message on Eric's answering machine, so if he calls in for his messages he'll know you're coming."

Her heart was doing a fast slide to her stomach. How could she have been so careless with something so precious? Eric's phone *was* answered by a machine, and just hearing his recorded voice caused goose bumps to leap to attention along her arms. She waited for the buzz, then said, in a tone tight with anxiety, "Hi, darling. I'm calling to tell you—" She stopped, uncertain how to proceed. "I'm..." She was going to run out of time! She blurted, in a rapid race of words, "I love you so much! I must have been crazy to stay away so long. I can only pray that you haven't changed your mind. I'm coming home, darling, as fast as I can get there." Cassie hung up, breathless and scared. She had to get to Big Sur. She had to get to Eric. Pray God it wasn't too late!

When Cassie arrived at Cliffhanger, she parked the car in the driveway and walked around to the front door. She didn't want to alter the ritual of homecoming in any way; she was afraid it would prove unlucky. She laid her palms against the warm wood of the door and leaned her forehead on it. Her quiet hello was drowned out by the hammering of her heart, which was in anxiety overdrive. She felt a new affinity to this beloved house. In many ways her own recent life could carry the same title: Cliffhanger. Boy, how she'd changed. Being perched on the edge of adventure no longer frightened her. After all, with Eric beside her she could handle anything. She had just reached for the doorknob when the door swung open.

Jake's big frame loomed over her. "Good afternoon, Cassandra, welcome."

She stepped into his hug. "Oh, Jake, you were right. I have been out of my mind!"

"Well, good for you. The first step to recovery is admitting the disease."

"It was just that I was so scared of making such an enormous change." She saw the skeptical look in his eyes. "All right. I was mostly frightened of such an overpowering love. It's something I never expected to experience."

Jake put his arm around her and closed the door behind them. "Loving someone with all your heart makes you terribly vulnerable, and that is scary. But not loving pushes us faster and faster to the death of our senses. And that's scarier."

She stopped and looked at him, her eyes round with anxiety. "Oh, Jake, what if he's changed his mind?"

"Well, now, honey, is that something you'd expect Eric to do in a month's time?"

Cassie took a deep breath, feeling some of the tension slide away. "No." For the first time in two days she was able to smile. "But he may be ticked off at me."

"Then I guess you'll have your work cut out for you. Have to butter him up a little."

"I won't mind that one bit."

"Why don't you go out in the yard and wait for him. He should be along any minute now."

Cassie's eyes rounded. "Really? Are you serious?" Her face split in one huge grin. "Jake! Did you call him?"

"Yep. Right before I opened the door." He chuckled. "I wouldn't worry too much about his being upset, if I were you."

Cassie gave a yelp of joy, kissed her grandfather, raced for the door and threw it open. She could hear the bark of the seals in the distance, punctuating the murmur of the quiet surf. Stepping outside, she turned to look up at the spectacular Santa Lucia Mountains, the glory of their curvatures highlighted by the deepening afternoon shadows, then spun around and gazed out over the glistening ocean, cupped by the glorious blue sky. She threw her arms wide and yelled, "I love you!"

"What?"

Whirling around, her startled eyes lighted on the figure that had appeared at the top of the driveway. Eric stood outlined in gold sun rays, his black hair blown by the gentle breeze. Cassie laughed aloud and opened her arms to him. "I love you!" she shouted.

Eric took off at a sprint, running toward her, his face split in a grin of pure happiness. Cassie ran to meet him, feeling the conspiratorial wind lift the last of her caution and carry it off to sea.

* * * * *

FOUR UNIQUE SERIES FOR EVERY WOMAN YOU ARE...

Silhouette Romance

Love, at its most tender, provocative, emotional...in stories that will make you laugh and cry while bringing you the magic of falling in love.

6 titles per month

Silhouette Special Edition

Sophisticated, substantial and packed with emotion, these powerful novels of life and love will capture your imagination and steal your heart.

6 titles per month

Silhouette Desire

Open the door to romance and passion. Humorous, emotional, compelling—yet always a believable and sensuous story—Silhouette Desire never fails to deliver on the promise of love.

6 titles per month

Silhouette Intimate Moments

Enter a world of excitement, of romance heightened by suspense, adventure and the passions every woman dreams of. Let us sweep you away.

4 titles per month

Silhouette Desire®

1989
IS THE YEAR
OF THE MAN!

What makes a romance? A special man, of course, and Silhouette Desire celebrates that fact with *twelve* of them! From Mr. January to Mr. December, every month has a tribute to the Silhouette Desire hero—our **MAN OF THE MONTH!**

Sexy, macho, charming, irritating . . . irresistible! Nothing can stop these men from sweeping you away. Created by some of your favorite authors, each man is custom-made for pleasure—*reading* pleasure—so don't miss a single one.

Mr. January is Blake Donavan in RELUCTANT FATHER by Diana Palmer
Mr. February is Hank Branson in THE GENTLEMAN INSISTS by Joan Hohl
Mr. March is Carson Tanner in NIGHT OF THE HUNTER by Jennifer Greene
Mr. April is Slater McCall in A DANGEROUS KIND OF MAN by Naomi Horton
Mr. May is Luke Harmon in VENGEANCE IS MINE by Lucy Gordon
Mr. June is Quinn McNamara in IRRESISTIBLE by Annette Broadrick

And that's only the half of it—
so get out there and find your man!

Silhouette Desire's

MAN OF THE MONTH . . .

MOM-1

Silhouette Special Edition

COMING NEXT MONTH

#529 A QUESTION OF HONOR—Lindsay McKenna
When narcotics agent Kit Anderson went undercover, she landed
"under the covers" with Coast Guard skipper Noah Trayhern!
Fireworks explode in Lindsay McKenna's Love and Glory series
celebrating our men (and women!) in uniform.

#530 FOR ALL MY TOMORROWS—Debbie Macomber
Ryder Matthews juggled friendship and guilt with his late partner's
widow—until the delicate balance tipped under the weight of his
unspoken love....

#531 KING OF HEARTS—Tracy Sinclair
When schoolteacher Stephanie Blair met dashing, evasive Morgan
Destine, he quickly became the king of her heart. But was this man of
mystery truly a prince among men?

#532 FACE VALUE—Celeste Hamilton
Beau Collins was frantic—where would he find a fresh face to launch
a national ad campaign? Then he noticed his next-door neighbor,
quiet, bespectacled Caitlin Welch....

#533 HEATHER ON THE HILL—Barbara Faith
Outgoing Blythe cared little for convention—her fatherless son was
proof of that. If she accepted proper Scotsman Cameron McCabe's
impulsive proposal, would centuries of tradition crush their new love?

#534 REPEAT PERFORMANCE—Lynda Trent
Years ago, Jordan Landry had broken their engagement—and Carley
Kingston's heart—to marry another woman. Now Jordan was back,
demanding a repeat performance!

AVAILABLE NOW:

#523 SOME LIKE IT HOT
Patricia Coughlin

#524 PHOENIX RISING
Mary Kirk

#525 AFTERMATH
Lisa Jackson

#526 CLIFFHANGER
Mary Curtis

#527 SHELTER FROM THE STORM
Victoria Pade

#528 IF THERE BE LOVE
Ginna Gray

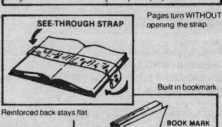

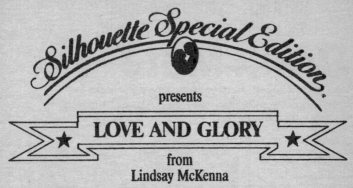

Silhouette Special Edition

presents

★ LOVE AND GLORY ★

from
Lindsay McKenna

Introducing a gripping new series celebrating our men—and women—in uniform. Meet the Trayherns, a military family as proud and colorful as the American flag, a family fighting the shadow of dishonor, a family determined to triumph—with
LOVE AND GLORY!

June: A QUESTION OF HONOR (SE #529) leads the fast-paced excitement. When Coast Guard officer Noah Trayhern offers Kit Anderson a safe house, he unwittingly endangers his own guarded emotions.

July: NO SURRENDER (SE #535) Navy pilot Alyssa Trayhern's assignment with arrogant jet jockey Clay Cantrell threatens her career—and her heart—with a crash landing!

August: RETURN OF A HERO (SE #541) Strike up the band to welcome home a man whose top-secret reappearance will make headline news . . . with a delicate, daring woman by his side.

Three courageous siblings— three consecutive months of

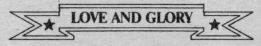

★ LOVE AND GLORY ★

Premiering in **June**, only in
Silhouette Special Edition.

LG-1